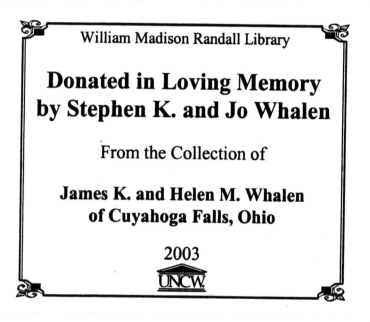

CLOUDCRY

CLOUDCRY

Sydney J. Van Scyoc

Published by
BERKLEY PUBLISHING CORPORATION

Distributed by
G. P. PUTNAM'S SONS, NEW YORK

For
Sandra

CHAPTER ONE

It was apparent to Verrons as he concluded his initial argument that more than a plaston shell separated him from Disposition Officer Jurgens. Although Jurgens inclined his glazed head in a distracted pantomime of attentiveness, his soft-focused gaze was canted well to the left of Verrons' tense face, and he perched on the conference bench molded into the exterior surface of the isocube shell poised for retreat. Verrons' jaw tightened. Three weeks encased in a transparent isocube in the isolation wing of Authority hospital satellite Britthold had infected him with a steadily mounting sense of helplessness. He was free to request adjustment of temperature, of diet, of wardrobe, even of spatial orientation of the cube itself, but he was entirely dependent upon isolation ward personnel for implementation of his wishes. And although Jurgens had promptly acceded to Verrons' request for a final interview, the disposition officer's studied preoccupation negated any sense that actual communication was in process.

With growing frustration, Verrons remustered his arguments, articulating each word sharply, the better to breach the walls of Jurgens' professional detachment. "I am scheduled to rendezvous with my party on Rumar in five weeks, Officer. We have just three years to complete our initial evaluation of the dominant life-form and to submit documentation of emerging intelligence to Authority. The time factor wouldn't be so critical if I'd had funds to sign on highly experienced personnel. But without scholastic credentials, without academic standing in any specialized field—"

"You were fortunate to obtain funding at all," Jurgens commented with a noncommittal nod.

"Exactly." But twenty years service with Authority Exploration Service had invested his argument that the big man-leopards of the Rumarian grassplains stood at an evolutionary crossroad with a certain weight. Even without academic credentials, he had obtained funding sufficient to permit him to hire a small party and to outfit it. With completion of Authority service, his status as a retired exploration officer was sufficient to assure shipping privileges to Rumar for party and matériel. Ironically it had been his retirement physical which had turned up evidence of bloodblossom microorganisms in his bloodstream. He frowned, channeling his thoughts past the dangerous topic of his own ultimate mortality. "If I can't meet my party, command will necessarily pass to Dr. Naas. And while his academic qualifications are good, he's never gone into the field before. Given his inexperience—"

"If you would like, you may withdraw authorization for the party to be transported to Rumar without you, Commander."

Verrons' gaze narrowed upon Jurgens through the transparent shell of the isocube. He shook his head irritably. "And see the planet turned over to the mining interests? They had already drawn provisional permission to strip the foothills when I filed for a delay. If my group is more than ninety days late beginning the study, the strippers can request termination of our permit and begin work in the hills immediately." And the man-leopards could continue to evolve toward intelligence only if they were left undisturbed, if in fact Rumar were ultimately granted reserve status. *If.* Helplessly Verrons' fists tightened on the molded counter of the isocube. "Officer, you know the statistics on susceptibility to bloodblossom. There is virtually no chance any member of my party will pick up the infection from me. But just to be on the safe side, I'll arrange to eat and sleep separately, to handle my laundry separately, to keep a physical distance at all times. There is no need—"

Jurgens' narrow shoulders rose, then fell in a regretful sigh. Reluctantly his eyes intersected Verrons'. "Your request for an exception has already been denied, Commander. As I told you earlier this week, you have been assigned to the isolation colony Selmarri Home. Selmarri is located less than five days downlane from our present coordinates. It is a small world, gravity slightly less than earth-normal, atmospheric composition and conditions quite similar to Earth. The colony is small—"

"I've audited the orientation tape a dozen times already."

"Then you realize—"

"I realize that I intend to file a formal request for another series of tests," Verrons said flatly. "And if my request is not honored—"

Jurgens' lacquered head barely inclined. "Med Division has already run every indicated test half a dozen times, Commander. And while the tests themselves are not particularly costly, the workload involved in the overall screening program makes it necessary to set limits on retesting of confirmed cases." A deliberate shuttering of his gaze dismissed further discussion of Verrons' demand. "As you know, Authority maintains isolation colonies on a dozen planets, not just to facilitate transport of infectees but to keep the colonies small. Beyond certain population densities, an institutional character develops. In addition—"

"In addition, if you let the colonies reach certain densities you have created a leper-pool of too many talents, too many capabilities, and too many skilled hands capable of constructing weapons that could knock Authority drop ships and monitor ships right out of the sky," Verrons said with bitter emphasis.

A tense frown bracketed Jurgens' pale lips. "Authority has never suffered an infectee insurrection on any isolation world, Commander. And as I have emphasized previously, Authority is devoting every possible resource to isolating a cure for the infection. Each new infectee is advised of that fact immediately. Research centers located in every arm of Authority territory—"

"I'm not interested in a cure at some indefinite future date," Verrons interrupted harshly. "My concerns are immediate. I want you to file a second request for variation on my behalf, making my position and my intentions completely clear. I am willing to travel to Rumar in my isolation shell and to utilize it as living quarters if necessary. Physical contact between myself and my party can be held to an absolute minimum. I—"

Jurgens' pale gaze skittered past Verrons' isocube to the neighboring shell. His varnished hair catching light, he unfolded his uniformed limbs. "Permission has already been refused, Commander. There is no point in filing a second request."

"Authority maintains other isolation patients on unpopulated worlds," Verrons argued, standing. "I can cite you cases."

Jurgens shook his head. "No exception can be made in the case of bloodblossom patients." Again he sighed deeply. "You are sked to be loaded aboard the drop ship in three days, Commander. The Ehminheer's cube will be loaded at the same time." Absently he glanced toward the adjacent isocube, where the Ehminheer perched awkwardly, his brilliant plumage bristling. "Your study party personnel have already been apprised of the facts. Communication will continue to be forwarded to them at your request." Reluctantly Jurgens' eyes panned back to meet Verrons'. "Messages from family and associates will be dispatched to you on a priority basis. If you wish—"

Angrily Verrons' fist hit the counter, a blow that communicated jarring force up his arm to the base of his skull. Jurgens' pale eyes widened and briefly Verrons had the satisfaction of feeling that full communication existed. Then the disposition officer blinked rapidly and stepped back from the isocube. His gaze slid down the corridor past the Ehminheer's isocube. "If you need to speak to me again before departure, Commander—"

"To what end?" Verrons snapped.

Jurgens' gaze returned to meet Verrons' again, a reluctant pilgrimage. His head dropped. "Commander, theoretically I have disposition of all Britthold patients. But when bloodblossom is involved, I have no options beyond deciding which isolation colony will be utilized. Exceptions and variations are forbidden by executive order. All I can provide is basic orientation material, an opportunity for ventilation and some—perhaps inept—counseling. Beyond that, I am as helpless as you are."

And, Verrons realized reluctantly, he was as uncomfortable with his helplessness. Sighing, Verrons extended a hand in a gesture of reconciliation. "If there is nothing you can do—"

"There is absolutely nothing," Jurgens confirmed.

Verrons shrugged. "Then back to the orientation tape," he said grimly. "And thank you for your time." If for nothing else.

Jurgens accepted dismissal with a silent inclination of his head and disappeared into the sterilization lock. Gazing down the empty corridor as the lock closed behind him, Verrons confronted despair again. But when he closed his eyes to face it down, a brief flicker of alien color illuminated his field of vision, distracting him.

Bloodblossom: he should have recognized the initial symptom of infection months ago. But his first glimpse of the ghostly Mazaahr spots had been so fleeting he could not remember now when it had occurred. And recurrences had been widely spaced until very recently. Only after he had been recalled to Britthold for retesting had the significance of the brightly tinted flashes of illumination become clear.

Verrons paced the isocube, glancing briefly at the Ehminheer in the adjacent cube. Jurgens had instructed the avian in use of the intercube talk channel, but the Ehminheer refused to activate his receiver. Instead he perched awkwardly in his chair, long-limbed and yellow-beaked, brilliant blue plumage bristling from the cuffs and collar of his custom-tailored dutysuit. His eyes were yellow, the pupils shimmering in tightly focused alertness. Yet he stared at Verrons without response.

Shrugging, Verrons slipped the orientation cartridge back into the viewer. A shrill banner of music issued from the speaker. "The deportee's first impression upon approaching Selmarri is that of a small globe covered almost entirely by dense jungle growth," the insistently optimistic voice informed him as the camera dropped toward a slowly emerging clearing set with opalescent domes. "Forty-two years ago Authority selected Selmarri as an isolation site because of its temperate climate and because of the absence of higher vertebrate life forms. Although jungle growth is heavy, confining residents to colony grounds, a sense of freedom has been attained through—"

Frowning, Verrons paced away from the viewer. *A sense of freedom.* But it was the substance which concerned him. And the tape made it clear that while the community provided security, comfort and a familiar social framework for the majority of its residents, personal mobility was limited. If dense jungle growth itself did not discourage residents from wandering from the immediate colony site, the colony administration did. Gov-

ernment was quasidemocratic, both the governing and the governed drawn from infectee ranks. Nevertheless limits were
plainly demarcated and travel beyond them discouraged.

And Verrons had never learned to honor limits. Early in life,
before he had ever come down from the hills of his native Eu-
bakker III to walk village streets, he had recognized boundaries
as walls cast up to restrict individual vision. Just as early in life
he had recognized a personal need not for security, not for comfort, not for salvation from hunger, cold or death but for free
movement, free vision. To exist within artificial boundaries
meant to endlessly examine man and his limitations. To live
without them was to study the contours of life as it ebbed and
flowed across the stars, cresting on this world, troughing on that,
entirely absent on another.

Restlessly Verrons paced off the limits of the isocube, a tall
man, his face burned dark on half a hundred worlds, his eyes instinctively seeking a distant focus. All they found today was the
Ehminheer in the adjacent isocube, his shimmering gaze intently
tracking Verrons as he paced.

Deliberately Verrons switched off the viewer and turned to
assess the yellow-eyed avian—although time had rendered avian
a misnomer. Once Ehminhee had been a forest world, its sul-
phur-yellow sky striped by the glossy white trunks of the perch
trees and, far overhead, laced by the soaring forms of Ehminheer. Then the trees had fallen victim to virus, their brittle
sunfeeders turning soft and black and falling to the forest floor.
Soon the trunks themselves had blackened and slumped in
death. Hungrily forest underbrush had swelled into a bristling,
thorny mat. And over a period of several centuries, Ehminheer
wings had evolved to no more than tiny nubs pulled taut by useless pectorals.

Ehminheer farsight and the keen Ehminheer navigational
sense remained intact, eventually making Ehminheer invaluable
members of Authority Fleet interstellar crews. Neither gift, however, had ever been successfully employed by Exploration Service. The veneer of civilization that Ehminheer donned along
with Authority uniform was dangerously thin. Until recently, Ehminheer had lived as solitary predators, restlessly wheeling the
yellow skies, beaks equally ready to slash prey or rival Ehminheer. Shipboard there was little to key alive ancient re-

sponses, but aground natural stimuli quickly eroded the tentatively established habits of civilization.

And when the Ehminheer set foot on Selmarri, when his shimmering gaze scratched passage up heavily mossed tree trunks to the sky?

Verrons dropped to the molded bench and rested his forehead in his hands, letting Mazaahr spots dance across his closed eyelids. Did his own civilized overlay extend any deeper than the Ehminheer's? The avian, in his natural environment, was driven by hunger and territorial instinct. Verrons' basic need was different, but it had propelled him from the arms of civilization across the star system. And the fact that he had functioned frictionlessly within the context of Exploration Service for twenty years was indicative of nothing. Explo had tapped Verrons' talents and met his need for mobility, for freedom from externally imposed bounds as fully as Fleet had served the Ehminheer's need to fly.

Grimly he activated the viewer again. Near the end of the tape, the camera and its human guide moved briefly out into the jungle. There damp black soil gave birth to dark tree trunks furred with velvety moss. Foliage blocked sunlight, casting multi-layered shadows upon the creepers that tangled treacherously across the jungle floor. And freedom was not illusion, not promise, but reality. Verrons ran the brief jungle passage twice, his eyes narrowed as he groped for a full sense of the environment. He would need to spend a few days at the colony to pick up necessary data on local predators, climate and natural foodstuffs. Then. . . . Pacing, his thoughts already ranging through dense undergrowth, he realized the Ehminheer stood at the shell of his own isocube, green-taloned digits spread flat against the transparent surface that separated them. His yellow gaze was intent upon the viewer.

Silently Verrons slid the viewer to the end of the molded counter and flicked the jungle alive again. As the narrator expounded, two pair of eyes evaluated shadow and undergrowth keenly. Two pair of eyes tested the jungle for peril, for promise. And when finally Verrons flicked the tape off and met the Ehminheer's shimmering gaze again, a flicker deep within the yellow eyes told him that despite the avian's refusal to activate the talk channel, communication had finally passed between them.

CHAPTER TWO

It was midafternoon when chill air revived Tiehl. His green-lidded eyes flashed open. The poorly fitted parachute harness bit deeply into his pectorals, but that was minor irritation compared to the spike of rage that crystallized in his throat with returning consciousness, jagged, ready to slash cartilage and flesh and let his pale Ehminheer's blood spray death across the still indistinct junglescape below. With a cry, he twisted his crested head. But the technician who had fogged his isocube with the choking gas that had immobilized him was beyond reach. The ship that had dropped him already receded into the sunshot reaches of the stratosphere, the Authority symbol glimmering blue on its silver flank. Except for the human who twisted to life in his own harness meters below, Tiehl was alone, the icy air of altitude biting his glossy lids and rime-slapping his lightly-downed face.

The assault roused him to the full heat of rejection. Ehminheer were not susceptible to bloodblossom. The isolation of the characteristic ciliated microorganisms in an Ehminheer's pastel blood was unprecedented. Yet he had seen the evidence himself. The diagnosing officer had projected slides on a treated wall and hundreds of tiny organisms had swum to life. Stunned, Tiehl had immediately been quarantined in the isolation wing of Britthold. And now the isolation colony Selmarri Home lay below.

Straining, Tiehl could see it through broken cloud. He rejected its reality with a bitter cry, whipping his indignant yellow-irised gaze wider over the vista. The world he settled toward was as dark with jungle as the orientation tapes had indicated. Quickly he brought his farsight to focus and swept the panorama of jungle and distant mountains. Peering intently, he detected a steep-sided mesa rising from the tangle of vegetation halfway between the colony directly below and the mountain range. On its flattened pinnacle was set a complex of pink structures that caught afternoon sunlight and shattered it to rosy fire. Tiehl adjusted his vision to define greater detail. From the center of the complex, a single soaring tower pierced sky. Tiehl twisted against the parachute harness, his heart suddenly surging with an unanticipated primal outpouring. The tower impaled his vision, a massive marble trunk. Instinctively Tiehl's feet clawed air, reaching for purchase.

But the mesa was many kilometers mountainward of his trajectory, and the chute homer would not let him leap sky toward the pink prominence. And as he scoured the tantalizing marble perch for full detail, a disturbing element appeared in the distant sky. A single form darted the puffy clouds mountainward of the mesa, throwing a swiftly moving shadow against the white of cloud. Tiehl strained, but he was able to distinguish nothing beyond the fact that the form flew.

That was enough. Abruptly, of its own volition, Tiehl's entire body mobilized, crest flaring, beak clacking. Straining, he flexed the muscles that should have set his own wings to flight. But he had no wings. Even the muscles that should have spread them were generations withered. Tiehl's legs pumped air furiously, trying to launch him against the distant form, but the homer anchored him to a plumb line of descent, and the flying form had already joined its shadow in the arms of cloud. An involuntary cry of indignation broke from Tiehl's throat. From below, the human peered up at Tiehl as the human's feet sank into cloud.

Moments later, Tiehl's feet slapped cloud. He inhaled the chill air, trying to dispel the singing fury of his aroused instincts. With a soft gobble, he regained control of renegade limbs. But the intensity of the total response was not so easily dampened. It continued to suffuse him. When he broke cloud cover moments later, the human's parachute was already spread across the dark soil below. Other humans surrounded the cleared circle of ground where he had landed. Tiehl's feet arched instinctively and he landed running, a hoarse dive-cry hawking from his throat. Startled humans swept aside, but Tiehl's swiftly collapsing chute tangled around a stack of shipping crates, yanking him to the ground.

A moment's stunned silence followed his swift scramble back to his feet. Then a plump capon forged way through the group of humans and approached, his face ashimmer with perspiration. "I have the safety key to your harness, Technician k'Obrohms, if you would flip up the lock shield."

Tiehl complied and when the harness was unlocked he shed it and turned back to whip a green-hooded gaze at the assemblage. The human had been freed of harness too. "I am Head Resident Davis Dublin," the plump man informed them both hurriedly. "We have just received a very optimistic report on progress toward the cure. We receive a full status-of-research communiqué each drop day, you see. But you'll hear more about that later, when you are settled into quarters."

"Will I?" Tiehl demanded. Peering around, still fueled by the glandular distillate of instinctual response, he made quick appraisal of his immediate surroundings. The target circle was located half a kilometer beyond the collection of milky domes that comprised Selmarri Home. Gravel walks connected the domes and planting beds contained individual specimens of indigenous plants. The damp tangle of the jungle was held back by broad swaths of scorched soil.

Briefly Tiehl's gaze intersected the dark eyes of the human who had been dropped with him. Ignoring an unspoken question, Tiehl turned and scrambled up the rank of packing crates his parachute had caught upon and flared his farsight wide. It was obstructed on all sides by jungle and cloud. But he knew in which direction the mesa lay. The sun's position as he descended, the angle of its rays as they shattered from the pink prominence were clearly recorded in his mind. So was his intended course of action, suddenly a function not so much of individual decision as of racial necessity.

He descended from the crates, chuckling uneasily as curious humans edged near. Dublin pushed forward again, anxiously. "I don't know how complete a briefing you received aboard Britthold, Ehminheer. I'm sure you know that the bloodblossom organism entered the human bloodstream half a century ago on Mazaahr V. A volcanic world, I'm told, where the stones grumble and roll, half alive. Even semi-aware, according to some.

"Unfortunately before it was realized that the infection existed, the microorganism had been carried across the entire galaxy by the first infectees. Bloodblossom: I like to visualize it as a marine entity progressing through a series of interconnected tributaries—our own human bloodstream. Whenever it enters a fresh human—and now Ehminheer—streamlet, it lies relatively dormant for nine years. But in the tenth it blooms, with invariably fatal results. And unfortunately the disease is contagious even through the extended dormant period. Only the fact that such a very small percentage of the human population is susceptible and that the disease can be detected from its earliest stages by standard blood-testing procedures has prevented a broad-sweeping tragedy."

Weeks of confinement had acid-bathed Tiehl's speech, stripping it of tonal refinements. "With me it has swept broad enough," he snapped irritably.

"Of course!" Dublin's mobile features flowed in instant empathy. "But you have the same assurance that sustains each of us here, Technician. Authority personnel are at work around the clock in a dozen locations, trained men and women dedicating themselves—"

Impatiently Tiehl slashed air with his beak. "I was told all that aboard Britthold. But no one has ever claimed that the human cure will be equally safe for Ehminheer."

Dublin's features fell. "There are fundamental metabolic differences, I suppose. But if the ultimate serum does not—"

"If it does not, how much time, how many personnel will Authority allot to manufacturing a separate serum for the only Ehminheer ever infected?" Tiehl demanded.

Dublin did not have to reply. The answer seared air between them: little, few.

And there was nothing to hold Tiehl here, nothing to anchor

him to a colony of humans, not even for a single night. Sighting
the pink prominence had brought his intentions to a peak of urgency. His talons closed on the chest of his orange duty suit. Impatiently he parted the stick-plaques. When he ripped the orange fabric away, blue body-down emerged, dark and thick
across his chest and abdomen, flaring to feathery luxuriance at
the genitals, then pale, lighter, tapering from his full chest down
his lean, spidery limbs.

His abrupt disrobing visibly agitated Davis Dublin. "I can see
you are anxious to be taken to quarters, Technician. We brought
only one vehicle, intended to transport your special furnishings.
However—"

"I do not intend to quarter here."

Dublin's plump body stiffened. "Technician, no exceptions can
be made. Quarters have been provided and your own special
furnishings will be installed well before dark."

Tiehl chortled, gesturing impatiently toward the trees. "Every
furnishing I require has already been provided—there."

Dublin cast an unbelieving glance into the encroaching jungle.
"K'Obrohms, we are all prepared to assist you in your adaptation
to the community. If you must—"

But Tiehl had no time to hear him out. It was midafternoon already. Soon daylight would begin to fade and somnolence would
overtake him. He aborted the human's insistent monologue with
a slashing clack of his beak. Dublin froze, perspiration turned to
rime on his staring face. Tiehl wheeled and paling humans
parted for him like a curtain. He sprinted easily from the target
area.

"K'Obrohms!"

Tiehl did not respond. A blue dart, he crossed scorched earth,
ignoring the telltale flashes of alien illumination that momentarily obscured his vision. Beyond the colony, the trees were
mighty gnarled bulwarks smothered in moss and vine. The smell
of the jungle was thick and green, the air heavy with moisture,
dark with shadow. Brush grew in bristling clumps that bullied
aside occasional soil-hugging advances of tender vegetation. Bitterness and elation hawked from Tiehl's throat in tandem. His
years with Authority Fleet had provided him with dazzling mobility. He had unreeled his farvision across the universe and
charted his ship's course into the heart of the unknown. But in
all his years of service he had never felt soil underfoot, nor had

he ever raced between massive trees, any one his own for the taking. Halting, he tossed back his head and flared his farvision up through thick foliage. He clawed sky with it, tore at cloud and mist.

But only figuratively. Dense foliage obstructed his vision. The withered muscles that should have swelled deep across his chest contracted spasmodically. Squawking, clacking, his cry acrid with elation, Tiehl ravaged the damp tangle of vegetation with his running body.

His initial euphoria was brief. Isocube confinement had bled his muscles of tone. Too quickly his legs were weak, his breath painful. He launched himself at the moss-slimed trunk of a massive tree, grappling his way through close-grown limbs. Minutes later he sat at tree's top, a slash of blue against the grey sky. His chest flared as he fanned his farsight toward the distant mountains, hungry for a second sighting of the pink prominence that had inflamed him earlier. But this bottom layer of troposphere was too dense. He could see neither mountain, mesa nor rising pink structure. He could see only leafmass and cloud.

And despite the bright prospect that lured him, he could see emptiness in his future. Somewhere beyond Selmarri, space still stretched, its star-spattered walls towering into infinity. Somewhere Authority ships still moved, crewed by humans, Ehminheer and half a dozen other, lesser species. But Technician Tiehl k'Obrohms would not harry infinity across the galaxy again. He would not whip his instrument-amplified farsight through star swarms and vast dust clouds. Disease had crushed his Fleet prospects, shattering his ship-wings and blinding his instrument-eyes.

Helplessly his lids snapped shut. A mourning cluck, deep and liquid, bubbled in his throat. On Ehminhee the ancient forests were dead, the gaudy wings withered. And now space as well as sky was denied him. Grief clucked thick and wet in his throat. He struggled to partition it, to extinguish it, but it possessed him.

Presently however its flow was interrupted. "K'Obrohms?"

Tiehl's crest flared. The voice was human, young to judge from its timbre. Composing himself, Tiehl swung down through the tree. A youth in ice-blue coverall stood beneath the tree, his hair white, his eyes snow-pale. His face was a white circlet targeted against jungle shadow. Unexpectedly, stinging acridity flooded

Tiehl's throat, the onset of hunt fury. His beak clacked involuntarily.

The reaction was as unwelcome as it was unanticipated. Humans were not prey for Ehminheer, not even when they appeared in the guise of the snow-savage. Swiftly Tiehl spidered back up the tree. Swinging limb to limb, he threaded himself beyond reach of temptation, a gaudy floss of color that disfigured the muted afternoon pattern of shadow on leaf.

When the bitter taste of hunt fury receded, he taloned back to the treetops. He snapped his lids shut and hunched tight, unsettled by the events of the past hour. Confined aboard Britthold, he had planned his escape from the infectee colony coolly, with reason. Human companionship held no compelling interest for him, nor any benefit once he learned to feed himself safely from the jungle. That would require a few days, perhaps a week. But, descending, he had sighted the stone perch and his long-buried primal instincts had betrayed him, puppet-stringing him prematurely through the jungle on twin leads of hunt fury and perch passion. Slowly he unlidded his gaze and peered with forced calm into the late afternoon sky. If he returned to the colony long enough to learn what local game he could safely consume. . . . But his breath hissed noisily through his beak as long-dormant glands fed fresh excitation into his bloodstream.

Then he heard the crackle of boots beneath his tree. The human from Britthold had joined the snow savage youth. Both peered up at him with tight-lipped keenness. Quickly he noted that the youth wore a single heat pistol at his waist, the other man two. "Resident Dublin asked us to tell you that you are not required to return to the colony immediately if you need time to get your thoughts in order," the older human called up the tree. "But we are required to return you before noon tomorrow."

Had he misread the human's intentions shipboard? Warily Tiehl handed himself down to the lower limbs of the tree. "And if I do not choose to return with you?" he probed.

An ironic smile touched the human's lips. "I told Dublin I could bring you back if anyone could." His glance, flickering away from Tiehl, evaluated deepening shadow. "Apparently there are boundary markers out here somewhere, red banners mounted on metal poles. So long as you don't lead us past those, we're within permitted bounds."

The snow-savage shook his head. "We crossed the boundary half an hour ago, Commander."

The older human's brows rose quizzically. "This close to camp? Not a very roomy run."

The youth spoke cautiously, his pale gaze shuttered. "Camp Authority discourages wandering. And few residents care to go even as far as the boundaries."

Again the older man's smile was ironic. "Then we could consider ourselves lost—if we didn't have Ehminheer to chart course back to camp. How long have you been assigned to Selmarri Home, Wells?"

Meeting the other man's gaze, the youth weighed his reply carefully. "I was dropped three months ago."

The older man grunted. "From one of the snow worlds, obviously. Did they net you on Ice House II or Wolfman's Point?"

The youth stiffened visibly. "I am a seventh-generation Talberonese. Before blood screening, I completed my radius-five survival trek. I was one of fifty selected to make the radius-six trek next year, to qualify to enter Academy." Bitterness tinged his voice. "This year now."

Tiehl skipped down a branch, his interest engaged. So the youth was not a barbarous descendant of the survivors of early exploration parties to the snow worlds. Instead he was birth-heir to the legend of Talberon, a harsh mining world of glaciers, mountains and snow plains which the Talberonese intended to eventually transform from cold hell to garden planet. *And why had not his own Ehminhee dedicated itself to educating breeders of virus-resistant perch trees?* But the answer to that lay in his own glands. Too few generations separated the Ehminheer from their solitary predatory state. Ehminheer were just now learning to cooperate with their own kind. Carefully Tiehl crept another branch lower.

"Trek? Then you've had a fair amount of field-survival experience. Have you had much chance to use it here?"

Again the youth's gaze was shuttered. "A group of us was permitted to explore to the north of the colony last month," he said noncommittally.

"And you found?"

"Very little beyond the ruins of a village. We—"

Sharply the older human expressed Tiehl's own surprise. "Village? According to the orientation tape, there is no higher life form on Selmarri. In fact—"

"There is not now," the youth corrected. "But the planet was inhabited once—by humanoids from all indications. We found a few small stone structures, most of them collapsed, and a scatter of implements and artifacts—but nothing to give us a clue to what happened to the inhabitants of the village."

"No remains?"

"None. We hardly had time to make a complete search. The site was extensively overgrown, and Dublin only gave us five days. It wasn't enough to yield anything substantial."

"And you never returned to make an extended study of the site?"

Wells frowned, his white brows drawing together. "Dublin had never authorized a group to pass the boundaries before. He's made it clear he won't grant permission again."

"Casualties?"

He shrugged tautly. "Presumably. We woke up one morning a man short. We never found him, although there was no sign of violence. Another member of the group contracted a fungus condition that hasn't yielded to treatment."

The other man grunted noncommittally. "And no one knows how long the putated humanoid race has been extinct?"

"Nothing appears in the records beyond the fact that it once existed. Apparently Authority performed only a superficial planet study before setting up the isolation colony." Briefly the youth considered. "Do I understand correctly that you're an officer of Authority Fleet?"

The other man shook his head. "K'Obrohms served with Fleet as navigation technician. I'm Cheram Verrons, Authority Exploration Service, retired. I spent my service years leading study parties aboard peripheral planets, dealing primarily with grant groups from academic centers and resource survey parties." Frowning, he turned to Tiehl. "Ehminheer, did you sight anything of interest from the air?"

Involuntarily Tiehl's beak snapped shut. But he could not hoard information, not if he wanted the human as temporary ally against the jungle. With effort he forced his reluctant body to the ground. "Between here and the mountains there is a group of structures," he said.

"More ruins?" Verrons probed.

"They did not appear ruined. And they are not primitive. They are raised on a tabled land mass, constructed of pink stone. The central structure—" But he bit off his words sharply. Initial cooperation was necessary; total betrayal was not.

Both human gazes were tightly focused on his face. "How far is this group of structures?" Wells demanded.

"I've never traveled jungle before," Tiehl said defensively. "If you want the distance in kilometers—"

"I'm more interested in your intentions," Verrons interrupted. "Are you planning to set course toward this set of structures immediately? And if so, have you learned something about local game and vegetation that I don't know, Ehminheer? Something that will permit you to live off the land without poisoning yourself?"

Tiehl's eyes shimmied wildly at the challenge. The human had touched the very heart of his quandary. He sought the unpromising vegetation, hunger already making his talons curl. He knew absolutely nothing of this world. Here even fresh-killed game could be lethal to an Ehminheer.

As if reluctantly, Wells spoke to Verrons' question. "Several of the early residents were biologists from the second Mazaahr V study team. Before they died they classified almost every plant and animal out here and performed extensive tissue analyses. I've had three months to study their compilation."

Verrons' dark brows arched. "And you have studied it?"

Defiantly the youth met his probing gaze. "I've committed it to memory—text, illustrations, even the index." He studied the older man tensely. "I suppose you have a strong background in jungle survival."

Verrons nodded. "But from what you tell me, I won't get a chance to exercise it if I wait for Davis Dublin's permission."

"You won't. He has an effective-life term as head resident and he doesn't blossom out for another six years."

And suddenly, without warning, Tiehl found himself impaled upon twin gazes, dark and pale. Their intensity discomposed him. A series of harsh chuckles rattled from his throat. "I do not intend to live in a plastic bubble," he declared defensively.

"Could you keep him alive out here, Wells?"

The youth's hair slid forward across his forehead, a smooth banner of white, as he nodded. "If he can tell me what elements of a normal human diet he can handle, yes. Almost half the species out here are edible. I've done extensive reading in human nutrition since I arrived and paper-structured what should be a safe local diet."

"With an eye to deserting Selmarri Home?" Verrons probed.

"Eventually," the youth admitted.

"For any particular reason?"

Wells' tone was defensive. "To make a substitute radius-six. I planned to triple the distance covered, to compensate for the milder conditions here."

"And then? When you had completed your trek?"

The youth shook his head. "I hadn't planned beyond that."

Verrons nodded, his gaze passing from Ehminheer to Talberonese and back again. "Then it appears to me that we have interlocking purposes. Wells has had a trek in mind. K'Obrohms has sighted a suitable destination. And I'm prepared to exercise everything I know about jungle survival. If there is no need to return to camp for supplies, spare clothes, medicinals—"

"I've already planted a survival kit a little south of here," Wells volunteered. "A few implements, first aid supplies, several cartons of nutrition caps. And we have heat pistols for protection —or for cooking game."

"I'd almost forgotten." Verrons unbuckled the extra holster from his waist. "Dublin issued one of these for you, Ehminheer."

Involuntarily Tiehl retreated from the proffered weapon. Hunt fury had very nearly driven him against the Talberonese less than an hour before. If he had been armed. . . . "I carry my own weapons," he said, flexing his talons.

Shrugging, Verrons buckled the weapon back at his waist. He turned back to Wells. "Dublin wasn't expecting us back much before noon tomorrow. Will he dispatch a search party when we don't return?"

"He may but he doesn't have anyone competent in jungle tracking," the Talberonese responded promptly. "And the monitor ship won't drop personnel to search for a group of three."

"Then we can travel at our own pace," Verrons concluded. "Ehminheer, do you want to accompany us to retrieve Wells' survival pack?"

Tiehl peered at them through the rapidly deepening gloom of the jungle. "I sleep at dusk," he reminded them.

Verrons' eyes narrowed. "You require sunlight to maintain wakefulness?"

Tiehl nodded, his tinted eyelids already heavy. "Shipboard my day can be extended by use of artificial lights. Here I will be somnolent once the sun sets."

Verrons turned to Wells. "We'll have to pick up your kit and make our way back here for the night then. Wake us at dawn, Ehminheer. We want to put ourselves well ahead of anyone Dublin sends out."

When they had disappeared into the dense growth, Tiehl climbed back into his tree and threaded himself upward limb to limb. Settling to a high perch, he closed his eyes. Immediately images of the slender pink tower blazed before him. He counterposed images of the humans and himself against it. A warning rattle sounded in his throat. No Ehminheer shared his perch, not with members of his own species, not with members of any other species. If necessary he would lead the humans to the mesa, but he would never permit them to claim the pink shaft from him. That resolved, he hunched at tree's top, his eyes drawing dusk from the sky and thickening it into night. Briefly his throat opened and he mourned his ship again, clucking and cawing his melancholy, warming himself with it. Then the last faint illumination faded from the sky and he slept.

CHAPTER THREE

Sometimes when night closed its jungled paws around Aleida, when she crouched silent and hard-eyed between her mother and the stone wall until sleep could wrestle her resistant senses to oblivion, a tormenting dream overtook her. In this dream, she walked under the sullen morning sky toward the greylizard nestings, a trapping net and game bag in her hands. As she neared the mudbank, flashes of brilliance suddenly lanced down at her, bathing her in sensation so intense, so unexpected, that she clawed at her glowing face and opened her mouth in an agonized scream. Her cry, however, was always silent. Dropping the trapping net, flinging aside the woven game bag, she ran.

She ran, driven, until the torturing light withdrew into the sky. Then Aleida heard a bellowing cry echo toward her, mocking laughter from a distant throat. It lay somewhere above, muffled in grey morning cloud. In response Aleida's body arched and her own throat opened with a terrible thick cry. The two cries joined, intertwining sinuously like streamsnakes mating on the surface of the water, and miraculously Aleida's feet left the ground. A quick downward glance revealed that the ground receded beneath her.

A quick upward glance showed that the dark underbelly of cloud lowered toward her. Aleida felt its dark weight descending. Her cry withered to a thread. Her only defense was to clasp her fingers above her head in a very special configuration that seemed to come to her from another time, another circumstance.

It was defense enough. The clouds ceased to lower. Instead Aleida pursued them upward until her face slapped into their moist underbelly. Blinded, she rose through the damp-clotted air.

She emerged on a plain of blinding white. There a different order of light from any she had ever before experienced advanced upon her, clean, hard and yellow, born of sun, undiluted by atmospheric contaminant. Its stiff beams scrubbed her flesh, searing and abrading it. She threw back her head, another cry erupting from her throat.

This cry was not of pain but of fusion. With the bristled touch of sunlight, insulating layers of flesh were scrubbed from her, and she, sunlight and sky were inexplicably fused into one. Aleida found herself suddenly infinite and tall, limitless in the radiant force of her energy. Breath became superfluous, sensation diffuse. Her earthly vision blurred, but she knew everything, knew infinity through the bobbing, busy molecules of her airy body. She fell across the world in yellow sheets, she shone with radiance unmatched, she swept at land and water with tearing winds. She looked out at her universe through an aura of orange brilliance.

While she existed in unity, she arched and dove, then tossed back her head and arrowed upward into the highest regions of the sky. As she soared, a second cloudcry reached her. It was not the thick mocking laughter of the fat lower clouds. The cry was piercing and sweet, drawing her helpless in its thrall.

Toward what goal? How could she know when the search was never consummated? Urgency drove her too swiftly. She flashed at the high cirrus, outspeeding the forces that gave her flight. Suddenly the power of flight failed and gravity wrenched at her. Panicked, she loosed her hands from the special configuration and she fell, a foreign object plummeting through the thin air.

She woke with a shrieking start that brought mutters from her parents.

They did not wake. Her parents seldom stirred or sat during the dark hours. They huddled flaccid and still around their pallid dreams like small animals. Sitting, the sense of dream still panoplied about her, Aleida measured herself against them. She was taller than either parent already. And she was different from them, from her siblings, from all the others who slept in the stonewarren, in other ways too. Her hair was rough, a wiry mass that bristled out from her head, while theirs was limp and fine. When she walked, when she ran, her movements expressed an urgency that had never driven any other member of the little band, even in youth.

Troubled, Aleida leapt up from her sleeping mat and picked her way across sleeping bodies. Emerging from the stonewarren, she raced under the gloomy predawn sky. But grey layers of cloud separated her from the bright regions of dream. She was outcast on the ground, no longer a part of anything but herself.

She returned to the dim stonewarren then and sat on her mat watching the other members of the small band that lived among the tumbled stones of the dead city. They were not many and during their waking hours they scurried like so many timid animals. Even their speech was plaintive, like the brush-call of a lonely stickletail. None of them, she knew, had ever ridden the clouds by night. And none of them had known the other dreams either, the darker and bloodier dreams of strange powers. She was the only one. She was apart from all the rest. How much apart and why she did not know yet but one night, surely, her dreams would tell her. *One night.* Hugging herself against doubt, she lay back to doze again.

Later morning poked dim fingers into the stonewarren, tracing patterns in the dust on the floor. The air was rank with the night's confinement. When the others chattered out to meet the day, Aleida hunched in mutinous silence while her mother roped and knotted her hair. The painstaking taming of her hair was a ritual of her new maturity, a maturity she scorned.

Her hair scorned it too. By the time she reached the mudbanks, it had swollen free of the knot—just as the night's dreamsense of power threatened to swell free of her mind. Last season, before her body had given sign of readiness, Aleida's sense of power had always evaporated with dawn. Now when she sat from sleep, it remained with her, a bare foggy tendril that expanded until it was a pressuring internal cloud. If she ever found the mechanism for releasing it, it would mist the acrid air of the warren, sheathing her in opacity.

Even contained it clouded her sight and altered her perceptions, heightening her realization that even her thoughts were not of the same order as any other's here. That became increasingly clear as she matured.

Now she waded downstream, scanning the warm mudbanks for nestings. Her morning pleasure was to crack brittle-shelled greylizard eggs and to let their salty viscosity coat the inside of her mouth, then ooze down her throat. Afterward she liked to scrub away the salty thickness with stalks of bitter-grass uprooted from the edges of the mudbank. But this morning her attention was distracted. Earlier she had heard footsteps in the undergrowth as she raced from the stonewarren. Now the same footsteps sucked mud behind her. Every time she turned to dart back notice of her displeasure, their perpetrator slipped into shadow.

But not before his thrusting hips had gestured her his intent.

To that she did not react with any of the emotions the other females reported. Her organs did not clench in a bursting wrench of excitation. Her skin did not burn, her eyes sear. Certainly she felt no ripple of pleasure course up her spine. No. She knew her father had sent her brothers telling of her new desirability when her readiness first evidenced itself. She knew the ritual message they chanted into male ears. She had countered by dispatching her own message to male eyes: *I am not receptive, not to you. Not to any of you.*

Now one of the band's males followed her anyway. She halted and seared the bankside trees with her scorn. But when she moved on, his footsteps continued to dog her. Aggravated, she felt her annoyance and her still-swollen sense of dream-power combine and sweep quickly to storm stage. And although she experienced her power as an inner cloud, its true colors were darker.

Bloodier.

She flashed a hot-eyed gaze over the turbid stream, then behind. Deliberately she twisted her stiff hair back into a knot. It was the ritual signal of female acquiescence.

She heard his excited titter. She teased him then, slapping

along the mudbank until she found sign of a fresh nesting. When her shadow fell over the tiny hole, a greylizard arrowed out and slid into the muddy stream. She waited, then knelt and sent two fingers probing the grass-lined interior of the nest. Her fingertips encountered eggshell.

Darting provocative glances back, Aleida made a leisurely breakfast: two salty eggs, several clumps of bitter-grass, a handful of yellow minna bulbs, a long drink of cool water. Then she washed her hands and face, patted mud into her hair to hold it, and strolled on her way. Her pace, her posture, flaunted the dark swellings of her new maturity.

And how could he know, following, that Aleida was not a little lizard for his game bag? That instead of tender morsel, she was stalking hunter and he the prey? They crossed the stream and moved into dense jungle. Spreading branches created a river of shadow that flowed torpidly beneath the trees, eddying sluggishly in the brush. The leaf-filtered light that submerged her matched the shade of Aleida's feeling, dark, drowning. Bloody images flickered from the deepest recesses of her mind.

Other things surfaced too as she led him toward the mating bower, things she had never before salvaged from dream into consciousness: postures, stances, configurations. Moving through the brush, Aleida's muscles rippled in new knowledge, bringing her sense of power to fresh, sharp focus.

The power existed. It lived somewhere inside her—and also somewhere outside her. It flowed, a diffuse wash having neither destination nor organization. But there were means for giving it coherence, for shaping it into a beam that would flash and sear, that she could wield like a weapon. She held those means within her own muscles. An arching of her back, a stretching of leg muscle, a tortured twining of fingers. . . .

Shadow deepened. Undergrowth caught at Aleida's feet. Pads of flocculent moss swelled thick and soft from tree trunks. It was convention that when the female crawled through the narrow tunnel-mouth of the mating bower, the male would wait an interval before following. Then he would linger in the plaited tunnel, emerging in the main chamber only when his eyes had adapted to darkness.

The bower nestled beneath protective trees. Aleida entered and waited, her body tense with expectation. By the time she heard the faint snap of stem under the male's knees, she stood at the center of the moss-choked bower, soft leaf-rot fluffing her feet, her body arched back in a very special way. She had torn her hair from its knot and whipped it into a stiff halo around her head. Then when she saw his eyes gleaming, her arms rose, hands sweeping high, fingers dancing like streamsnakes, boneless, predatory.

He reached the chamber and his glistening eyes widened to startlement, then fear. Aleida recognized him immediately: Pystarr, her eldest brother's agemate. Now she looked at him through surging veils of power that suddenly hung in the close air like sheets of orange light. They moved and swept from her dancing fingertips, vivid, vibrant. She was a being, her eyes, her stance told him, while he was an animal. And she did not mate with animals.

The terrified Pystarr tried to turn in the tunnel mouth, tried to voice his fear. All he uttered was a squeal. The tunnel heaved, rattled and burst. Emerging, Pystarr shrilled away into the brush, his stubby legs pumping as if possessed.

Aleida scrambled free, her fingers darting angrily, her own mind suddenly charged with baffled impotence. For with Pystarr's squeal of fear, the veils of light had winked out. So had her sense of the ability to command them up again, instantly. Fiercely Aleida arched her body and let her arms sweep and writhe again. No orange curtains danced around her. And after a brief fury of frustration she realized—too late—that when Pystarr reached the warren, he would chatter and cry to his agemates about what had happened, and from them word would infiltrate every segment of the small band until everyone knew.

Knew what? What unnatural power had she summoned up? And why had it been invested in her? She had no answer for any of those questions. She had seen dread in her mother's eyes this season. And she knew there were certain dark secrets that had not been shared with her yet. They were secrets that were traditionally whispered from adult to maturing young, creating a thread of fear that wove all generations into one. But Aleida had no hint of the content of the secrets. And after Pystarr told what she had done, would her mother whisper the secrets to her? If they were withheld, what did it mean? Aleida touched her stiff hair, her sense of apartness an opening chasm. She had never known any people but these, although she knew other bands haunted the ruins of other cities. If she was not of these people, if they would not share the secrets with her, who or what was she? Did she stand alone in this world?

She thought for a long time outside the deserted mating bower. Finally she elected to protect herself in the only way she could devise. When Pystarr's chatter reached the adults, Aleida would claim that she had never seen Pystarr today, that she had been nowhere near the mating bower. Instead, she would say, she had been hunting in the dense brush at the other side of the stream. Pystarr slandered her from thwarted desire. Everyone knew she would not mate with him, not until he became more a man, less a stickletail.

Accordingly she ran through the trees and waded the stream, seeking game for her bag, game to bolster her claim. Shortly after sun's zenith, she carried her filled bag back to the stone-warren. Her mother sat on the rubbled plaza, tiny brown hands moving swiftly, now selecting a reed from the bundle beside her, now wetting it against her tongue, now working it into the pattern of the sleeping mat she wove. She was small and dark with age. Even the mud dressing she worked into her hair every morning failed to give it body. She peered up at Aleida's approach. "What are you bringing, Ale'a?"

"This! I have spent the entire morning hunting. There is enough here for everyone today." Before the little woman could question her further, Aleida tossed the bag at her feet and darted away. Now let Pystarr squeal!

Beyond the stonewarren, the deep tunneling basement where the band slept, a single tree grew from the broken surface of the plaza. Exhausted, Aleida scrambled into a high mossed crook to snatch an early afternoon drowse.

A short time later she woke abruptly. A voice shrilled below. Aleida looked down to see the smallest of her litter-brothers fleeing across the plaza. Quickly Aleida swung from her place. "Where are you running, lizard?"

"Devils!" he yelped, his eyes distended. "We have seen devils coming through the trees. Hide!" Darting away, he disappeared into the nearest doorway as if pursued.

Alerted, Aleida distinguished other cries of fear. Quickly she abandoned the tree and pattered to the spot where she had left her mother. She found only strands of reed. But from the stone-warren she heard frightened voices. "Devils . . . running this way! Demons unleashed from the jungle!" She peered around, but she had no time to choose her course before an electrifying cry reached her from the jungle beyond the plaza. It clawed her, harsh and deep. She whipped around.

Three creatures stepped to the plaza. They were so alien, their appearance so unexpected, that Aleida's eyes did little more than slide over their utter improbability. Suddenly her mouth was useless, her own startled shrills lost inside her.

Her feet were less helpless. After a brief, frozen pause, they moved. Aleida bounded away and leapt into the stonewarren. She found its musty chambers illuminated by pale fingers of midday sunlight—and by fear that glistened in the air, its odor choking sweet.

Fingers tugged her. "You saw the devils, too, Ale'a?"

"I saw them," she panted. But her initial panic dissolved quickly as she crouched with the others. From outside she heard the harsh voice again, then another, milder voice.

Excited whispers ran through the warren. "Do you hear it? It speaks words—devil words."

Her brother tugged her arm. "You hear it speak, Ale'a?"

"I hear." She also heard the scuffle of feet on stone, the rattle of rock. And she heard her own intentions speaking clearly from within her. For she was no animal to cower in a fear-misted cellar. When both voices passed, Aleida bobbed up and ran to the door. A single frightened plea, her mother's, followed her from the stonewarren.

Silently, dodging wall to wall, she trailed the intruders through the rubble-strewn plazas. The taller was an unsettling blue being with head, arms and legs exaggerated in proportion. His companions had body form and facial features very closely resembling her own. The slighter wore a pale blue garment that covered most of his body, leaving only his strangely pallid hands and face exposed. His smooth white hair caught the sun. The second was taller, heavier and darker, clad in brown. But that was only physical appearance. It told her almost nothing. Where did these three come from? Why were they here?

Silently she followed them through the city. Talking, gesturing, they explored abandoned stonewarrens and climbed piles of tumbled stone, casting alien silhouettes against the afternoon sky. The farther Aleida followed them, the greater their disparity seemed. The tallest was brilliant-hued, his movements abrupt. The others were slower, more deliberate.

It was the tallest who made the kill when, near the far reach of the plaza, their approach sent a stonehog yammering from cover. With a swift surge, the blue creature rode the screaming hog to the ground and slashed its throat with the horny weapon that protruded from his gaudy face. Then he skinned the hog with swift precision and the three divided the kill. The slightest pulled an instrument from the waist of his garment and pointed it. A streak of orange crackled at his meat. Aleida moved nearer, drawing a strange odor from the air.

They sat to eat. Abruptly, partway through his meal, the tallest being tossed aside his portion of meat and darted at Aleida's hiding place, uttering a paralyzing cry. Aleida's reaction was instinctive. She sprang from hiding. Her back arched and her leg muscles stretched, bringing her to her toes. Her arms flared up, fingers writhing. Through surging orange veils she saw the blue being halt, saw the other beings rise from where they sat. Her fingers danced, pulling skeins of light from the air, drawing them into heavy sheets, hurling them like game nets at prey.

None of the three fell. None writhed and cried—as her dreams had told her all should. None twitched and convulsed in agony. Neither did they flee. They stared at her, frozen. Then the tallest moved toward her again, his long limbs flexing in exaggerated slow motion. Immediately Aleida's confidence was shattered. Did she only imagine she commanded orange veils from the air? But Pystarr had seen them. Pystarr had fled them only a few hours before.

Pystarr had not fallen screaming to the ground, had he? So perhaps he had only run from the unexpectedness of her bizarre posture in the dim bower, from the scare-halo of her hair. Aleida's arms fell. With a yelp, she turned and bounded away across the plaza.

Their awful voices followed her, one shrieking, two calling. She successfully evaded them, finally throwing herself into an abandoned stonewarren. There she lay for a long time after their voices faded into the distance. The thick air grew stagnant in her nostrils. Her sense of the power had been so real.

It *was* real, an insistent sense of her own being contended. The strangers were simply immune—because they *were* strangers, creatures never intended to respond to her net of light. Under stimulus of this reassurance, Aleida rallied and crawled from the warren. The strangers had gone, leaving only a spatter of blood and a clatter of bones at the perimeter of the plaza. Swiftly Aleida ran back to her band's stonewarren and flung herself through the rubble-choked door. Her parents, her brothers, the others still crouched in the shadows. They had dewed the subterranean chamber with the sweet odor of fear. It hung in the air, a choking mist.

"The devils?" old Narnar demanded, raising his head to peer fearfully at Aleida. His words ended with an anxious whine.

"They are gone!" she exulted.

"Gone? Gone?" It was a breathy whisper through the warren. Aleida's mother touched her arm. "They are gone?"

"Gone. Into the jungle," she boasted. Did it matter that they had not fled at her command?

A second word whispered in the air. "Back? Back? Will they come back?"

Aleida cast commanding eyes over their bedraggled heads. They were small, pitiful. For the first time she felt protective of them. "They will not come back here," she pronounced.

"No, no?" her mother pressed hopefully.

"They will not."

Her mother's hand crept up Aleida's shoulder. Quickly the little female withdrew it, spat on it, then reached up to pat Aleida's hair. "You did it, Ale'a?"

At the servile query, Aleida's charitable mood evaporated instantly. She leapt back from the damp caress, her back arching. Of their own volition her arms flashed up in the gesture she had employed twice already today.

Her mother's reaction—the sharp intake of breath, the sudden dark mist that glistened on her face—stopped her. Aleida jumped back, quelling her writhing muscles. *She had seen fear in her mother's eyes this season.* She realized now when she had seen it: when her mother had touched her and she had sprung away; when her mother had groomed her and she had spat; when her mother had whispered to her and she had answered with stinging words. Aleida fanned a gaze over the band. In almost every face she saw some reflection of her mother's fear.

A scalding surge of vindication swept her, heating her body to the fingertips. Her hair seemed to stiffen from her head and a soft sound moved up from her throat. It did not need to be loud or harsh, not when fear was already so plain in every face.

Driven, Aleida lunged for the door and flung herself into sunlight. Her eyes found the underside of cloud, sparse today, glinting white. She raced across the plaza and from her throat welled the cry she had uttered in dream a hundred times. It curled up the afternoon sky like a twining snake, sinuous, thick. Orange veils of power swept with it, whipping around it.

Today there was no answering cry from above. There was only sunlight on her shoulders and stone under her feet as she ran. For a while it was enough.

Then it was not. Urgently Aleida ran the ruined city twining her fingers in the special configuration she remembered from dream. She shrieked at the sky, she bellowed at the clouds, but she could not gain unity with the upper forces. She remained separate, cast down. Despairing, she pattered to the mudbank and splashed into the stream, determined to join the water's flow instead. A natural force in her own right, she would wash at the stream bed. She would gobble up dirt and mud, swirl around snake and lizard, drown them and gnaw the flesh from their fragile bones.

But despite the urgency of her need, water would not yield her its power. Enraged, Aleida ran from the stream and threw herself into the mudbank instead. She rubbed mud into her stiff hair. She rolled in it. It was thick and slippery and warm.

It was separate from her. She was separate from it. She was separate from everything, everyone.

Then a certain sensation demanded her attention. It was not related to water or mud, to cloud, wind or sunlight. It was related instead entirely to herself, to those organs which had not welcomed Pystarr's courtship. Now, unaccountably, they began to engorge and pulsate and send sprays of sweet agony through her entire body. *Why?* Driven by a new urgency, Aleida splashed clean in the stream and loped back toward the warrens. As she ran the sensation grew stronger, sweeter, overloading her nervous system and making her skin alternately ripple and draw.

When she neared the stonewarren, there was alarm again. Her people congregated on the plaza, shrilling in fright, pointing to the sky. "A devil comes there! A devil comes from the air!" Aleida halted and stared up, searching the clouds. She saw nothing, but the pulsation grew stronger. Impulsively she swept her arms together and twisted her fingers.

"Devil!" Her family tried to flee, but Aleida did not budge.

Her brothers tugged her arms, her mother squealed in panic, her father danced a futile little frenzy on the stone. Fear-ridden, they struggled to pull her to shelter. "Ale'a—come! Come with us! The devil!"

"No!" Her eyes, her hands were for the sky. Finally her resistance defeated them and they abandoned her, skittering to shelter after the other members of the band.

Then he came from the sky. At first he was no more than a silhouette against cloud, then he swooped lower and took flesh. He was darker than Aleida, much darker, his arms and legs longer and more muscular, the fingers of his hands—twined! And in a configuration Aleida knew. Her own arms swept together again. Her writhing fingers imitated his and her legs stretched as her entire body arched for the air. As he drew near her need was great, her need was terrible. It seared every nerve ending, consumed every muscle fiber.

With a crackle of air, he arced across the plaza, low enough for her to see his face, to meet his eyes. They glowed a devil's green, and between them, recessed into the almost black flesh of his forehead, was a large green crystal that flashed with the same brilliance as his eyes. Briefly it swept a swath of green light over her.

Despite her impassioned effort, Aleida's feet would not leave stone. She uttered a cry that tore the air, an inarticulate demand. He did not acknowledge it. Instead his green gaze briefly scorched her and then he swooped back upward. His black form shrank until he was a silhouette again. Disappearing, he rejoined cloud.

And he did not return. Enraged, Aleida bellowed her fury until her throat was raw. Then she threw herself defeated to the stone of the plaza. Her despair blackened around her, a yawning hole that swallowed her.

Gradually she became aware that the members of the band crouched in ranks around her, keeping their distance. Their eyes were large and wet, and every face dripped the dark sweet moisture of fear. It puddled on the stone, its odor cloying. After a while her mother crept forward and dabbed at Aleida's hair, spitting into it and licking it with her tongue. This time Aleida huddled tight under the unwelcome grooming. The day had been replete with event. Despite her frustration, she must take time now to draw the strands of new experience together and weave them into some coherent pattern. For today, she knew, the fabric of her life had been radically altered. And until she understood the full nature of the alteration, the ashes and dregs of bitter discontent would be her lot.

CHAPTER FOUR

It was morning of the sixth day when Tiehl ruffed his crest from sleep, flared his farsight toward the mountains, and was impaled upon a shard of pink brilliance, a shaft of sunlight reflected into his eyes like a spear of pure energy. It slashed the damp air, Tiehl's first sighting of the perch since he had parachuted toward Selmarri Home. Stiffening, he struggled to focus the vision, but thick air obscured detail. Swiftly he swung to the ground, ignoring the waking sounds of his human companions, and splashed his plumage across morning shadow. Eight years before, when he had donned Fleet uniform, his body plumage had thinned to down. Now, stimulated by exposure, it thickened back across his body. Soon it would match the feathery luxuriance of his crest and genital crop. Soon it would be full-fledged plumage to flaunt against the sky—when he claimed perch.

And the fact of perch spoke in his shimmering eyes. He had tailored his pace to the humans for six days, depending upon

Wells to protect him from possible poisoning and upon Verrons' astringent assumption of ascendancy to counter the rising tide of his own primal instincts. Now he had absorbed enough of the younger human's dietary data to sustain himself, Verrons' dark eyes were still hooded by sleep, and perch would wait no longer. It drew him on a beam of light.

As he ran through the dawn-dewed trees, the Selmarrian jungle receded from his awareness, becoming no more than a dark framework for flashing visions of his own Ehminhee. The Ehminhee sky rose up hard and yellow, an enameled wall. Giant trees striped it, white-limbed, their sparse yellow-green sunfeeders drinking harsh sunlight. The pattern of white tree trunks against hot yellow sky was stark, but a single winged Ehminheer softened it, lacing the sky in a soaring arc, his spread wings powerful and bright.

This of course was an Ehminhee Tiehl had never known except in tale, except in dream. But now, in the racing passion of his inflamed instincts, he seemed to breach some invisible barrier and flatten himself against the painted yellow sky. His crest flared wildly in the suddenly altered sunlight. He tugged at withered pectorals and pain tightened across his chest, stinging his eyes. Then although, fantasy borne, he did not successfully realize the reaching power of wings or the slap of dry air against his face, he seemed to glide up the yellow sky until he reached a high cross-limb he recognized instinctively as his accustomed perch. Possessive fury boiled in his glands, distillate of centuries of life as master of the forest. He settled to his perch puffing his plumage and declaring his ownership loudly to every point of the sky.

But today it was an empty victory. His grasping talons did not curl around solid wood. Instead they closed on a substance that immediately turned liquid and flowed from his grasp. Startled, he watched his fresh-claimed perch run down the enameled sky, a stream of thin white paint. An indignant shriek slashed his throat. Struggling, squawking, Tiehl tumbled back through the barrier between worlds.

Submerged in the shadows of Selmarri again, Tiehl threw himself up a tree and glared at the sky, trying to reimpose his vision of Ehminhee upon it. He obtained only a glimmer of yellow, bare of striping trunks, barren of soaring Ehminheer.

Shaken by the spasm of passion that had driven him, he tried to dampen the still-surging fury of his blood with the cold reality

of fact. There were no soaring Ehminheer in this sky or in any
sky because there were no wings now. And Ehminheer were in
themselves to blame for that fact. It was their shame among intelligent species, a shame that could do little even now to alter
their conduct. When the ancient forests of Ehminhee died, flying
game quickly evolved into ground species and for the Ehminheer, wings became maladaptive. What extra speed they
offered for the chase was more than offset by their encumbering
awkwardness when the prey went to ground in brush or bad-
lands. Consequently, given the genetic malleability of their species, as generations passed greatly decreasing numbers of Ehminheer were born winged. Those found that the frustrated
perch-passion of their newly unwinged brothers had evolved
perversely to include a new and dangerous element: fierce jealousy of any individual or species endowed with the obsolescent
gift of flight. Although their germ plasm had surrendered physical claim on the sky, their more slowly evolving emotions could
not accept the loss of supremacy. Ehminheer jealousy bred killing hatred and winged Ehminheer were hunted like prey. Unable to take refuge at treetop—for all the perch trees had long ago
slumped in death—fewer and fewer winged Ehminheer survived
to reproduce until finally there were none.

Before being relegated to Selmarri, Tiehl had seldom experienced a raw surge of killing jealousy. The time of his youth had
found the yellow skies of Ehminhee empty. Later, shipboard,
there had been nothing to stimulate jealousy. He had been
satisfied to remain aboard the craft even when his human ship-
mates took liberty leave. The ship, after all, was his wings, his
cabin, his perch. All his primary needs were met there. But now,
remembering the flying form he had sighted darting the mountainward clouds, his talons curled and possessive fury flashed
alive in his breast again. What being, commanding flight, would
leave the pink perch unclaimed? None. Driven by urgency, Tiehl
scrambled down the tree.

Even the quest however could not thread him through the jungle faster than arms and legs would carry him. He wove a zigzag
path between massive trees. Creeping vegetation clawed at his
talons, tripping him. And finally, some hours later, despite his
loud-hawked protest, dusk dissolved the world from under his
feet. Despite his urgency, his eyelids sank, hooding his vision.
Angrily Tiehl scrambled to the treetops to sleep.

When morning touched his eyelids, he raised his head, flared

his farsight, and sleep-numbness dissolved instantly. The pink
perch rose resplendent ahead, a tapering shaft of polished stone
jutting from its mesa-top setting amid a cluster of domed structures. The angle of observation, the slow boiling of morning
mist, did not permit him to distinguish much of the detail of
those structures but that was irrelevant. Tiehl descended the
tree, blood hissing, beak snapping.

He paused briefly to make a meal of a hapless little broad-
tailed animal. Then he surged through the jungle. The sun approached zenith when he finally emerged upon the bank of a
sediment-choked stream. The dark water was torpid, the apron-
ing banks of mud thick and warm. The mesa rose from the far
side of the stream, vegetation a competitive tangle of scarlet,
green and black on its steep sides. And towering from its tabled
top—Tiehl's heart died, every chamber slashed by a piercing vision of stone. For once no cry formed in his throat. There was
only a deep, choking bubble of awe.

He was not so stricken however that he overlooked the foot-
prints on the opposite bank of the stream. Leading from the
weed-choked gully that cut the mesa wall to a bend of the stream,
they were little more than a narrow track across the smooth mud.
Nevertheless they represented threat. Tiehl hesitated, torn. But
his ascent to the pink perch was to be a culmination. He would
not have it marred by the distracting sense of details left un-
investigated.

Mud sucked Tiehl's feet as he forded the stream and followed
the trail. A kilometer downstream his searching eyes distinguished
five humanoid forms burrowed into the mud of the streambank.
Tiehl froze, thunderstruck at their intrusive presence. Circling the
group silently, he assessed sleep-slack faces intently. Bifurcate
nostrils bracketed round oral orifices. Curtains of crepey violet
tissue flowed from the lower arcs of the round oral orifices. Two
of the five slept curled around half-devoured branches of yellow
berries. All were naked—of clothing, of hair, of plumage.

Tormenting uncertainty filled Tiehl's craw with gravel. He uttered a harsh, cawing challenge. When none of the humanoids
responded, he stepped forward and deliberately slashed his
talons across one bare back, drawing lines of black blood.

The injured humanoid struggled half upright, round eyes open
and astonished. His round mouth contracted soundlessly, twitch-
ing his violet lip-veil spasmodically. Tiehl leapt back, crest flared,

plumage puffed. But the humanoid did not respond to the challenge. Instead he slumped dully back to the mud. Tiehl sprang again, slashing more deeply this time, uttering a crowing threat.

With a quiver, the creature hunched away from him and collapsed back into sodden sleep. And his four companions recognized Tiehl's challenge with nothing more than random muscular twitches. Tiehl retreated, reassured. These five seemed to offer no threat, unless they were starvling outcasts from a larger group. Withdrawing, Tiehl slapped mud to the gully that led up the mesa wall. The climb was perilous. Vegetation clung perilously to the thin soil and loose rock slid beneath his feet. But a beacon of pink guided him.

He emerged from the gully upon an expanse of solid ground. And across a hedonic tangle of grass and vine, past a spreading pink shimmer of polished stone plaza, past a stately progression of colonnades and splendid-domed structures, the perch rose like a declaration of power, a solid pink shaft that ruptured the sky. Tiehl's stringy chest swelled. He whipped his gaze wide. Planet-east, moist air veiled the vista. To Tiehl's west, mountains thrust at the sky. He unreeled his farsight dizzily, skimming it toward them. Cloudy white faces puffed from behind dark stone shoulders, pouting. With an exultant crow, Tiehl whipped his vision back, reeling it past a cavernous area at the base of the mountains where steam rose from the ground in silvery plumes.

Returning his gaze to the mesa, he caught the perch in his whiplashing farsight. Briefly it occupied his entire field of vision, mammoth stone blocks reaching to infinity. Then he drew in his farsight, but the perch still consumed his entire attention, a primal object. His talons dug soil.

There was order to the progression of domed structures across the polished pink plaza. There was symmetry to the march of columns, to the rise of stone steps. Tiehl did not notice. He hawked through the complex, his cry a strident warning to anyone who might try to obstruct his passage.

It was an unnecessary warning. No one intruded upon the mesa. No one occupied the stone perch. Tiehl raced through the bright-domed structure that fronted it, emerged in a walled courtyard, and found himself alone at the broad stone base of the perch. Unlike the trunk of a perch tree, it was not a solid shaft. At its foot were four arched portals. Entering, Tiehl peered up a mirror-polished stone chimney hundreds of meters high. Sunlight shone far above. Tiehl flared his vision swiftly up.

Abruptly fury gripped him, squeezing a sharp shriek from him. Even using his farvision to magnify the interior surface of the shaft he could find no handhold. There was not the thinnest seam to offer him a grip. Tiehl dodged outside. There block fitted precisely upon block, again providing no purchase for talons. Incredulously Tiehl flung himself at the glossy surface of the perch. His talons scratched stone and slid down it impotently. He glared up, his pectorals taut with frustration. He claimed this perch—and he was completely powerless to mount it.

His outrage flung him from the perch and around the complex, his farsight clawing the clouds, his beak clacking fiercely. An hour later, rage spent, plumage bedraggled, Tiehl huddled at mesa's edge. Nothing had prepared him for this unwelcome denouement. And no matter how calmly the reasonable side of his nature counselled him, he could not accept his impotence. The pink shaft rose from the plaza like a stalwart trunk, inviting conquest. Yet conquest was impossible.

When he heard his name, his crest flared weakly. The youth Sadler Wells scrambled from the gully, coverall muddy, unnaturally pale face taut. His eyes rested briefly on Tiehl, then slid quickly past, the multidomed complex swimming to focus on the surfaces of his eyes. The second human appeared then and his eyes too quickly became mirrors. Tiehl's beak clacked with resurgent possessiveness as he measured the perch's power upon dilating human pupils.

Verrons was first to cast off the spell. "Have you had time to look around up here for other life forms, k'Obrohms?"

Tiehl's crest flared. "There is no one here."

"No one at all?" Verrons frowned intently. "Then we have five stray humanoids burrowed into the mud below and no larger group to connect them with. Have you checked out the structures, Ehminheer? The stone shaft—"

Almost with volition, Tiehl sprang to his feet. "You will not approach the shaft," he warned quickly, his voice distorted.

Verrons' dark brows arched quizzically and Sadler Wells' pale eyes narrowed. "Is there some reason we should avoid the area?"

Tiehl chuckled warning. "There is one reason and that is because I have told you not to approach it." Shimmering eyes impressed the threat behind his words.

Verrons tongued his lips thoughtfully. "You're staking claim to the shaft? Exclusively for yourself?"

With effort, Tiehl stripped his words of the primitive ferocity that bubbled within him. "The shaft is my perch, Verrons. You will not approach it, even when I am not in the immediate vicinity. It is inviolable."

Slowly Verrons nodded. "I suppose we can honor your territoriality, so long as it doesn't extend too far, Ehminheer." He glanced across the stone plaza and then studied the western sky. "We have several hours before dusk to make an initial evaluation of the area. Will you join us?"

Tiehl paced away from them. His gaze flashed over the structures that confronted them. But only the perch keyed a live response in him. And with their arrival he suffered keen unease at leaving it unguarded. "Not now," he said, hoping the noncommittal refusal camouflaged his consuming preoccupation with the pink perch.

Verrons' gaze was keen, but the two humans withdrew to circle the perimeter of the mesa without further question. Quickly Tiehl hurried across the complex to the courtyard wall that encircled the base of the shaft. He scrambled atop the wall and paced its length, his plumage puffed to catch sunlight. Uneasily he kept the humans in sight from his vantage point as they explored the structures atop the mesa. He was uncertain what his response would be if they approached too closely, if they attempted to enter the courtyard he patrolled.

Fortunately the problem did not arise. The humans filled the remaining hours of afternoon with their exploration and at sunset withdrew to a small domed structure. When he realized they did not intend to emerge again, Tiehl settled more easily upon his wall.

Dusk brought a spontaneous bubbling of Ehminheer from Tiehl's throat. Suddenly, in the vicinity of perch, there were ancient tales to be warbled, ancient warnings to be hawked, expressions that welled from a layer of Tiehl's mind that had never been touched before. Frustration and anger were forgotten as he sang the sun behind the mountains.

Later his sleep was disturbed by an auditory phantasm, a random sounding of notes, distant, disorganized. Puffing his plumage, Tiehl expelled the dream and huddled deeper into sleep.

CHAPTER FIVE

For a time the setting sun made the distant mountains a ridge of ragged teeth against the western sky. Then the dying globe itself succumbed to the granite bite. Shadow that had been diffuse etched black chasms against stone plazas. From the upper level of the complex, the Ehminheer's song clucked to silence. The air was chill.

So was the floor of the small temple where the two humans had settled for the night. Sadler Wells slept curled against one wall, his hair a streak of white gleaming from shadow. Verrons sat in a corner, his arms wrapped around his knees, wakefully resurveying his surroundings. A single chamber twenty meters by twenty comprised the interior of the small temple they had chosen for shelter. Walls and floors were of the same stone employed in the plaza and exterior features of the complex. Only the figured interior dome of the grand temple several levels above gave relief from the splendid monotony of polished pink stone. The interiors of the smaller temples were flat-roofed and without motif.

Verrons hunched forward, preoccupied with the day's developments: their discovery of the second group of humanoids burrowed into the mud downstream; the Ehminheer's possessive fury later when they topped the mesa; and finally the presence here of this complex of structures, out of time, out of place, an anomaly on this deserted jungle world.

But it wasn't a deserted world, was it? Since leaving home they had sighted six humanoids representing two distinct races. And the squealing panic in the undergrowth four days ago, when they entered the ruined city where they encountered the young female, had made it clear she was not an isolated survivor.

But survivor of what? What had decimated the two races? The state of the ruined city certainly did not point to warfare. What damage existed appeared to have been inflicted solely by time and encroaching jungle. And the temple complex? Verrons slumped down the cold wall, pinpointing the incongruities he had noted on initial survey of the temple ruins. In the first place, they were not ruins. They were splendidly preserved, each structure intact. In the second place—

Verrons pushed himself erect. In the second place, there was the sound of flutes on the chill air, a plaintive scatter of notes, random, thin, now washing to silence, now resuming. A quiver ran down Verrons' spine. Not a likely manifestation in this coldly splendid setting. And equally unlikely: the tonal quality suggested not primitive reed or wood flutes but metal instruments.

In the hands of primitives? There had been nothing in the humanoids' sleeping area this afternoon to suggest that they owned anything beyond their own muddy hides. He and Sadler had made a thorough search. Teased into action, Verrons jumped up, hand on his pistol grip.

He briefly debated waking Sadler. But the very unlikeliness of the phenomenon demanded the flexibility of a solitary investigation. Verrons emerged from the temple. Disorganized notes led him across the shimmering plaza, his shadow dissolving stone before him, leaching from him the suddenly tenuous sense of self-reality he commanded. As he passed the courtyard wall, he paused. The Ehminheer gripped the stone wall with green talons, glossy plumage puffed, beak tucked into his folded arms.

He did not stir when Verrons slipped past. Soon the sound of

flutes brought him to a high-walled courtyard at the upper perimeter of the complex, one level beyond the stone needle.
Drawn, Verrons sprinted toward the yard—and halted abruptly,
suddenly aware of the soft corona that graced the air above the
enclosed area. It was faint, blue-white, totally unexpected.
Quickly he took cover in the shadow of the courtyard wall.
Glancing up, he found misty blue radiance surging brightly in
the air beyond the wall, dimming the stars. He paused, momentarily paralyzed by the ebb and flow of illumination. Then,
doubting his senses, he closed his eyes, pressing the lids tight.
The swift flash of alien color upon his eyelids bore no resemblance to what he saw in the chill air. It was no phantasm of infection, no exaggerated manifestation of Mazaahr spots, that
stirred in the air above the courtyard.

As silently as possible, Verrons edged the length of the wall
and slipped around the corner. Now he traversed the mountainward wall that incorporated the courtyard entry. Reaching it, he
caught a quick breath and tested the stone-sheet door with an extended hand. It did not yield. Frowning, he pushed more insistently, then slid nearer to examine the door's polished surface.
He found metal hinges but neither handle, knob nor any other
device. Apparently the door was secured from within.

Dissatisfied, Verrons peered at the light in the air. Violet and
green joined blue now, not blending but moving easily around
and through each other. The multi-colored glow seemed less like
light cast by a moving source than an active surge of energy
through the air, light only one of its manifestations.

And the nature of its other manifestations? He would never
learn from this side of the wall. Verrons backed away, measuring
the wall with his eyes. It was too tall to vault, too smooth to
climb. Nor was there any overlooking structure. This isolated
courtyard represented the high point of the complex and apparently it was inviolable

Frustrated, he slipped across the plaza to the arcade that
marked the mountainward boundary of the complex. According
to Sadler, Authority briefing had consistently assured new ar-
rivals that Selmarri was entirely devoid of surviving higher life
forms. While early infectees had ranged into the jungle and dis-
covered ruins, their recorded reports had never mentioned this
set of structures. Yet now they encountered not only temples and
humanoids but metal flutes and unaccountable illumination. Ver-

rons squatted and considered possibilities, none of them particularly credible.

His feet slipped into hibernation and his fingers numbed, but the glow of light above the courtyard wall remained tantalizing, the sound of flutes tuneless. An hour later, discouraged, Verrons stretched out, his head pillowed on his arms.

The sky was grey when the rasp of hinges brought Verrons fully awake. Quickly he dodged to shadow—and found himself sharing it with Sadler. Wordlessly they watched the five humanoids they had sighted sleeping on the streambank the day before emerge from the courtyard. Afoot, they appeared even more likely to pass abruptly into delayed extinction than they had previously. Painfully gaunt, grey-hided, they shambled across the plaza. Their round eyes were dull, their gait disorganized. But in their bifurcate hands, Verrons caught the glint of metal. His heart accelerated unaccountably. The glance he shot at the Talberonese was brief, distracted. "Coming?"

Sadler nodded, already on his feet, poised for pursuit. Together they slipped across pink stone after the humanoids. The five led them across the barren complex to the gully. As the humanoids disappeared over the rim of the mesa, the sun struggled above the horizon, a captive bound in skeins of cloud. Silently the two humans allowed the humanoids time to get halfway down the gully, then lowered themselves into its weed-choked mouth.

The descent was treacherous, rocks and vegetation slippery with dew. When the two humans emerged at the bottom of the gully, the humanoids had already disappeared around the bend of the stream. Tracks led to a brush-choked bog where the humanoids fed, tearing down branches of berries, stuffing horn-lined mouths with brute concentration, grunting and mumbling. Juice, yellow, scarlet, strung through violet lip-veils and puddled on gaunt concave chests. The smell of berries was pungent.

Verrons and Sadler watched from cover as the humanoids ate until their lean bellies bulged tumorously. Then they trekked upstream, their faces stuporous. When they reached the area where the humans had sighted them the day before, they burrowed into the mud. Verrons and Sadler watched for a quarter hour. None of the five stirred. And nowhere was there sign of flutes.

"Evidently they cached them somewhere between the gully mouth and the feeding ground before we caught up with them,"

Verrons said, withdrawing from the mudbank. "They had no time to go afield. More indicative, their tracks didn't go afield." And he knew he would not be satisfied until he had examined one of the metal flutes.

Quickly they backtracked to cover the humanoids' path from gully to berry bog. Restlessly Verrons' eyes probed shadow for the glint of metal. "Nothing," he admitted finally, disappointed. The flutes could be anywhere, tucked into the crook of a tree, hidden under a sheaf of moss. And why five such apparently degenerated specimens should possess sophisticated instruments. . . . Frowning, Verrons peered around the dense growth. "I suppose while we're down here, we may as well take game."

Pistols in hand, they stalked the brush until they had made their breakfast. Then they napped in nested brush. Troubled by dream-fragments of swirling light, Verrons woke at noon and sat listening to the sounds of the jungle: a cry, a call, the rattle of brush. The odor was thick, an uneven mingling of the odors of stagnant water, warm mud and exuberant vegetation. By now Naas was completing final arrangements for the Rumarian study party. With what degree of competence? Before leaving Britthold Verrons had messaged the academic to retain a retired Explo officer to guide the group in its initial survey of the grassplain. But he was not confident Naas would appreciate the qualities a good Explo man should bring to the job.

Restlessness. Inability to tolerate limitations. An instinctive attraction to the unusual, however subtle or bizarre.

Frowning, Verrons realized that Sadler had wakened and was silently evaluating him. Deliberately Verrons quelled the unease the youth's thin-lipped snow-savage countenance inspired in repose. "Ready for the hunt?"

Sadler assented. He stood and peered around, the jungle reflecting darkly on his pale eyes. "I'd like to locate a second ascent route to the mesa top if we have time."

Verrons acceded and they spent the next two hours exploring the eastern foot of the mesa as they filled crudely-woven game bags. However they found no satisfactory secondary ascent route. The wall of rock was steep and harsh, the gully its only vulnerable point.

Returning to the mesa top late in the afternoon, they found the Ehminheer absent from his courtyard wall. Wordlessly they ascended to the plaza's highest point. By waning daylight the rectangular courtyard from which the humanoids had emerged at dawn was totally barren. Tossing down his game bag, Verrons paced it off with sharp dissatisfaction.

"There's certainly no sign of any possible light fixture here," Sadler observed, poised near the courtyard entry.

"There's no sign of anything here," Verrons agreed. There was only dust and a half-open stone-sheet door. Dissatisfied, Verrons emerged from the courtyard and gazed over the complex. From its eastern boundary, plazas, arcades and walled courtyards joined a succession of progressively more imposing temples. The climax of the complex lay a single level below them, an elevated domed temple that seemed to join the sky in the light grace of its structure. The towering shaft of stone that rose from its courtyard made thrusting counterpoint to the grace of the temple's design.

Standing on the brink of dusk, Verrons surveyed barren stone with discontent. He could comprehend the lack of structural damage, the absence of day to day life. The ascent to the mesa was too steep to permit casual invasion by jungle fauna. And there was neither game nor vegetation here to sustain life. But the disturbing sense of stones that had never been walked, of walls that had never housed activity, disturbed him. "I don't think this place was ever used," he ventured. If it had been, where was the inevitable litter and clutter of habitation or worship? Where were the altars, the urns, the casks, the sacred objects and representations? Or conversely the implements, tools, containers and miscellaneous castoffs of secular existence. "I can't imagine any race constructing such an elaborate facility without having a use for it in mind."

"But the humanoids carry flutes," Sadler pointed out obliquely.

Verrons did not have time to pursue the thought. A gargle of sound interrupted him. Verrons' gaze snapped over the complex. The Ehminheer emerged from the mouth of the gully, stringy limbs flexing. His beak snapped and tore at coming darkness. His plumage was a splash of color. He taloned across stone plazas and launched himself at the courtyard wall. Topping it, he thrust out his head, crest flared, to fill the air with a complexity of clucks and cries. At moments the compelling spill of notes seemed almost like song.

At other moments it was less pacific. Verrons stood captured by the poetic incongruity of the moment: the sun sinking behind the mountains, barren temples and plazas dissolving into dusk, the Ehminheer defying the alien night with his cry. Finally Verrons turned attention to the courtyard again. "We could simply establish ourselves there and wait, although the humanoids might consider our presence an intrusion and retaliate."

"With what? There was no sign of weapons in their sleeping grounds."

"There was no sign of flutes either," Verrons pointed out.

Nevertheless his suggestion stood. Soon twin moons appeared upon the horizon, their faces bright and cold. As the Ehminheer's evening song died, Verrons and Sadler returned to the courtyard and established themselves in the rearmost corner.

Soon they heard bare feet on stone and the first humanoid appeared. He paused at the courtyard door. By moonlight, the vacancy of his gaunt features was chilling. Dull eyes found the humans. Lip-veils quivered weakly. Warily the humanoid sidled into the yard and hunkered at its center, his face turned to Sadler and Verrons. His gaze fixed, he raised a forked hand. The flute he held was gracefully formed, its metal barrel ornate and untarnished. The humanoid's nostrils flared. Lip tissues rippled as he mouthed the instrument. The flute yielded a tuneless sign.

Other members of the band followed. Finally all five humanoids hunched, their dull eyes fixed on Sadler and Verrons. The humanoids mouthed their flutes tunelessly, dark spittle stringing down through their fluttering lip-veils. But by that time, Verrons was little aware of the unprepossessing mien of the players. Because as flutes sounded, there was another presence in the courtyard.

It came as a cloud of light that gradually brightened until it filled the yard with soft, shadowless radiance. As it brightened, metal flutes glowed. Verrons stared as bony fingers groped aimlessly up and down luminous instruments. There was neither order nor beauty in the sounds produced.

Yet those sounds somehow caused the cloud of light to birth a single tenuous light-presence. It darkened slowly from the heart of cloud, taller than human or humanoid but similar to both in form and proportion. The presence glimmered across the courtyard, radiantly blue, its natal cloud luminous around it. It bowed before the huddle of humanoids, extruding long arms of blue light that it slowly wound and wove about itself and reincorporated. Then long arms rippled free again. The apparition arched into the air, threw itself backward and cartwheeled about the yard, passing easily through the hunched humanoids, light-limbs flickering.

Flutes continued to sound. The apparition flung itself erect at the center of the yard, light-limbs spiraling around its body. Helplessly Verrons was drawn into the vortex, his consciousness absorbed and irradiated. Faintly he could tell that there were other light presences in the yard, violet and green. But the blue entity claimed his allegiance.

Then the first moon appeared above the courtyard wall, a flat white disk. The apparition at the center of the yard brightened visibly, changing form. The guise it assumed was flame: licking arms, surging head, consuming maw. Initially it was an intense blue flame that seemed to flare from a rupture in some other dimension. Then it spread, brightening fiercely. Verrons groaned as fiery arms licked him. Desperately he tried to gain his feet, a silent scream filling his mind. The humanoids grunted in agony.

An eternity later, when both moons hung halfway up the sky, flame drew back and began to spin, drawing fiery arms after it, until it was a brilliant wheel of light that arced around the yard. As it spun, fiery red became orange, orange yellow, yellow green. Reaching the end of the visible spectrum, the progression of color reversed. With effort, Verrons extracted one corner of consciousness from the dazzle of light. He licked dry lips. *What are you?*

The entity answered in a silent tongue. It was a wheel of light. It was turning, drawing his awareness back, reclaiming it. Verrons arced and spun the yard forever, his consciousness joined with the brilliance of light. Then the wheel began to fade. Verrons shuddered, the ragged sound of flutes swimming back into his awareness. He peered around, eyes burning, face inflamed. There remained only a diffuse cloud of light in the yard.

The tallest humanoid sprawled forward, his head touching the stone pavement, his flute still clutched in hand. His fellows stared at him, their own fading instruments forgotten. One reached forward and jammed the flute between his quivering lips.

Play! The word was a scream in Verrons' mind. The humanoid's mates battered him with brutal hands, equally impatient.

But he did not respond, and flutes were forgotten in grey-hided hands.

Released from fascination, Verrons gained his feet. Overhead the moons were haughty white twins. The stars glittered with manic brilliance. Regaining control of his own limbs, Verrons sucked an icy breath, standing away from the scene in the courtyard. The pavement was far, the humanoids small. Stumbling, Verrons pushed at the stone-sheet door and fled the courtyard. Dimly he realized that Sadler followed.

Outside he clutched himself tight, ignoring the stumbling youth. When he emerged from behind the courtyard wall, when the complex spread from his feet again, he saw manifestations he had been blind to the night before. Halos of light swept across the complex, bestowing brief, misty glory now upon one structure, now upon another. There was a glow of light trapped in the stone needle. It shone from the top of the shaft, shrieking light-energy into the night like an imprisoned princess. And other manifestations rode the chill air. It was no longer empty but aquiver with—

—life? Verrons clenched his teeth and dropped a hand to his belt. The metal grip of his pistol was as solid, as cold as the stone beneath his feet. And, with an exercise of will, he dismissed ghost-light from the complex. He was alone except for Sadler. No mysterious radiance touched temple walls with life.

He was not comforted. Nor, he saw, was Sadler. He peered into the Talberonese's shock-masked face. "Commander, the light—"

"I can't explain it." Never on any world, had he been drawn into a vortex of pure light. Never. At the weak sound of flutes, Verrons spun to peer back toward the courtyard. Again light swirled in the air above the wall. A rising sense of urgency touched him, almost drawing him back toward the courtyard. Instead he stepped back, turned and moved quickly away across the plaza, retreating not from light, not from the unknown, but from the mindless compulsion to rejoin it. If he permitted himself to be sucked back into the vortex tonight—

"I'm sleeping below," he said harshly, leading way across moonlit stone toward the gully. He needed time to assimilate tonight's experience, time to build defenses against the drowning fascination of light. Tomorrow would be time enough to walk gleaming stone again, to dare the maw of light.

CHAPTER SIX

At dawn Verrons crouched in the brush at the foot of the gully. Nearby Sadler still slept in a nest of brush. Above, the sound of flutes had died a quarter hour before. Verrons squeezed moisture from his cuffs and shifted uncomfortably. The mysterious light phenomenon had occupied him throughout the night. If he could get a close look at the flutes, if he could determine their source, learn where the humanoids had obtained them. . . . Frowning, he reviewed the course of action he had decided upon.

A scatter of rocks alerted him. Moments later the humanoids tumbled from the gully. They gained their feet and straggled away down the streambank in rough file, flutes in hand. When they rounded the bend of the stream, Verrons followed. Some meters beyond the bend, they angled into the jungle, five grey bodies merging with the bleak shadows of dawn. Their progress was stumbling, brutish.

It was also purposeful. A quarter kilometer from the streambed, the tallest knelt at the base of a dead tree. He dug into a heap of rotting debris, then reached into the moist hollow he had created between the tree's roots and brought out an oblong object half a meter long. He pried at it with forked hands.

It opened. Moving near, Verrons watched the five humanoids fit their flutes into a scarlet-lined case. His pupils dilated. Steeling himself, he stepped forward, one hand extended. "Why don't you give me a look at those?" he asked conversationally. His other hand rested lightly on the grip of his heat pistol.

His words had the desired effect. Slowly five heads turned. Five pair of eyes converged on Verrons. Bifurcate nostrils flared and crepey lip veils rippled. But the humanoids' response did not develop beyond dull startlement until Verrons stepped forward and snapped the flute case from the kneeling humanoid's hands.

His action precipitated a wave of agitation. The kneeling humanoid struggled to his feet, lip veil switching, his eyes weakly aglimmer, a spark of swamp fire trapped at their depths. Alarm, fear, even weak menace grunted from the throats of the band.

The menace was very weak, and when Verrons backed away, the humanoids made no immediate effort to recoup the flute case. Verrons heeled back toward the gully, where he shook Sadler awake. "Flutes," he snapped, exhibiting the case.

It was enough. The Talberonese was up, running with him to the gully mouth.

Pursuit was neither swift nor hot, but as they mounted the gully, the five humanoids stumbled around the bend of the stream, grunting angrily. Satisfied, Verrons scrambled upward, flute case in hand. Reaching the top of the gully, he dodged to cover behind the base of the curving colonnade that marked the southern perimeter of the complex.

Beneath caked mud and vegetable matter, the flute case was black, molded from a heavy plaston material. Verrons pried at its seams, quickly explaining to Sadler how and why he had obtained his booty. He found the scarlet fabric of the interior liberally smudged with mud. "But there's no sign of fabric deterioration," he remarked.

"A synthetic of some kind?"

"Appears to be," he confirmed, testing the glossy fabric with his fingertips. There were recessed spaces for eight flutes in the case. Three spaces were empty. Gingerly Verrons selected a flute and polished damp fingerprints from its barrel. Silvery metal gleamed, its surface silken to his closing fingers. But this was not the moment to succumb to the sheen of metal. Quickly Verrons slid the flute back into the case. He peered around concealing stone.

The humanoids emerged from the gully and took disorganized stance at the edge of the plaza. Their distress apparent, they half-loped after their leader across the plaza. Verrons glanced around to see the stone needle draw the sun's dawning brilliance to focus and disperse it over the complex in iridescing shards. Pink stone took fire. The humanoids were incongruous against the splendor of domed temples, their gait untidy, their gaunt bodies barely erect.

"It should be instructive to see what they intend to do about their lost flutes. Let's go." Sliding the case behind the base of the colonnade, Verrons jumped up to follow the band.

The humanoids did not progress beyond the fourth level of the complex before Sadler touched Verrons' arm. "Commander, the Ehminheer."

A blue streak had materialized from the main temple and flamed across polished stone toward the starvling band of humanoids. Verrons drew a sharp breath. "Ehminheer," he cried, "let them pass!"

Momentarily the Ehminheer paused. His gaze shimmied across the plaza. But possessive fury defeated reason without contest. The Ehminheer raced toward the humanoids and bowled them down the stone steps, his beak slashing air. His cry was a raw declaration of ascendancy.

Verrons' reaction was automatic. It carried him swiftly across the plaza and up the steps. He seized the Ehminheer from behind, careful not to exert undue pressure upon the avian's fragile bones. The Ehminheer responded with a sharp twist backward that raked his beak across Verrons' jaw. Verrons recoiled and the Ehminheer leapt free to fling himself at the humanoids again, crest flared.

Panicked, the humanoids toppled over each other across the pavement and down the steps in retreat. Mercilessly the Ehminheer targeted the tallest and pursued him, ripping the flesh of his back with beak and talons. The humanoid gurgled in fear.

Verrons threw himself at the Ehminheer again. His tackle bounced the avian free of the humanoid and knocked him to the pavement. Doggedly Verrons hugged the avian's bucking torso. Arching, squawking, the Ehminheer slashed futilely at his human encumbrance.

Verrons maintained the enforced embrace. "Ehminheer, listen to me. I maneuvered the humanoids up here deliberately. They're obtaining artifacts somewhere, objects much too sophisticated to be of recent local manufacture. Haven't you heard the flutes at night?"

With effort the Ehminheer twisted to face Verrons. Slowly the fury in his eyes subsided. "I sleep at night."

"And you haven't wakened even briefly and heard the sound of flutes from the upper courtyard?"

The Ehminheer's blue crest sagged perceptibly. His eyelids, which had deepened to midnight green as he charged the humanoids, faded. "I have heard, briefly," he admitted.

Verrons released him and stood back. "Then consider the facts, k'Obrohms. There are five humanoids living below, no more. They sleep and feed by the stream—and come here by night to blow flute in the mountainward courtyard. They use metal flutes, Ehminheer, sophisticated instruments they store by day in a plaston case." Grimly he held the shimmering gaze, determined to reach past the Ehminheer's inflamed instincts to his intelligence. "That means they must have access to artifact stores. And that access may lie right up here."

Slowly the avian's plumage flattened but his stringy body remained flexed. "So?"

"Aren't you curious? Logically, if there are storage vaults, they should be located right beneath our feet." Assaying his audience carefully, he advanced his own theory. "I doubt very much that this mesa is a natural land feature. It's completely out of keeping with the region. There is no other prominence between here and the colony—and probably none west of here until you approach the foothills. I'm inclined to believe the mesa was erected here— to create protected repository space."

Briefly the Ehminheer's full interest appeared to be engaged. Then his gaze sheered giddily away. "That may be," he said, "but this is my perch, Verrons."

Verrons' brow creased. "The entire facility? The three of us set out together. As far as I'm concerned you're entitled to claim territory here, but not the entire complex."

The Ehminheer's beak clacked. "This is perch," he said obdurately.

"And you don't have any interest beyond claiming it? You don't want to know why the mesa was constructed? By whom? And why we've already sighted two separate races of humanoids on a world where we were told there were none? You don't want to find what is probably hidden directly under our feet?"

Yellow eyes shimmered fiercely, rejecting his argument. "Curiosity is a human principle, Verrons."

Verrons' brows arched. "Oh? And what do you claim as an Ehminheer's animating principle?"

Uneasily the Ehminheer danced back, his talons chattering on polished stone. "Flight, the hunt—and perch."

Verrons frowned, intently assessing the avian. "Then we'd better negotiate a compromise, Ehminheer," he said finally. "You spent enough time with Authority Fleet to know that humans evolved from a territorial background too. And living under primitive circumstances can trigger reversion in both our species. I suggest that instead of attempting to claim the entire complex, you settle for a single area and designate the rest public space, open to Sadler, myself, the humanoids and anyone or anything else we care to bring up here." He measured the slow resurgence of the Ehminheer's crest. "Why don't we designate the stone shaft and the courtyard where it stands your territory? Sadler and I are willing to forego claiming separate areas, so the remainder of the complex can be considered public."

The glistening surfaces of the Ehminheer's eyes rippled. "If I agree—" he said tentatively.

"If you agree, the shaft and courtyard are inviolable," Verrons promised.

The Ehminheer's reluctance to compromise was clear in his rising crest, in his darkening eyelids. But Verrons refused to yield. Finally, with a half-intelligible squawk of assent, the Ehminheer turned away. His talons clacked on polished stone as he retreated to the main temple. Moments later his perch cry tore air from the courtyard wall.

"Can we count on him?" Sadler demanded, a taut frown bisecting his white brows.

Verrons shrugged. "We can count on him to be unpredictable, even openly hostile if we push him too far." Verrons sighed. "Meanwhile our humanoid subjects have fled the scene. So we don't know if they came up here hoping to find us—and the stolen flutes—or because they have some way of gaining access to flute stores from up here. We'll have to play the waiting game—and hope they come back."

Crossing the complex, they threw themselves to cover again at the base of the colonnade. The flute case lay where Verrons had left it. Grimly he slid it beyond reach.

An hour later a series of grunts alerted them. The humanoids emerged from the gully as distraught, as disorganized as before. The coarse grey flesh of their leader's back was flayed and oozing. He hunched stiffly on the verge of the complex, lip veil switching as he surveyed barren stone.

This time no shrieking Ehminheer disrupted the band's untidy advance. They hobbled along the southern perimeter of the complex, taking the circuitous route to the mountainward courtyard. Verrons and Sadler followed inobtrusively. When the humanoids disappeared into the courtyard, the humans edged through the stone sheet door and flattened themselves against the courtyard wall.

Their presence was noted, then ignored. And if the humanoids had expected to find the missing flutes in the yard, their search was unfocused and they were an undue interval in recognizing disappointment. They shuffled around the yard dully until their leader withdrew, despair apparent in his gaunt body.

When Verrons ascertained that their second destination was the main temple, he ran ahead of them. As he passed under the broad portico that led to the interior of the temple, the Ehminheer shrieked from the courtyard wall. Quickly Verrons crossed the temple floor. K'Obrohms leapt from his wall, feathers bristling. But his clacking talons halted short of the courtyard entry to the temple. Human gaze and Ehminheer met across glimmering stone. Verrons did not yield. With a dissatisfied cry, the Ehminheer retreated to the base of the stone shaft, beak slashing air.

As he hurried back toward the portico, Verrons' glance was distracted upward. The vault of the dome was lofty, its interior surface brilliantly patterned with interlocking geometric forms. The patterned surface was divided into wedge-shaped quadrants by intersecting ranks of wheels of light. Verrons sucked a sharp breath, his attention immediately absorbed. Despite their physical immobility, the inlaid wheels appeared to move across the surface of the dome: orange, yellow, gold; blue, indigo, violet; silver, red, green. A red wheel meters in diameter dominated the center of the dome, multiple arms flaring from its central body, streaks of moving brilliance.

Orange, yellow, gold; blue, indigo, violet; silver, red, green. Vivid hues surged across Verrons' retinas, numbing him. But the humanoids were entering the temple. Grimly Verrons threw off the fascination of moving color.

After initial frozen apprehension, the humanoids straggled aimlessly across the temple floor, their eyes sliding dully past Verrons and Sadler. Their quest was as unfocused as their search of the mountainward courtyard. Then, as if struck, the smallest member of the band suddenly crouched, his head snapping up. His gaze zigzagged across the patterned ceiling and his lip veil began to switch. With a grunt, he hopped across the floor, still crouched. Reaching the center of the dome, he slowly stood and gazed directly upward, as if presenting petition.

Verrons caught a sharp breath. For as the humanoid stared up, the central core of the red wheel of light that dominated the ceiling slowly lowered from the dome surface. With a faint hum, it glowed alight, encapsulating the paralyzed humanoid in a column of intense red light. His face glowed and his eyes flared, puddles of fire. His switching lip veil fell limp.

Intense light bathed him for an interval of seconds. Then the red column dulled and receded, taking light with it. The humanoid's head fell forward. He stared around numbly. After a moment, he began to flex his legs, to bob up and down, grunting insistently, almost angrily.

His performance stimulated the band's leader to knuckle him aside and address his own petition to the dome ceiling. Verrons watched, breath caught, pistol grip in hand, solid insurance against too overwhelming an involvement in the mesmeric pattern of the ceiling. Again the central core slid downward. Again a faint hum announced a column of intense light. The second humanoid was as helpless within the beam as the first.

And as disappointed when the core withdrew. He whipped his gaze wide and began to grunt, to slap stone with forked feet, to glower upward almost in demand.

Each humanoid claimed a turn in the beam of light. The leader claimed several. Each time the reaction was identical: disappointment, anger, protest. The band shuffled around the temple in patent frustration, alternately seeking the polished floor and peering at the distant ceiling, grunting and muttering unintelligibly.

"What do they expect?"

"I don't know." Verrons stepped forward, his advance stimulating an agitation of lip veils. Ignoring the humanoids' forbidding grunts, he strode to the center of the floor. Dropping one hand across his pistol grip, he let his head fall back.

Wheels of light surged across the ceiling, intense, restless. Verrons hardened his jaws, willing flaming arms to immobility. But by then the red core of the central wheel had extended and a humming vibration obliterated volition. Verrons tried to suck breath, tried to impose will upon suddenly lax muscles. But he stood helpless, only faintly aware of the light that bathed his face and glared from the reflecting surfaces of his eyes.

Then light was gone. Sensation returned. Verrons' head sagged forward.

"Are you all right, Commander?"

"Apparently. I—" His answer seemed to come from a distance. Dumbly, before he could analyze his condition, Verrons watched a barricade of pink stone rise around him, a hollow column, richly grained, himself enclosed at its center. He fought brief panic as stone girdled him, rising to his waist, to his chest.

There it halted. Verrons peered across the unexpected barrier at Sadler, at the five humanoids. Their deep eyes simmered with emotion. Frowning, Verrons examined his prison. He stretched out his arms, able to half-extend them. Then a curving section of stone moved smoothly aside at waist height, revealing a polished pink cavity. A black tongue, a small plaston oblong protruded from the cavity. Frowning, Verrons gripped a second flute case, smaller replica of the one they had abandoned at the colonnade. He stared at it, stared at the slowly receding stone column, stared, when his trembling fingers had breached the case, at the enclosed two metal flutes. Even in the dim temple, their silvery surfaces found light to shatter against his retinas. Clumsily Verrons extracted an instrument from the case. Its metal barrel communicated an electric thrill to his fingertips.

Simultaneously the flute brought him intense apprehension. He stood at the center of a closing ring of humanoids, his protective stone barrier receding into the temple floor. Ten dim eyes converged on the flute in his hand. Lip veils flopped emphatically. Meeting Verrons' glance, Sadler drew his pistol.

"No, let's head them back to their own instruments." Quickly Verrons slapped the flute back into the case and aimed himself at the circle of humanoids. He broke it, tumbling grey bodies to stone. A gabble and a cry rose after him as he set trajectory down the temple steps. Without looking back, Verrons sprinted across the complex to the colonnade where he had half-concealed the humanoids' flute case. Quickly he retrieved the case and placed it in the path of the pursuing humanoids.

The diversion proved successful. While the humanoids reclaimed their flutes, Verrons rejoined Sadler and they backtracked toward the upper reaches of the complex. Below the humanoids hunkered briefly over their find, then made scrambling exodus into the gully. The two humans were alone again—with the fiercely chuckling Ehminheer and two metal flutes.

Settling under the portico of the main temple, Verrons reopened the plaston case and withdrew a single flute. It was lightweight, little more than twenty-five centimeters in length. Turning the instrument, Verrons found fine lateral seams. He tested them with a thumbnail. But he did not want to open the instrument now. There was a more confounding paradox to be investigated. "Let's have another look inside."

In the temple, he circuited the glossy pink floor thoughtfully, drawing first the toe of his boot, then the tips of his fingers across it. "Can you find the seam in the stone?"

After a brief exploration, Sadler's index finger described an arc across the stone floor. Kneeling, Verrons traced the fine seam. He grunted. "Now I'd like to know why I was able to activate the mechanism when the humanoids were not."

"They must have activated it before, at least once," Sadler pointed out, his pale eyes circuiting the structure.

"Yes, when it dispensed them the flute case," Verrons agreed. "And how significant do you consider it that our case contains exactly two flutes? One for each human in the temple at the moment I activated the mechanism."

Sadler's eyes narrowed. "You think that was programmed?"

"I think it's a possibility we should check out. Do you want to be the test animal this time?"

Sadler glanced reluctantly at the red wheel of fire. "I'll try it." But when he placed himself at the center of the floor and gazed up, his experiment was prematurely truncated. The red core extended and there was a brief humming vibration, a flash of red light. Neither lasted more than a few seconds before the red core slid back up into place. Blankly Sadler peered around. No hollow column rose from the floor.

Verrons paced around him, frowning. "So we're non grata now, too." He stared up at the ceiling, considering. "Presumably what we have here is a scanning beam, activated either by the pressure of our weight or by some more esoteric means. So why don't you qualify for the full beam?"

Sadler shrugged. "Why don't you try again?"

Verrons did, stepping to the center of the floor and peering up. This time his reception was no warmer than Sadler's had been. "Of course it's already made one full reading on me today," he mused.

"It made three full readings on the leader of the humanoids—within a quarter hour."

"Agreed. So there must be some other disqualifying factor." But what?

Sadler stared at the flute case in his hand. "Commander, maybe it knows we already have flutes."

"*Ah.*" It was a possibility just farfetched enough to be plausible. "Let's check it out. And just to give ourselves a better picture of the situation I'd like you not only to remove the flute case to the portico but to stay there with it."

Sadler did as instructed, and this time the red beam numbed and held Verrons again. When it was gone, pink stone rose from the floor and a third flute case dropped into his hands.

"Commander?" Sadler demanded, returning.

Verrons displayed the open flute case in answer. It contained a single instrument. "You were beyond range of the detection system when the beam came down," he said slowly. "I was the only qualifying individual on the premises."

"But qualifying—how?" Sadler insisted, examining the lone flute.

Verrons shook his head. He stood at the center of the glossy floor, his own words returning to haunt him. He was convinced that the mesa was no natural land feature, that it had been erected here, the temple complex set atop it like a tantalizing jewel. But by whom? Why? To dispense flutes in carefully measured quantities, one flute to each human present? Why not—today—to each humanoid present? Verrons turned to peer across the courtyard at the Ehminheer, his plumage fiery at the base of the stone shaft. If the avian stepped to the center of the floor, would he draw down the red beam and summon up the stone column?

And there was the matter of his own intentions. Now he had flutes. Unfortunately he still had no understanding of the phenomenon the flutes activated in the mountainward courtyard by night. All he knew was that light was compelling, motion irresistible—and that he would learn little more without returning to the courtyard. "Are you game to blow flute with me? Tonight?"

Sadler's eyes evaded his. The youth's voice was husky. "I—no. Not yet."

Shrugging, Verrons paced away to peer over a vista of jungle and cloud. Nothing drove him to face the compelling force of light either. Nothing but his own curiosity. Nothing but his own restless intolerance of the unknown. With a second shrug, he slipped the double flute case into his pocket. "I'll use one of these tonight."

CHAPTER SEVEN

Aleida hunched in the dark mating bower. Soft leaf-rot cushioned her knees, its promise close and sweet, but her mood was acrid. An angry hand whipped to her hair. Mud-dressed, knotted tight, it tugged her features back into a hard grimace. She had failed again to draw him into the bower. Whoever he was, he had scampered after her eagerly enough while she fished the nestings. Later she had heard the snap of stems under his feet as she hunted the tangles and the brush. But when she had teased him with her swinging gait, leading him deep into the jungle, he had not dared follow her into the bower. She had Pystarr's whisperings to thank for that.

She had the whisperings of all the others to thank, too. Since the day the male had appeared to her from the sky, every eye that encountered hers skittered swiftly and fearfully away, a greylizard flushed from its nesthole. Every face that peered up and found her face near fell back with a strangled yelp. Fear perfumed her days, a near-tangible effluvia that rose whenever she accosted any member of the little band. Even her own mother did not touch her anymore. At night, wherever Aleida stretched her mat, isolation blossomed. If she defiantly picked up her mat in the middle of the night and flopped it near the others, she woke in the morning to find herself alone. The others had edged away in the dark, abandoning their mats.

Their exodus was never pointed, but the effect was. Aleida was a person apart from all the others. She had known that since her first dream of power. Now the others knew it, too. And she could not even retreat to her dreams for comfort, because now the dreams had changed, too. Before the flying male had appeared, they had been episodes exultant with power. She had arrowed at the clouds and fused herself with the forces of upper air. She had swept the sky, infinite, radiant, a being beyond all others.

No more. Now if there were power in her dreams, she did not possess it. Instead it possessed her, savagely. It twisted her, tortured her, racked and ravaged and ruined her.

Every night. Because every night a black form flashed from the skies of dream, the devil's green of his eyes searing her with a compelling beam that choked shrills from her throat, that arched her reaching legs, stretched her impatient feet, that flung up her hands in the writhing configuration that had become so familiar.

It had also become futile. Before the male's appearance, she had arced the sky of her dreams almost at will, soaring triumphant. Now her feet clung to the stone plaza, and he refused to join her there. She was gravity bound, he was free. As he flashed and soared over the crumbling city, Aleida's organs engorged, raying her with agony. Desperately she ran the rubbled plazas, twisting her stiff hair into a knot, smearing her new swellings with mud that thickened them into hard prominence. Pursuing him, she seized a plaited reed cape from unseen hands. First she covered herself with it, then she whipped it away, teasing. She strutted, she flaunted, she shrieked, she cried.

Nothing—*nothing*—could draw him from the air. And nothing could free her from the torment of her own earthbound impotence, except waking. Even then only the physical agony was dispelled. The mood remained, violent in its intensity, quickly perverting into a vengeful ecstasy. Wakened, Aleida reared up on her solitary mat and hunched forward like a predatory beast, her eyes measuring the members of her little band for the kill. She ached to flash them awake with the orange flame of her power. She burned to toss them screaming and kicking across the dusty floor, to twist them into hideous choking convulsions. She hungered to see them die in her thrall.

Her vision of their demise was so vivid that she gobbled sweet death-fear from the air of the warren, spiritual nourishment. In reality the members of her band continued to sleep, limp hair trailing in the dust. In her mind they died horribly, sacrificed to the killing intensity of her power.

The power existed. But why? From what did it stem? Why was she its focusing agent? Who was the flying male? Aleida knew there was a strand of dark mystery that tied maturing young to the parent generation. Mother whispered of it to daughter, father to son. Her agemate Gherrmi had already been bound to his parents by the whispered secrets. Aleida had not.

So she hunched in the mating bower tracing the thread of her own dark thoughts instead. It always led back to the secrets. Her mother would not impart them to her now. She knew it. She read it from the cowering fear in the little female's eyes. But there were other members of the band who held them: Gherrmi, Pystarr, every member of the band older than herself.

Every *male* member older than herself. Because with the males, she had goods to offer in barter. And if the bartering failed, *when* it failed the target male would be alone with her, isolated in this close, sweet bower. She had only to throw herself up and arch her back, blocking his exit with her body. Then her arms would writhe, her fingers would dance, and she would fling orange veils of power around him like trapping nets. And when his small body arched and bucked in agonizing convulsion and he cried for mercy—

Yes, then the secrets would pass freely. She would know.

She *would* know—if she could ever once lure a male into the bower. So far she had met only failure. Now, fiercely, she reached to snatch her hair from its knot. But her head whipped away from her angry fingers. *No.* Mobilizing herself, she crawled from the bower.

Noonday sun pricked through dense foliage, littering the brush with needles of light. There would be males, she knew, hunting the nestings, trapping the brush, wading the stream. So stalk them, little lizard, she admonished herself. Hunt them. Bring them tittering through the brush to the bower. *Strut.*

Aleida ran through the brush until the smell of the mudbanks were near. Emerging at streamside, she swooped down upon a deep wallow and smeared glossy brown mud across the ripe swellings of her readiness and massaged it into her knotted hair. She danced to dry the mud. It made the knot of her hair as heavy as a helmet.

She strutted. And she found a covey of males in the bog where dyeberry grew. They crouched in a circle under the ripe berry bushes playing chuk-chuk: Pystarr, old Narnar, eldest male of the band, her brothers Kislik and Lelar and three others. Caped in shadow, Aleida stood watching as they poked the odd-shaped chuk-rock from player to player. "Chuk-chuk, chuk-chuk, chuk-chuk." The refrain was a husky whisper on the air.

Kislik rolled the rock to Narnar, Narnar to Dartak, Dartak to Pystarr. The little male's jabbing stick glanced off the rock's irregular surface. Frantically he jabbed again and sent the rock rolling, but it was too late. The rhythm had already been disrupted. Squealing, he jumped away from the circle.

The others pursued him and Lelar brought him down. This time the refrain was shrill—"chuk-chuk, chuk-chuk, chuk-chuk"— as they tangled their playing sticks in his long hair and pulled. Pystarr squealed in protest that was half delight.

Quickly Aleida stepped from cover. She threw her body erect, flaunting her mud-packed swellings, tossing her stiff-knotted head high. "Do you know any other games? That a female can play who has no poking stick?"

Her sudden appearance stimulated a frantic scramble of bodies. A few minutes later the seven males reassembled, huddled in a pack under the dyeberry bushes, staring out at her with huge eyes. Fear cloyed the air.

"Now see the little greylizards run from my shadow," Aleida taunted, striding down upon them. Her shadow was dim, foliage-fragmented, but when she threw it across the pack of males, they shuddered with dread. Her brothers Kislik and Lelar burst free of the huddle and dodged past her. She let them go. For when she twisted her hips and arched her body, the others became still, very still.

Old Narnar's desperate whine was barely audible. "Ale'a, your mother wants you."

"She is calling you," Dartak urged, squirming behind the older male. "Hear her?" He pitched his voice high. *"Ale'a! Ale'a!"*

"Ha!" Aleida's tight-drawn features twisted into a fierce grimace. "Listen closely because I hear someone else calling. *Dartak! Narnar! Pystarr!"* She mewed the names tantalizingly. The two oldest males quivered, unable to pull their eyes from hers. But Pystarr leapt up and tried to scramble past her. She blocked his path, her spread legs a barricade. "I hear someone, Pystarr," she insisted. "She is calling from the bower. She needs a strong little male to please her. Hear? Hear?" She caroled his name, rotating her face hypnotically around the axis of her calling mouth. *"Pystarr! Where are you, Pystarr? Are you coming, Pystarr?"*

Pystarr's eyes dampened and his face misted. His mouth sagged in helpless dismay. "Ale'a. . . ?"

She held him helpless. Her eyes flashed to the others. They peered at her from oozing faces, from shadowed eyes. She reached out to tug Pystarr's fine hair. "Chuk-chuk!" she teased and danced away.

Helplessly he toddled after her, little legs pumping, face dripping with fear. "Ale'a?" he beseeched.

"Come to the bower, Pystarr," she hissed and darted away into the trees.

But she did not run ahead heedless. A short distance away, she scrambled into the lower branches of a tree to be certain he came. He lurched after her through the trees, limp hair flopping. From her perch, Aleida could see her name tumbling from his lips, half-formed. Quickly she jumped down and ran after him, angling through the trees to reach the bower before him, to be ready for him. And the sound of the others calling his name, the crackle of their feet through the brush did not alarm her. They could not stop Pystarr. She could almost hear her own voice summoning him from the depths of the jungle.

But when she crouched in the bower again, waiting, no little body rattled the reeds of the tunnel. No face appeared from the dark tunnel mouth. Aleida waited, her fury growing. Still Pystarr did not come.

This time she did not stop her angry fingers from yanking her hair free. She rubbed the mud dressing to dust, shaking her head violently until her hair stood in a bristling halo. With vehement nails she raked dried mud off her body. Her fingertips tingled malevolently. So no one of them could be isolated. The others would always prevent it if fear did not.

But with the power coming to focus through her burning fingertips, she did not have to isolate one of them to learn the secrets. She did not have to play little lizard or bower-hungry maid. Her body arched back and her arms flared up. Surging veils of power materialized around her, vivid, vibrant. She cast them across the small bower, roiling the leaf-rot that carpeted the floor, searing the woven reeds and branches that screened the bower. Flame burst from her fingertips. With a flash of her hands, she spread it. With another flashing motion, she ripped open the exit tunnel and raced through it.

Behind her the bower flamed. Choking clouds billowed up until within minutes the bower was no more than smouldering rubble.

Aleida detected a sound behind her. She spun, her eyes penetrating shadow. Nine of the band's males crouched in the dense brush: Pystarr, his face engorged; her brothers, Kislik and Lelar; her father; Narnar and the others who had played chuk-chuk in the dyeberry bog. Lelar and Dartak physically restrained Pystarr.

Aleida's anger was immediate and intense. It brought her to her toes, her fingers snaking into the air. "I called Pystarr," she said, the menace in her voice as muscular as her writhing arms. She had called Pystarr, but her own brothers had betrayed her. Her own father had followed her into the jungle, preventing Pystarr from crawling into the bower, preventing her from flashing from him the secrets that should already by right be hers.

And she would not be prevented. She flung her hands through the air, and the power shrieked around their heads. It curtained their shoulders, it netted their torsos, it paralyzed their legs. Nine voices shrilled. Nine bodies were tossed and tumbled by the firestorm of surging orange power.

But Aleida did not burn and twist them all, as she might have. She had no use for nine shrieking animals. She had use for one. And so after the first numbing play of power, she narrowed its focus, pulling the orange curtains tight around Pystarr. His body leapt from Lelar and Dartak's restraining arms and flopped across the ground toward her, as if yanked on strings. His eyes bulged helplessly. His fine hair tangled in the whirlwind turbulence of her power.

The others were as brave as she had calculated. With a yelp and a shrill, they disappeared into the jungle, abandoning Pystarr to his fate. But that was not so cruel, was it? Aleida had no use for Pystarr dead. She released him from the power immediately and he flopped storm-tossed to the damp ground, his hair snarled. "You know the secrets," she purred, bending, fingering fear-syrup from his lax jaw. "Now you can tell me the secrets your father whispered to you."

Pystarr moaned. His eyes blinked rapidly, sending fresh rivulets of liquid down his face. "Ale'a?" he quavered.

He was a useless little animal. She stroked his hair. "You know the secrets. Now tell Ale'a."

Numb of lip, he struggled to appease her. "The sun," he moaned.

"The sun? I see it every day. What is the secret there, stickletail?"

The stunned Pystarr made an obvious effort to assemble the information she demanded. "The setting sun," he specified. "Never go to the setting sun. There is—there is something against the setting sun. Something that—"

Aleida's eyes enlarged. "What is against the setting sun? Another city? Like ours?"

"No-no, no-no." His head began to roll. "There is something else against the setting sun. But no one knows what. And no one must go there or the light-that-is-death will come again. It—" With a quick intake of breath, his eyes enlarged. "The light—" he gasped, staring at her in fear-choked realization. His body stiffened. Desperately he struggled to escape her.

Aleida restrained him easily with wiry arms. "I want to hear all the secrets, Pystarr. The secrets belong to me, too," she insisted mercilessly.

The argument did not calm him. Squealing, he fought her, his body arching and flailing desperately against her grasp.

A useless animal. "I hold light too, Pystarr," she reminded him, hurling herself atop him. "You know what my light does to silly lizards. I want to hear all the secrets."

Pystarr's limbs fell limp. He sucked an agonized breath. "There is light," he babbled. "Light-that-is-death. There is the setting sun. There is something that stands against it. There is someone who can ride the sky." The words spilled from him in a verbal glut. "There is light, light-that-is-death, there is the setting sun, there is—"

"Those are all the secrets? That is everything?" she demanded incredulously.

"There is light, there is the setting sun, there is something that—"

Her hair a scare-halo, Aleida leapt away from him. Precious few were these secrets. Did she not already know that there was light? Did she not already know that there was someone who could ride the sky?

But since there *was* someone, why could she not ride that same sky? She soared it in dream. But her physical body had never left ground when she had willed it, and she knew that it would not leave ground now either. Why not? Why did gravity bind her, despite her sense of power, despite her will to fly? Was the answer to be found against the setting sun? Was the power of flight to be claimed there?

Although the secrets were few, perhaps they were enough. Standing back, Aleida watched Pystarr scramble away from her and skitter into the brush. Drawing herself to her toes, Aleida swept up her arms. Her posture, her elastic muscles were a declaration. She commanded power. She was a being beyond all others here. She was a being beyond Pystarr, beyond Kislik and Lelar, beyond her mother and her father, even beyond old Narnar.

And so she would not remain here. She would hurl herself at the arms of the setting sun and she would claim whatever additional power lay there. She would claim the sky. Taking heel, Aleida ran through the dense jungle, pursuing the arcing, soaring freedom of her dreams.

CHAPTER EIGHT

Stars studded the carapace of night, and twin moons glided up the horizon, cold and white. From concealment of the colonnade, ignoring the play of Mazaahr spots across his field of vision each time he blinked, Verrons watched the humanoids stumble across the plaza toward the upper levels of the complex. The Ehminheer voiced no protest; his evensong had concluded in a drowsy gobble a quarter hour before. When flutes sounded from the upper reaches of the complex, Verrons gathered his own flute cases and moved silently across silver-washed stone. The dome of the grand temple was resplendent by moonlight, beckoning. Impulsively Verrons elected against joining the humanoids in the mountainward courtyard. Tonight he wanted to test the flute phenomenon alone.

Within the grand temple, the stone floor glistened palely, but the upper reaches of the dome were lost in shadow. Verrons' footsteps echoed lightly as he moved along the eastern wall and sat. Bracing himself against cold stone, he opened the double

flute case. The first instrument came to hand, its metal barrel
cool. It was little more than an ornate barrel with fingerholes, a
mouthpiece at one end and a flaring belled extrusion at the
other. But when Verrons placed the flute to his lips, when he
blew, the air clouded brilliantly before him.

And he was captured. Numbly he raised his head. The figures
on the dome surface took fire and began to move, color and line
merging and flowing with hypnotic sinuosity, wheels of light rotating, their streaming arms creating a cloud of rainbow brilliance in the air. Staring up, Verrons was barely aware of the instrument in his hands, of the breath he nurtured it with. He was
aware only of the writhing ceiling and of the slow resolution of
cloud-brightness into light-being.

But this was not the featureless blue being of the night before.
This was a golden creature who, materializing, draped herself in
the remnants of her natal cloud with a graceful sweep of long-
fingered hands. She moved across the temple on long muscular
toes that splayed from the tapered ends of her legs. Her drapery
of light concealed nothing, but her body, a sweetly tapered
sheath of flesh, was in turn marked by no suggestion of profane
function. Her face—oblique eyes, arcing mouth—was a compelling composition of golden light. A separate cloud of light
enveloped the upper arc of her head, faintly iridescent.

Verrons continued to flute, the sounds he produced distant,
divorced from the reality of the moment. Overhead the inner
surface of the dome became as broad as the sky, as deep—and
suddenly as dark. Light wheels detached themselves from the
dome surface and spun down through forever, arcing, weaving,
fusing the air. Smaller luminescent figures flowed after them,
cascading in brilliant confusion.

Chaos engulfed Verrons. His flute glowed with colors he had
never seen before, colors he did not see now but felt in his burning fingertips, in his suddenly sensitized scalp and hair. From the
depths of confusion, his golden creature arched and sprang upward. She arrowed sleekly through an eternity of dark space,
flexed her body and flattened herself against the distant black
surface of the dome, arms and legs elongating. She hung there,
dimming, becoming tenuous. Then she resorbed her fading limbs
and contracted until she was a gaudy yellow sun in a black sky,
burning. Suddenly her limbs exploded outward again. Rippling,

she launched herself downward, swimming air to where Verrons cowered.

He was overwhelmed by light figures that darted and flexed around and through him. They glanced off the staring surfaces of his eyes, dazzling him. The golden creature swooped to penetrate his chest and disappeared into the temple wall behind him. A moment later she reemerged from the wall meters away. She swooped up again and danced over the melee of light, threading the living forms upon her long arms, impaling them with her legs, ordering and taming them. Then with them she created a pyramid in the air, circle upon triangle upon hexagon upon octagon. Finally, with a sweeping motion of arms and legs, she directed them back through the air in a gaudy stream. They flattened against the surface of the dome again, surrendering motion. Only the wheels of light continued to spin.

The golden creature flowed near and hovered, sweeping robes of light around her. *I am.* The words were blown into Verrons' mind. *I live again in the precincts of your power.* Muscular toes arched and curled. Fingers rippled air, sinuous extrusions of light.

Verrons struggled to form words of his own, questions to probe past the barrier of her insubstantiality. Instead the sound of his flute increased in volume.

She brightened, her features becoming distinct, her halo coruscating and condensing into a crown of jewels. *I waited in the matrix of light. I waited to live in your power. Now it moves me.* Eagerly she arched backward. Her limbs joined and elongated, and she became a golden parabola that spanned the temple floor. She wagged her head and shook free jewels that fell away from her into eternal darkness. She flung herself up again, fingers soaring to the upper point of the domes, toes holding the floor. She dwindled slowly, becoming brighter, until she had resumed her original stature.

Unexpectedly a second cloud appeared in the dark air of the temple and surging brightness condensed into a second being, dark, violet, his body powerful. His features contained less flow and more force than the golden being's. He moved on long, thick toes, striding through the remnants of his cloud, gathering them around him grandly. Then, flexing himself, he cast his light-body straight into the air and began to spin swiftly.

Verrons extracted his gaze from the violet being's plane of rotation with effort. He found the five humanoids crouched in a semi-circle a few meters away. One of them had rifled Verrons' flute case. The stolen instrument glowed in the humanoid's grasp, lighting his grey face and casting shadows through his lip veil. Verrons stared at the humanoid, helpless to defend his property. The numbness of fascination held him too strongly.

And as he hesitated, trying to mobilize resistant limbs, a faint remonstrance whispered into his mind. *I waited to live again.*

He shuddered. Distracted, he had let the flute slip from his lips. His golden dancer dispersed into mist. Verrons jammed the instrument back between his teeth and exhaled with will. His dancer flared bright again, her eyes suddenly glowing a brilliant tawny-gold. Exultant, she sprang again, tossing herself up—

—and into the spokes of the violet wheel that flashed across the temple dome. Quickly she arched her body to form a second wheel. Together the two spun through the air, feature and limb obscured by the fiery speed of motion.

Gradually, as the two wheeled through the reaches of the dome, Verrons became aware of a third light entity, the blue being of the night before. He precipitated from the air, flared brilliantly, and flung himself into union with the other two. Verrons managed to pull his glance aside. The tallest humanoid blew his instrument intently. The remaining three cradled theirs, crepey lip veils limp, horn-lined mouths gaping. Light—golden, violet, blue—reflected across the surfaces of their eyes.

Verrons' attention was drawn back to the three-lobed storm of light that sundered the interior of the temple. After a time the three entities separated. The golden being resumed her original form and arced near. Recklessly she swooped through the stone above Verrons' head, to reappear from the opposite wall of the temple moments later. She glided to a halt before him, exultant. Her voice rang in his mind. *When I had flesh, I ran the stones on toes that flexed like springs. I flew with sparks in my hair and between my eyes I wore a jewel that caught sunlight and made it a cleaving sword.*

Verrons' mind was lanced with intense light. He groaned. Into his consciousness flashed a vision that raced the stone pavement, a crackling mane of hair sparking behind her. She tossed a glance back and he knew her face, knew the line of mouth and eyes. But now she wore flesh instead of light, her young body supple and brown. When she turned again, her eyes were as tawny-gold as the flashing jewel recessed into the flesh between them. Impulsively she whipped her gaze to the sun. When she swung back, the jewel slashed a blade of light at Verrons. He grunted in pain.

With a leap she soared into the air. They rode above a city of stone structures set in broad aprons of contrasting stone. At the edges of the plaza jungle crawled dense and damp. *I flew. But my power was weak because I was unmatured. I sank down again, unsatisfied.*

They did sink, until her muscular toes touched stone. She landed running. *But I knew my power would strengthen because my line is strong. My male parent crossed the jungles and the mountains many times by night and returned with fire still flashing in his jewel. My female parent rode the high strata, a flesh-deity, until the day she was caught by storm and torn to her death. I knew it was in my line to soar the sky.*

I flew. Again she launched herself. This time their journey was longer. They darted invisible currents, her sensitive fingers testing the air and conveying its essential characteristics to both their minds, her hair crackling as she swung it around her shoulders. They soared above the city, riding waves and troughs. Reaching the jungle's edge, they swooped high. Trees grew small below. Leaf and vine tangled. Suddenly, fiercely, she arched her back and dove.

They accelerated crazily at the treetops. Verrons uttered a cry that emerged from his flute a harsh note. Only a moment separated them from collision when she swooped up again and arced swiftly toward the puffy white clouds. Moisture slapped Verrons' face. He tasted it gratefully. Then she dove again, this time carrying them to rest at the edge of the city.

I flew. But I walked, too. My feet carried me on my seeking course. I tasted, I smelled, I looked, I touched. My mind grasped and grew and my hair caught current from the air and transformed it to fire. I was a force in my time.

Verrons was drawn into a whirl of activity as she flung through the city, testing and examining, trying and discarding. In her eagerness, she seemed to bounce off her world, leaping from situation to situation. The scene she led Verrons through was a running blur. He saw color, saw pattern, saw objects and structures, saw others of her kind—and not of her kind. But she moved too swiftly for him to resolve anything into detail.

I was, she echoed in his mind. *And now I am again. I take life from your power. I leap, I fly.*

She leapt. For a brief moment she was suspended in her fleshly body against a background of brilliant light. Then she began to recede until Verrons held her at a distance, an apron of darkness wide around her. She stood, hair crackling, her arms thrown back to embrace a giant crystal that broke light to shards upon its faceted surfaces. Throwing her head back, she faded against the crystal, dissolving into it until she was no more than a golden gleam somewhere deep beneath its flashing facets. She hovered there, immaterial.

Then she emerged again. But somewhere within the crystal, she had shed flesh for light. Her hair was a cloud of radiance. *I am!*

She was. She arced about the dome, flashing through darkness like a manic sun. Then she swooped back. *When I had flesh. . . .*

Verrons followed her back through the crystal into flesh again. He lived with her her maturing years, her urgent search for a mate, her frantic sorting and testing of males, her ultimate selection. Then two brown bodies arced the skies, darting and racing, golden jewel and red flashing. Wind-torn deities, they mingled crackling manes and joined arching bodies. When their union was consummated, they returned to their separate lives.

Verrons lived with her the subsequent months while she carried the products of conception to term. Then he fled with her through the cloud-smattered sky to the mountain cavern where she ripped her four young from her own dilating cervix and hissed first life into their gaping mouths. Somewhere beyond the stone birthing chamber, steam pounded, thickening the air with sulphur. Verrons emerged with her when all four young breathed and whisked with her, two young on either arm, tiny hands clinging to her hair, back to the city to find an underling to suckle and tend them.

The young grew. First hair appeared, but only one of the four sprouted a stiff little mane of power. The others grew hair silky and limp. Her fury was wild. She flashed the clouds, venting her anger upon the air, diving and bellowing until all that remained was an acrid residue of bitterness. Then she tore to a dark plaza where she abandoned her ungifted three. She darted away without looking back. *Let whatever scuttling little person wants them claim them. Let them be reared to dig and weave, serve and tend. With their dead hair and their powerless minds, they are none of mine. Instead they will serve mine.*

She bore her remaining daughter into the clouds. Child in arms, she cometed the sky until the shadow of the mountains was dark below, until the smell of sulphur was thick even at altitude. When they returned to the city, her daughter's eyes glowed fiery red.

That was the color of the jewel that, in secret ceremony, was recessed into infant flesh upon the anniversary of the birth. *And I bore my daughter up and taught her. And power flashed between us, an enduring umbilical.*

Verrons followed her through her subsequent years, through the quests and victories of her ever-developing power. He conquered with her and commanded with her that portion of her world she claimed as her own. Her flesh was sun-darkened until it gleamed ebony and her eyes were fierce golden jewels gleaming from twin caverns. Scuttling little people wove and cleaned and served and tended all around her—and when she flashed fire into their weak eyes, when she pulled surging curtains of light from the air and flourished them wide, they moaned and cried and begged to serve her more.

When I had flesh. . . . Her words no longer rode the wind into his mind. Now they came bold and clear, instrument of command. But gradually as she flung through her years, Verrons' strength waned. His mental responses dulled and the sound of his flute grew ragged in his ears.

He was exhausted, drained, but there was no way to communicate his utter depletion to her. Nor could he permit himself simply to let his eyes close, to let his head fall, to let the sound of his flute die. For somewhere in the long night he had ceased to exist as a self-determining entity. He had become as much an instrument as the flute. His dancer commanded them both, regally, mercilessly. Finally, as his head dropped toward his chest, she lived in a single dim chamber of his mind. She performed a shadow show there, flying, surging, commanding, reigning, a force in her time. Doggedly Verrons continued to supply the flute with breath.

Finally even that last lighted chamber of his mind darkened. His fingers laxed. He heard the flute clatter to the stone floor as he slumped unconscious.

Time was a well, deep, black, inescapable. Verrons struggled mindlessly in its dark hold. Much later his feet found purchase. He mounted perpendicular walls and opened unfocused eyes. He lay on his side on the cold stone floor of the temple, his muscles totally unresponsive to his efforts to mobilize them.

"Commander, it's light."

"Sadler?" The query was faint, his head light. Accepting Sadler's help, he sat, dizzily. His flute lay nearby. He closed possessive fingers around its cool metal barrel, passport to wonder. "The humanoids?" he wondered wearily.

"They just went down the gully. They were carrying their leader, the tall one. And they took your flute case and the spare instrument. I didn't try to stop them, but I could probably catch up with them if—"

With effort Verrons shook his head. Let them claim that small offering, especially since in place of the newly issued flute, the humanoids had left one of their own smudged instruments. Verrons retrieved it and muzzily burnished it against his daysuit. Painstakingly, as he studied the abandoned flute, he recaptured mental images of the night in the mountainward courtyard, of last night here. There were five humanoids in the little band. Each blew flute. But there had never been as many as five separate light-entities in evidence, not even when he himself had sponsored the golden dancer and one of the humanoids had launched the violet entity into the night air. There had been only three dancers, golden, violet and blue. Despite his thick-minded confusion, he produced a coherent conclusion. "They left this behind because it's dead."

"Dead?"

"It's exhausted, it's lost its charge, whatever," Verrons responded laboriously.

Sadler's eyes sparked with comprehension. "They damaged it —or depleted it, possibly just by overusing it. And for some reason they couldn't key the temple mechanism to issue them replacement instruments."

Verrons nodded. Stiffly he took his feet, jamming the discarded flute into a pocket. His legs seemed unnaturally long, unnaturally stiff. He stilted across stone to the plaza. From there he surveyed the morning-misted jungle below pensively. Perhaps on their trek here, they had passed through the very city from whose pavements she had first soared into the air. Perhaps those

distant trees were descendants of the ones they had almost intersected in flight. Certainly this sun, rising. . . . Verrons' hand
tightened on his flute. He had walked half a hundred worlds in
the course of his Service career, but he had never before risen
and looked over one as alive as this one today. Even with its for-
mer inhabitants dead.

Dead? When light dancers still cast their spell at the face of
night? But he had no capacity for critical evaluation of the flute
phenomenon today. Someone had packed his brain case with
plaston pellets. They shifted dizzily when he moved, making reality wax and wane around him disturbingly. "I'd better get
some sleep." Dully he rubbed his eyes, making brilliant Mazaahr
spots dance across his field of vision, merry wraiths of disease.

"I'll take the day to explore the western foot of the mesa,"
Sadler offered.

"Do it." Numbly Verrons selected a spot near the colonnade
where the rising sun would warm him and stretched out to sleep.
Vaguely he heard the Ehminheer's first morning cry from the
upper level of the complex. Then he drifted into dreamless sleep.

A few hours later he was wakened by an urgent stimulus. He
sat, sunlight lancing pavement around him, gripped by an agony
of hunger. He frowned at the sky. It was midmorning. He hadn't
eaten since the afternoon before. Even so the force of his hunger
seemed unusual, devastating.

Rubbery legs carried him to the gully. He descended treacherously, reaching its lower mouth on his back, his body sliding
out of control. He lay on the damp ground for moments, his
daysuit ripped, his legs still reluctant to support him. But the degree of his hunger was compelling. There was a ravening beast
in his belly, and it would devour him unless he made it offering,
substantial offering.

Despite his shakiness, an hour later he had brought down
game, skinned and cooked it, and satisfied the gnawing threat of
hunger. He was following a roundabout course back to the gully
mouth when he caught a gaudy ripple a dozen meters away.
"Ehminheer!" he called, the effort bringing a recurrence of dizziness.

The avian halted and his yellow gaze shimmered brilliantly
through damp shadow. But before Verrons could reach him, he
hawked away.

His brief appearance triggered speculation. If Verrons could bring the Ehminheer to attempt to trigger the temple mechanism. . . . He frowned intently. Did the red beam perform a brain scan? A metabolic analysis? Or a sophisticated anatomical survey? Would the mechanism dispense a flute to the Ehminheer even though his oral structure made it impossible for him to use the instrument properly?

But what constituted proper? Certainly Verrons had played with no particular skill. Was a stream of exhalate, however composed, however directed, sufficient to bring light and motion to the air? Or were there compositional criteria? Heat criteria? Must the stream have a certain force, a certain coherence, to activate the flute?

One thing was clear. He had experienced much last night, darting and striding the world with his golden dancer, but he had gathered virtually no hard data. The temple complex remained a mystery. Had it been constructed solely as a playground for light dancers? And the dancers, his golden dancer— why, powerful as they had been, were they extinct now?

Were they extinct now? But could they be otherwise with the cities falling to rubble, the skies empty of arcing brown bodies? Verrons returned to the mesa top and peered reflectively across silken pink stone, measuring the seductive proportions of plazas, colonnades, temples and courtyards with a hard eye. Tonight, he knew, he would return to the temple, return to the world of his golden dancer. When he did, he could again rule her ward with her, again share with her the fascination and power of her time. Or he could take steps toward obtaining more hard data about this place and these extinct dancers.

But what steps? An obvious answer was to expose himself to a variety of dancers, to sample, to pick and cull, obtaining a variety of viewpoints, comparing them coldly. But could he bring that degree of control to the flute experience? Could he deliberately move from flute to flute, voluntarily terminating one experience, initiating another?

It was a question that would have to answer itself. Decided, Verrons mounted the ascending levels of the complex and penetrated the shadow-cooled main temple to milk the mechanism of flutes.

Half an hour later a dozen flute cases were pyramided under the portico and an unreadable Ehminheer was poised near. "You have obtained artifacts." The statement was strained through gravel.

Glancing up, Verrons assessed the beaked face sharply. Each morning the Ehminheer's sunrise song was more fiercely jubilant, each evening his protest at sunset more raucous. Even his speech was reverting, becoming harshly interlaced with chortles and shrieks. Cautiously Verrons extracted the humanoids' discarded flute from his pocket and proffered it for inspection. "We've come across something very interesting here," he confided. Carefully noting the avian's reaction, he detailed the experience he had undergone, first in the mountainward courtyard, then in the temple.

At mention of the golden dancer's first flight, the Ehminheer's yellow eyes lit hectically. When Verrons' narrative wound down, the avian's head flicked back. He scanned the midafternoon sky, guttural sounds warbling from his throat. "And these dancers flew without wings?" he demanded.

Verrons frowned, trying to analyze the sharp insistence that lay behind the question. "They did. Flight seemed to derive from some inherited power to focus and harness solar energy, some innate capacity that developed as the individual matured. Each dancer carried a gem focus recessed into his or her forehead. Apparently—"

"That is what you expect to find below?" the Ehminheer demanded. "The focusing gems?"

"I—I hadn't considered that," Verrons admitted. "I've been thinking primarily in terms of relics." Certainly he had encountered enough such relics in the course of last night's experience. But the flow of images had been too swift, his attention too intensely absorbed by his golden dancer to permit him to focus upon material furnishings. Now detail evaded him. "Certainly the gem seemed to have a central significance to the channeling of the inborn power. And consequently to the development of flight. On the other hand—" His voice died, victim of doubt.

"On the other hand?" the Ehminheer mocked acridly, his crest flaring. "Obviously the need for flight does not drive you."

"I *was* flying, if only at second hand," Verrons snapped back. Frowning, he studied the avian. "Ehminheer, you saw yesterday how the temple mechanism operates. Why don't you step to the middle of the floor and see if it will dispense you an instrument?"

The Ehminheer's glance whipped from the instrument in his taloned hand to Verrons' stockpile. "Why? Aren't there enough instruments here to accommodate your dancers?"

"Certainly, but I'd like a better idea of the mechanism's criteria for dispensing flutes. Sadler and I qualified. Apparently the humanoids did at one time, but now the beam refuses to recognize them. If you were to test the beam, it might give us some idea whether you'll be able to activate an instrument when the time comes."

"And why is the time not now?" Abruptly the Ehminheer jammed the humanoids' abandoned flute into his beak. He exhaled harshly.

Apprehensively Verrons stepped forward. "You're working with a dead flute, k'Obrohms. And by daylight the phenomenon—"

But the Ehminheer had no time for argument. His eyelids darkening, he flung aside the flute and seized one of the pyramided cases. Green talons broke the case open and a second silver instrument disappeared into his yellow beak. The sound the Ehminheer produced this time was no more than a querulous whisper. His pupils shimmied in agitation. Abruptly he hurled the second flute to the pavement, his beak slashing air. His talons clattered as he raced across the temple floor to penetrate the base of the stone needle. He shrieked back inarticulate warning from shelter.

Verrons shrugged helplessly. If there were some way to reverse the Ehminheer's growing alienation—but for now he had to think about tonight. If he were to wield control as he blew his way from flute to flute, he must sleep this afternoon. Wearily he retrieved flutes and moved his stockpile to safekeeping.

CHAPTER NINE

Control? Verrons wielded that tonight. Hunched within the confines of the smallest temple, his golden dancer sheathed in plaston and secured in a breast pocket, he tuned himself across a lost world with cool self-command. At the touch of his breath, light sundered darkness. Motion was born, a brilliant vortex, and narrative whispered into his mind.

When I had flesh. . . .

When she had flesh, when he had flesh . . . when sun-blackened bodies pierced cloud and stone cities dissolved below . . . when crackling manes whipped and sparked and cringing little people fell yelping . . . With Verrons' breath another time came alive. He had arranged the flutes in advance, placing them where spell-numbed fingers could grasp easily. As night passed, Verrons sucked his consciousness first from this light-spell, then from that, his fingers fumbling for fresh metal, raising it, mating it with his lips. Occasionally the sound of the humanoids' flutes reached him from across the complex. They occupied the mountainward courtyard again tonight.

Or the main temple. Or some other temple. *Did it matter when flashing gems blinded him, when time fled beneath his feet and those feet were long-toed, brown . . .*

. . . running . . .

. . . flying. . . ?

Then he realized his careful arrangement of flutes had been disturbed. He peered up and Sadler's ice-pale eyes met his over the glowing barrel of a second flute. As the Talberonese exhaled, green mist surged and a second dancer was born. The Talberonese's pale hair glinted, the bowls of his eyes overflowing with light, his life's breath lost in flute.

The distraction was brief. Almost immediately Verrons' consciousness returned to the world of the dancers. But gradually, involuntarily, the force of his awareness ebbed, drained away. With ebbing vitality, his limbs numbed, and his breath became no more than a dry whisper. *I live again . . .* his irate dancer shrieked, his cry whiplashing Verrons angrily as his violet aura faded. Verrons rallied obediently, but the energy spurt was as brief as it was labored. Abruptly the dimming flute fell from his fingers. Light became darkness, motion stillness, and Verrons' body slumped to the floor.

It was dark when he revived. He lay on his side, absently charting the shimmer of moonlight on stone, trying weakly to reunite the fragments of memory and anatomy. Arms and legs lay at a distance, unresponsive to his will. But somehow his body rested not inside the small temple where he had left it but outside.

Explanation hovered near, pale eyes intent. "I dragged you out here after you lost consciousness, Commander. Are you all right?"

Verrons' head was light, his body numb, his tongue thick. He managed to struggle to a sitting position. "I'm—I think so," he said indistinctly. "I'm—"

But Sadler's concern for his welfare was quickly appeased. The youth knelt, his features concentrated. "Commander, how many of those flutes did you activate tonight?"

Strabismic, Verrons' eyes scrabbled stone toward the small temple. He wagged his head dizzily. "I don't know. I drew at least a dozen from the temple. But I—" He pressed his temples, trying to force his thoughts to clarity. Instead the gesture stimulated a celebration of Mazaahr spots, a frantic flutter of brilliant, unearthly butterflies. He shook his head, trying to clear his vision.

"I cased up the flutes and put them out of sight," Sadler reassured him quickly. He leaned near, excitement kindling in the depths of his eyes. "Commander, have you followed a dancer to his death yet? Or through a crystal passage from one state to another?"

Verrons managed a muzzy frown. His golden dancer, flesh-clad, had splayed herself against a crystal as tall as herself the previous night and dissolved into it, to emerge in altered form, her hair a cloud of energy. Oddly, he realized, he had attributed no particular significance to the transformation. Yet now, considering. . . . Briefly, thickly, Verrons described her crystal passage and haltingly dredged up others he had witnessed tonight.

Sadler nodded eagerly. "But you didn't follow her to her death bed? Or any of the others?"

"No, not—not to my knowledge." But at this point he could not be entirely certain of anything. His mental processes were clouded, muffled in heavy fog.

"Apparently I was lucky in the flute I selected. My dancer was born with a congenital weakness. His life span was much shorter than normal. At first, in the earlier part of his life, I thought the crystal passages were purely symbolic devices for leading the awareness from one state of the dancer's existence to another. But later, after you passed out, my dancer went to what he called the dying house and took a small crystal in his hand. It was colorless, clear, about half the size of the first segment of my little finger. He went to a special room and held the crystal in his palm and—he died. Then the attendant returned and opened his hand—and the crystal had changed. There was a green fleck at the center of it. And the green crystal embedded in the dancer's forehead was dead. He didn't explain fully what was happening, so I'm not clear on the precise function of the smaller crystal. Maybe it was just a device for registering death, or a communicator to summon the attendant. But I'm inclined to think that when he died, something—some electrophysical expression of his personality—was absorbed into the crystal. A—a soulprint you might call it. Does that seem plausible?"

Numbly Verrons considered. The suggestion was incredible. Yet so was the power his dancer wielded. So was the gift of flight. "I—I wouldn't want to venture an opinion until I've passed through a death scene myself," he admitted. Because until he had followed his golden dancer down the passage to her own death. . . .

Tonight? Did he want to live her death tonight? Did he want to surrender the surge and power of her vitality to a crystal half as large as the first segment of his little finger? But her death would never be final, not while he held her flute in hand, her Lazarus-factor. Stiffly he stood, grasping after whatever data his dazzled mind had culled from his evening's experience. "One thing I think may be significant," he ventured, massaging his temples distractedly, "is the fact that although I passed over this portion of the jungle last night, the mesa wasn't yet present. We flew westward over the jungle from a city located the other side of the mountains and landed at streamside to drink. The profile of the mountains was unmistakable. The perspective—"

"Then that tends to support your theory that the mesa is an artificial land feature, apparently raised after the lifetime of the dancer you flew with," Sadler pressed.

"But when?" Verrons demanded. "I was in and out of half a dozen lifetimes tonight. I heard and saw absolutely nothing about the temple complex. And the humanoids—"

"You encountered them?"

"No, never. There wasn't a whisper of their existence."

Sadler frowned. "Perhaps they avoided contact."

"But how? The underpeople had small settlements scattered throughout the jungle. An entire race could hardly have escaped their notice, particularly a race no more canny than the humanoids."

"Then perhaps the underpeople did know about the humanoids. They wouldn't necessarily have communicated the fact to the dancers," Sadler argued. "Or possibly the humanoids are the mutated remnants of the dancer race. If they exposed themselves to too much radiation at altitude—"

Verrons wagged his head emphatically. "Humanoid form is the only point of resemblance between the dancers and the humanoids. And that's not enough." He rubbed his beard thoughtfully, reviewing what little he knew of the dancers and their command of solar energy. "The potential for power was inborn, but the crystal was implanted later. How it was obtained, precisely how it was implanted I don't know. But it was definitely the device that brought solar energy to focus and permitted the dancers to fly, to exercise control over the underpeople and later in their lives even over inert objects."

Sadler shrugged, moonlight glinting across the alabaster surfaces of his face. "It's too bad they never developed scruples to match their power. From what I saw, they didn't even consider the underpeople truly—human."

"Little people who scuttled and served?" Verrons frowned. Certainly the quality of mercy had not been strained in his golden dancer. She had exhibited little empathy for her inferiors, nor for those of her own offspring born without potential for power.

But the night before he had lived in her dominion, just as she had lived in his; he had ruled her ward with her, savoring the tang of her power with his own tongue as well as with hers; and he had not sickened, had he? No, because when she brightened from the instrument at his lips, her consciousness became his. His standards, his ideals were submerged in hers. And hers were grounded in the exercise of power.

He touched the pocket where she waited. Her will to live tingled in his fingertips, in his lips. She had waited in the bowels of the temple mechanism for his resurrecting breath for—how long? Centuries? She had waited to dance the night—tonight. He peered back into the darkened temple. "Are you ready to sample another flute?"

The Talberonese's gaze fell, instantly shuttered. "I—no. Not tonight."

Verrons nodded. He felt something of the same reluctance to place himself again at the mercy of a phenomenon he did not comprehend. But his dancer's mesmeric summons overrode caution. "I understand," he said, and turned back to the temple.

The small structure bore twin moons in its single arched window. Verrons sat on the chill floor and brought the flute to his lips. He tongued the mouthpiece, drew a deep breath and blew, ready to ride his breath to her time again.

But nothing appeared, nothing beyond a faint haze that draped dolorously in the air of the temple. Disconcerted, Verrons blew again, his fingers picking out a small tune no one had ever heard before. No one heard it now, no one but Verrons squatting alone in the chill temple, his lips suddenly cold, twin moons gliding icily across his glazed retinas.

Did she demand the company of her kind? Verrons thought

not. But when his internal timepiece had measured a leaden quarter hour and his breath still produced nothing but mist, he creaked to his feet and measured tread to the main temple.

Another night the hypnotic tumult of light might have claimed his awareness. The humanoids squatted around the walls of the temple, glazed eyes reflecting radiant chaos. But Verrons was not dazzled, not tonight. Stiffly he sat. Muscles clenched, he placed his own flute to his lips and blew.

Again she did not materialize. There was only the limp curtain of light he had blown in the lesser temple, forlorn, barren.

Later he barely remembered his staggering journey back across the complex to the colonnade. There, by gloss of predawn moonlight, his fingers found the silver flute's seams. They were fine, reluctant to part. He parted them anyway with his fingernails. Inside a complexity of miniature elements occupied the metal barrel: ceramic units, gleaming wires—and a single white crystal, half as large as the first segment of his little finger, at its depths a golden speck. *His dancer.* But the crystal was shot with fracture lines. When he probed it, it splintered.

Shattered. Verrons shook bright shards into his palm, loss throwing its pall across him. A soulprint etched in bright crystal; an electrophysical expression of the personality, captured at the moment of death and preserved with all its memories—but in a medium fatally fragile. Verrons had resurrected her to dance a single night. Then, exhausted, he had dropped her flute to the stone floor, shattering her crystal matrix. The clatter of flute on stone echoed in his mind, a sound that would never die from his awareness now.

He closed his hand around sharp fragments. He had destroyed the indestructible, slain the immortal. Some ceremony was demanded to mark the finality of the moment. Abandoning the violated flute barrel, Verrons crossed shimmering stone and lowered himself into the gully. He descended perilously, his dancer's shattered crystal cradled in one palm. Below he slipped into the night jungle. From the mesa the sound of flutes laced the night. Minutes later he emerged at streamside, the smell of mud thick in his nostrils.

I flew with sparks in my hair and between my eyes I wore a jewel that caught sunlight and made it a cleaving sword. Now his golden dancer cried to light the upper atmosphere of her world with a final crystalline surge. It was gross injustice to lay her to rest anywhere here: jungle, mesa, temple.

Then Verrons saw the shimmer of twin moons on the surface of the stream. His body tightened in recognition of appropriate entombment. With a flick of his wrist he cast the shards of her broken crystal upon the stream's surface, committing her to final rest. She broke silvered water lightly. Twin disks rippled briefly and she was gone, gone from the night, gone from the world. Abandoning the streamside, Verrons moved aimlessly through an empty jungle, his eyes intent upon an inner play of light, his hands clenched tight on nothing.

A rustle of brush startled him. Involuntarily his hand closed on his pistol grip. "Sadler?" But did the Talberonese have oblique eyes that held orange light at their depths? Orange light, furthermore, that intensified as the slender body unfolded from the dense brush, as the sinuous arms rose?

He did not. But despite obscuring predawn shadow, Verrons recognized the individual who emerged from the brush. His jaw sagging, he recognized her not once but twice. First she was the young female they had encountered days before in the ruined city. And second the crackle of her hair, the increasingly violent glow of her eyes told him she was sister to the dancer he had just laid to rest in the moon's disk. Verrons stared at her, sister to his golden dancer. But this dancer was here. This dancer was now. And Verrons was not prepared.

Nor was Aleida ready for confrontation. She had emerged at stream's edge at dusk to find herself confronting a tall land mass, an erection of rock, soil and brush like she had never seen before. And when she scrambled up a nearby tree, at the summit of the mesa she sighted a single towering finger of fiery pink stone glowing against the cloud-purpled sun. Instantly Pystarr's warning shrieked to mind. *Never go to the setting sun. There is something against the setting sun—light-that-is-death—someone who rides the sky. . . .* In her arrogance, Aleida had assumed that light-that-is-death was analogous to her own surging curtains of power and that any being who rode the sky was analogous to herself. But now she was here. Now this pointing stone finger— *raised by whom?*—accused the heavens. And now something more than Pystarr's frantic warning possessed Aleida. His fear possessed her, too, gripping her tight.

Who was she, after all, counterposed against this massive stone? She had lived her entire life in a tumbled stonewarren in the jungle, daughter and sister of whining little animals. She had not even been given the secrets at the proper time, in the proper manner. And her own light? It was a sporadic weapon. She had tested it on her pilgrimage through the jungle, withering brush and tree, twisting and searing stickletail, greylizard, stonehog, and other small game.

But not all these intended victims had been consumed by her power. Too often when she cast herself into strike posture, nothing at all flowed from her burning fingertips. She rose to her toes, she arched her body, and the air remained barren. Yet at other times, with the same gestures, she successfully commanded storm.

Why? She thought she understood. The power existed, both within herself and beyond herself. It was a property of her own nature and of the nature that existed around her. It flowed everywhere, a diffuse wash having neither destination nor organization. But she had found means, through her arching back, through her twining fingers, through some change this alteration of posture keyed alive within her own neurological system, to give it coherence, to shape it so that she could flail it around her like a weapon. Her means, however, were not totally reliable. It was as if she sat to play chuk-chuk not with a sturdy poking stick but with a green joint of stiffgrass. Sometimes her joint would send the chuk-rock rolling. Other times it would bend uselessly against the rock and she would be the butt. Her means of commanding power was no more reliable.

Was that, she wondered, why she could not leave the ground? Perhaps. But another question tortured her more. Could her lack of command actually be an inborn deficiency? Could she be inherently a lesser being than the sun-blackened male who had come to her from the sky? Could she be destined to enjoy only the first raw taste of power, never its refinements? Could she in fact be to the flying male and to the Aleida of her dreams what her siblings, her parents, the others of the band were to her? An animal? As darkness came to the jungle, she crouched in the crook of a tree, torn by doubt.

Doubt became fear when faint notes reached her from the mesa top. She bristled, listening intently. The sounds wavered through the damp air, weak, random, inexplicable. They were not the call of any animal. They were no natural sound at all.

The conclusion was inescapable: someone held the mesa top. But who? The flying male? His people? Or someone or something else, something she had never imagined? She visualized it fully now, grotesque with power, a devil beyond any her mother had ever whispered to her. Should she flee? Run yapping back to protection of the stonewarren? Her long toes wriggled, and swiftly she slid down the tree.

But when would she command her full power if she ran yelping to her mother now? When would her feet leave ground and her body arrow sky, clean and hard and surging? Never. Aleida rattled into the undergrowth at the base of the tree, hugging her fear to uneasy quietude.

The notes from the mesa were persistent, now unified, now separate, now louder, now weaker. From her hiding place, Aleida monitored them for as long as she was able. Then her exhausted body slept.

Sometime later her senses leapt awake abruptly. She sprang to her haunches and peered from cover at a dark shape moving through the night. Instinctively Aleida sprang to her feet. Her arms arched up, fingertips tingling.

But before the air crackled with light, she recognized the intruder: one of the creatures who had passed through her band's territory days before. And, she remembered instantly, he was immune to her power. Furthermore, here, who knew what power he himself commanded? Aleida's eyes met his for frozen moments. Swiftly Aleida threw herself into the brush and darted away.

If he commanded killing light, he gave no indication as he chased her through treacherous jungle darkness. Aleida flung herself through brush and vine, but he pursued her with nothing more deadly than shouts and pounding feet. Finally Aleida eluded him by scrambling to the treetops. There she clutched the frail upper branches, her heart throbbing, her breath a windstorm in her ears.

Apparently his ears did not detect it. He passed below her tree a dozen times, circling, looping and eventually returning in the direction of her original hiding place.

So—was this a being so imposing she did not dare follow him in turn? Challenged, Aleida crackled down from her perch and took earth between her toes. Moving as silently as possible, she tracked him to the place where they had originally encountered. He paused, then sat for a while on a small rise of ground, peering at nothing. Then, when first dawn greyed the jungle, he rose and led Aleida to the face of the mesa, where he disappeared into an eroded gully.

Aleida crept forward, tempted to follow. But before she had opportunity to mount the mesa wall, loose rock rattled and she looked up to see grey-hided bodies descending the gully. Shocked, she tumbled back into hiding. As she huddled in the brush, five emaciated grotesqueries emerged from the gully, dull-eyed, hunched, cascades of flimsy tissue flopping from their chins. The tallest carried black-scabbed lacerations on his back and shoulders. The five stumbled away downstream like demon-struck brutes.

Aleida felt just as demon-struck. Could this be the familiar world she had hunted, fished and trapped for her entire active lifetime? The world where she could name every plant and every animal? If so, how could there suddenly be three major varieties of beings she had never encountered or even heard of before: the grey-hided dullards, the pale-fleshed ones and—yes—the bright-feathered creature too? She shuddered. The first two might or might not command magic. The feathered creature's every extremity was armed with slashing talons. Stricken, Aleida burrowed deeper into the brush.

However there was no further traffic down the gully. At midmorning, stiffly, warily, Aleida dared the world again. Safely upstream from the mesa she fed on greylizard eggs, cutting the salty thickness with bittergrass. Later in the day she explored the jungle downstream. It was afternoon and her confidence was on the rise again when she stumbled across the burrowed greyhides and stood over their sleeping bodies, her fingertips tingling with the urge to destroy them here, where they slept. But the power was undependable. If she failed to draw killing light from the air, if the monsters woke and found her arched over them. . . . Wisdom returned her to her explorations.

They yielded her nothing. Her only hope of learning what lay at the mesa's top, she realized reluctantly, lay in ascension. And so at dusk, when she heard the grey-hides crashing through the undergrowth, she followed them, permitting them to lead her into the gully mouth. Ascending cautiously, she trailed far enough behind to escape their notice, near enough to feel herself under protection of their entourage. If there were attack, she would have precious moments' warning to find safety.

Fortunately that eventuality did not arise. When the last grey-hide disappeared over the rim of the mesa, Aleida hesitated briefly, then scrambled after him—and emerged upon another world. She stared around herself, wonder-struck. Polished stone glimmered from her feet, a pavement touched with magic. Columns, stairs, and fantastic structures marked the stations of this new world, all of it spreading from her eager toes.

And all of it was hers! Standing there on the perimeter of discovery, she knew that immediately. The slouching grey-hides were intruders here. So were the pale-hands. None of this had been structured for their eyes or laid for their feet. It had been erected to receive her, daughter of the jungle. Transformed, Aleida strode across polished stone, tall, powerful, her jungle litter origins cast off. She was a being of long limbs and strong toes, a being whose stiff hair was not unruly but charged with power, whose searing fingertips could wrap her in cascades of light and bring lesser beings flopping helplessly to her feet. *The power lived!* And she was its monarch.

As she rode her burgeoning exaltation across the plaza, the sound she had almost run from the night before resumed. It was little stronger and no sweeter tonight. But a sudden surge of light in the air and a brisk electrical excitation of her nerve endings tugged her irresistibly. Aleida ran, not from the sound but toward it.

The sound came from the interior of the largest structure. It grew from glowing instruments pressed to the lips of five grey-hides and two pale-hands. Drawn, Aleida hesitated only momentarily. And when she threw herself to the center of the temple, when she tossed back her head and her eyes caught the swift surge and flow of a hundred linear light forms, the sound was sweet enough.

Instinctively she arched to her toes at the center of the floor, her body spinning, impaled on an axis of light. As she moved—faster, faster—her outflung arms blurred. Her hands, her fingers were lost. Her hair belled out from her head and she heard it crackle sharply, saw the sparks it discharged into the surging air.

Why did those sparks take so long to fall? Because suddenly Aleida was as tall as the temple ceiling, as tall as the world. Because suddenly her head rode the heavens and the sparks from her hair formed a shower of stars bursting from a single mother-body—herself, the sun.

She beamed and she shone, her twirling body left far behind. But at any moment she could arc back to reclaim it. She could move it, she could fling it, then she could open it wide and draw everything into it, sun, moons, stars, universe. She could suck them all through her pulsating fingertips and absorb and hold them, a mighty reservoir as capacious as eternity.

And she did it.

But when she held all within herself, her mighty vaults ached for something more. Light sundered the air, light that shrieked a song she must hear, light that flashed a streaking rainbow against the black of night. She must possess that light. She must hold it and hear it and feel it and know it.

But she could not at once contain this light and the universe. So she spat the universe upon the floor. She disgorged sun, vomited moons, regurgitated stars in a gaudy sparkle. Then her vaults were empty again. She stretched out her arms, summoning, and the light surged in through her fingertips and flashed shrieking through every cell of her body. It burned her, froze her, tore her, recreated her. Then, its course run, each charged particle flashed away through her hair into the air.

To come again. To burn again, to freeze, tear, recreate again, then to shriek free once more.

But this was more than ecstasy. Each stream of light, as it transfused her, implanted strange and glowing wisps of knowledge in her brain cells. She could feel them accreting there, vivid strands of information, irretrievable, incomprehensible—but there. They almost seemed to contain the cry of voices from another time, the shadow of faces, the play of personalities and moods. Impatiently she plunged in after them, but they eluded her, fleeting fragments she could sense but could not examine, not yet.

Then, an eternity later, she found her body winding to the floor of a silent temple. The grey-hides and the pale-hands lay unconscious before her. And her own body was hardly stronger. Her knees were traitorous joints of stiffgrass, ready to bend.

Exhausted, she rode reluctant legs from the temple and stood at the verge of the stone portico, seeking the sky for dawn. Finally it came, the sun bearing her own victorious features into the regions of sky, proudly. And it seemed to her, in her weary exaltation, that she should follow it there. The universe was hers. Why not the sky?

Why not? This earth lay beneath her, inanimate, insensate, but she moved and tasted, thought and felt on behalf of all its lifeless particles. That was her function in the unity of their being. For not only was she of this world, she was its pinnacle, its ultimate expression. She was its culmination, and it recognized that and rewarded it. Why did not the sky? Aleida rose to her toes, reaching, twining her fingers.

But the sky refused to recognize her. She commanded power, but she could not bring it to proper focus to jet herself from the glossy pavement.

There was good reason for her inability to fly, she realized reluctantly. If she could only tap the information deposited in her brain cells by night, she would know what she lacked and she would learn how to implement flight. But hard as she strained, the vital information would not flow at her will. And so she was left only with the frustrating knowledge that it existed—and with this empty construct of stone.

This *un*empty construct. Because suddenly a harsh crow seized her heart. Instinctively she tossed herself to shelter of a smooth pink wall, fear suddenly shriveling her sense of transcendence. She had forgotten the other intruder, the blue-feathered creature armed with beak and tearing claws. Now she huddled in shadow, diminished by fear, unwilling audience to the song he hurled at the morning sun. Her reaction to his presence, to her own fear, was acrid resentment, bitter resolve. Today she cringed from this creature's Superior natural weaponry. But she would not always be at the mercy of this creature or any other creature. She would find the means for harnessing and directing the power.

She would be victim no more then, not even of momentary fear.

CHAPTER TEN

Days passed, days demarcated by brilliant sunrises and gaudy sunsets, warmed by midday sunlight and chilled with darkness. Tiehl passed the night hours in sleep, prisoner of metabolism. But at odd moments he swam to awareness, perched on his courtyard wall, the glistening stone shaft at his back. Each time he listened uneasily to the plaintive cry of flutes. And each time his crest surged and his plumage ruffed and he regretted that he had permitted the dull-eyed humanoids access to the mesa top.

Now dawn came again and when he had greeted it, he peered out over his violated domain with growing dissatisfaction. They had all gathered under the grand dome last night, humans, humanoids, and jungle female. Bristling, he hopped down from his wall and strutted across the courtyard to the temple, his yellow eyes shimmering. Humans and humanoids sprawled gracelessly across the temple floor. Tiehl gobbled scornfully. So this was how the humans flew, their unkempt bodies abandoned upon the stone floor, metal flutes clutched in their mud-clawed hands.

Puffing his plumage, Tiehl birdtracked around them, contrasting his full glossy plumage to Verrons' rough-bearded face. Were these the clever humans who had tricked him into leading them to perch? Who had then denied his claim to the entire mesa top and pared his territory to a single walled yard?

Contemptuously Tiehl raised a talon and traced the uneven line of Verrons' beard. Since the ship-wings of Authority Fleet had lured Tiehl from Ehminhee, humans had wielded their more highly evolved mentalities against him like so many weapons: slap, chop, slash. Shipboard, they had deliberately employed his own needs and drives to wrest performance from him, a betrayal that had masqueraded as altruism. And he had been helpless to outwit them. He had not even realized he had grounds for dissatisfaction until he had warmed his plumage upon his own wall, protecting the stone trunk that grew from the plaza floor. For years he had tamely permitted himself to be subverted.

But no more. Here the harshness of noonday sunlight, the cool sting of jungle mist, the reaching splendor of moss-trunked trees had stripped the blinders from his eyes. Here he recognized how he had permitted himself to be used and deceived. The knowledge did not inspire him with compassion for any member of the human race. And what use was the human brain-weapon when the human lay unconscious on the stone floor, his stale mouth agape, a blade-sharp Ehminheer talon tracing its tender lips?

Something restrained him, a last vestige perhaps of the weakness that had permitted him to live willing captive of Authority Fleet for eight years. And before he could blot away the taint of irresolution, he caught sight of motion from beyond the temple. His crest rising, he flared his vision to the plaza. It was the female again. With a squawk, Tiehl clattered across the temple floor, ripping air with his beak. He emerged to see her dart away to the lower level of the complex.

Gobbling, he patrolled the portico, inflamed by her repeated appearance in the vicinity of his perch. She had been timid enough the first day she had arrived upon the mesa top. The sound of his voice had sent her leaping for shelter then. But by the second day she had been bolder, and by the third she had stepped from boldness to audacity, circling his courtyard wall on long toes, her hair a thicket, her gaze a challenge some uneasy instinct warned him against meeting. She appeared defenseless. Yet there was an electricity in her eyes, a tension in her wiry body, a quality of restrained menace that she carried with her not like a shield but like a weapon.

Stirred to protective fury, Tiehl raced back to the courtyard and flung himself atop the wall. His gaze whiplashed the complex. The female darted to the open plaza and peered up at him, her oblique eyes defiant. Then she turned and strode away toward the gully. But Tiehl knew he had not exorcised this particular demon. She had only gone to make her morning meal.

His own demanded attention. Tiehl strutted the wall again, possessively, then with a glance toward the gully where she had disappeared, hopped warily down. He strode through the temple, where humans and humanoids appeared to be struggling feebly toward consciousness. With a possessive glance back at the pink shaft, Tiehl loosed an angry shriek at them. Then he hurried across the complex to the gully.

When he reached the base of the mesa, hunt fury hissed in his blood. It drove him through damp-clotted foliage, through claw-tangling vegetation, until his beak tasted blood and his senses dispatched notice that struggling bristle-tailed prey had become meat. He carried his catch into the trees then and tore it hungrily, riding a river of blood back to Ehminhee. There he sat at perch with his kill, plumage ruffed, his crest hot in the sun. Pale sunfeeders rattled against the hard yellow sky, chips of living parchment. The breeze was astringent. And in the air, soaring—

Abruptly perch petrified in his claws. While he sat leisurely savoring a fantasy world, where was the female? With a shriek, Tiehl scrambled down the tree and assaulted the gully. Ascending, he squawked indignantly across the plaza, his aroused instincts blaring alarm.

And if the female lingered in the jungle feeding, what brown body dodged from the grand temple at his strident charge and ran to hiding at the upper level of the complex? Racing through the temple, Tiehl clattered angrily around the base of the perch, his farsight enlarging the paving stones. Did this one carry a smear of mud from a long-toed foot? That one a single coarse hair? Was there a trace of dampness, a speck of fresh vegetable matter? From his own foot or hers? Furiously he examined each taloned claw. They were clean. Then he darted from the yard.

The humans still huddled in the temple, semi-conscious. Tiehl clawed Verrons' shoulder and the human's head rolled loosely.

Laboriously Verrons opened a single eye and mouthed an inarticulate query.

Tiehl's accusation was barely intelligible through angry chuckles. "The female has violated my perch!"

Verrons' second query was as indistinct as the first. His tongue contributed nothing to it, the words emerging unrefined from his throat. Vengefully Tiehl slashed the arm of the human's daysuit and clattered back to his yard. He patrolled his wall, directing acrid shrieks at the mountainward colonnade, where the young female hid. But his fury was not directed entirely at the female. It was Verrons who had insisted that Tiehl permit violation of the mesa top, with the stipulation that no one would be permitted to intrude upon Tiehl's courtyard. Verrons bore a large part of the responsibility in the matter.

The sun measured several degrees of arc and Verrons roused himself and appeared in the courtyard entry. His appearance was unpromising. He leaned against the stone arch, his shoulders sagging, his eyes misaligned. "We—you woke me, Ehminheer?"

Angrily Tiehl hopped from his wall and strode to confront him. "The female has trespassed upon my yard."

"She—she's been in here?"

"She was here less than an hour ago."

Vaguely the human peered across the empty courtyard. "Looks like you chased her away."

Tiehl bristled. "I do not want her here to be chased, Verrons. You promised that if I permitted you and the others access to the mesa top, no one would disturb my courtyard. Less than an hour ago she slipped in here and you did nothing."

Verrons grunted. "I was asleep, Ehminheer. I—"

"Are you rescinding your promise that the courtyard is mine?"

"No. No, I didn't say that. But I have no control of the girl. I didn't bring her here, I can't communicate with her. I—"

"You have heat pistols," Tiehl snapped.

Verrons' eyes widened. "Use them on the girl?" Muzzily he shook his head. "She can't damage the shaft, Ehminheer. She's defaced nothing. She—"

Outrage strained Tiehl's eyelids, darkening them to midnight green. "She trespasses in my courtyard, Verrons. And if you refuse to understand that—" But he was not ready to voice the threat, not yet. If Verrons would not deal with the female, if Verrons could not. . . . Indignantly he danced away from the bleary human, a slashing of his beak terminating the interview. He leapt to his wall and glared until Verrons withdrew.

Several minutes later the two humans emerged from the grand temple and straggled across the stone plaza. Keenly Tiehl's gaze danced over the pair of them. There was no mistaking their deterioration. Since their arrival at the mesa top, something had gradually neutralized their wit, rendering them a pair of stumbling automatons. He watched as they stretched out on sunlit stone and lapsed back into sleep. Then from the perimeter of the plaza Tiehl caught sight of the female, her oblique gaze trained upon him.

Tiehl chuckled fiercely. The humans grew weaker, the girl bolder. If Verrons would not defend the courtyard from invasion, Tiehl must do so himself. And if Tiehl could not catch the jungle female and dispatch her with talons and beak, he must destroy her with some other weapon. He crouched in the early morning sunlight, his throat rattling ominously.

A short while later he emerged from the temple and approached the humans. Vengefully he danced a bird step around them as they slept, tattered and muddy, bearded and dull. The Talberonese's belt buckle was exposed. Tiehl crouched, disengaged it and slowly inched the belt from under the inert body. Both Verrons' buckles, however, were beneath him. Tiehl hesitated, then boldly rolled the human to his back and snapped free his weaponry. Verrons opened a watering eye, which immediately quivered shut again.

Tiehl tossed one of the pirated pistol belts over the edge of the mesa. Then, deliberately, he strode toward the gully and disappeared into its rocky mouth, a pistol belt slung over each arm. Reaching the bottom of the gully, he crouched on the mudbank and used his beak to pierce new holes in both belts. Then he secured the weapons around his stringy torso, extending his attack capabilities well beyond reach of his beak and talons.

Purposefully he circled the base of the mesa until he reached its southwest face. Here the mesa was steep, treacherous with entangling vegetation that ripped free under his grasp. But the female would be watching for Tiehl to reappear from the mouth of the gully. She would not extend her vigilance to the southwest perimeter of the mesa rim.

Finally topping the rim of the mesa, Tiehl slithered to cover at the base of the colonnade and peered out. There was no sign of activity in the vicinity of the grand temple. But he was convinced that when he rushed the courtyard wall and flung himself over, he would trap the female violating perch. And this time. . . .

He had no chance to put his revenge into motion. His scanning eye flickered to the sky and an involuntary squawk broke from his throat. His crest erecting, he leapt from hiding. A dark form skimmed the clouds, riding the sky like an expertly tossed dart. Fiercely Tiehl unreeled his farsight and brought a sleek black body to focus. Hair a sparking thicket, brilliant green gem at his forehead, the body arced down toward the complex, fingers twined, and described a broad parabola about the summit of the perch.

Fury gripped Tiehl in a raucous burst. He hurled himself across the plaza, a gaudy streak of blue, and shrieked through the temple into the courtyard.

This time the female did more than simply violate his courtyard. She had penetrated the base of the perch and she crouched at its interior. Her head was thrown back. Unaccountably her glowing eyes cast vivid orange illumination up the inner shaft of the perch. Light reflected from polished stone surface to polished stone surface and back upon her face, masking it in glare. At Tiehl's shriek, she sprang to her feet, her oblique eyes flaring. Swiftly, malevolently, her hands climbed the air. The muscles of her arms writhed.

The bright curtain of light that danced from her fingertips had no more effect upon Tiehl's rushing fury than a waft of perfume or a snatch of melody. Enraged, he saw only exposed belly. He plunged at her, his beak ripping air.

But there was a greater trespass than the female's, and it deflected him screaming and squawking around the base of the perch. He gobbled up at the male who arced from the sky and glided smoothly to rest upon the upper rim of the perch, his black body gleaming. As if in rebuttal of Tiehl's shrieked malediction, a swath of green light rayed from the gem at his forehead.

Tiehl's blood hissed. Distractedly he registered the arrival of the two humans in the courtyard as he unholstered a heat pistol, released the safety and aimed.

A tight beam of heat-energy leapt from the barrel, but as Tiehl triggered the weapon, both humans threw themselves at him, jarring his aim from the midline of the black torso. With a furious gobble, Tiehl brought the barrel up again.

The heel of Verrons' hand smacked Tiehl's arm and the pistol clattered to stone. Fiercely Tiehl spun on the human, eyelids darkening, beak slashing. But before horn tasted flesh, the other human caught a pin-feathered arm and twisted it back. Light, fragile-boned, Tiehl was at an immediate disadvantage. Impotent, a restraining human on either arm, he glared up the stone shaft.

Vindication swelled his stringy chest. He had wounded the invader. The wound in his side was ashen white against the ebony of his skin. At first it appeared the male would slowly fold forward and topple down the steep side of the perch to his death. Then dark muscles rippled and he stood again, unsteadily, on the upper lip of the shaft. With obvious pain, he raised his hands and twisted the fingers together. The gem at his forehead glimmered palely as he took air.

This time he wobbled like a dart thrown by a drunken hand. He lost altitude over the western reach of the complex, barely topping the pink columns of the mountainward colonnade. The humans released Tiehl, and he ran after them through the temple. Emerging, they pounded to the highest level of the plaza. Tiehl flared his farsight after the escaping male.

He took altitude briefly over the jungle. Then his muscles seemed to lose tone. Tiehl enlarged the twined fingers with his farsight and watched them ravel and drop. The flying male followed, describing an uneven trajectory down into dense jungle growth. Tiehl's eyes fired with triumph. The enemy was down.

But other enemies still littered the mesa top, enemies who had shown their colors long before the flying male's appearance. Tiehl rounded on them, his beak slashing. Verrons' whiskered lips crackled open incredulously. The female recognized threat before either human. At Tiehl's onslaught, she rose to her toes, her arms writhing, her stiff hair a threatening crackle. With a squawk, Tiehl hurtled at her, beak clacking.

She squealed and long toes flung her away across polished stone. She dashed for the perimeter of the plaza. With an angry gobble, Tiehl hurtled after her, the fury of the chase singing in his blood. He harried her around the perimeter of the complex, his talons slashing air, never quite able to draw blood. In the fervor of the chase, he completely forgot the heat pistol at his waist.

Dodging around a colonnade, she tried to reach the gully mouth, but Tiehl raced ahead and blocked her path. With a frightened yelp she darted to one side, attempting to circumvent him. This time his beak ripped the flesh of her leg. Crying with pain, she retreated and raced back toward the upper levels of the complex. When she reached the vicinity of the mountain-ward courtyard, the two humans appeared to run ragged interference for her.

Their attempt at intervention accomplished nothing beyond corralling them for the final drive over the side of the mesa. Chortling furiously, yellow eyes glaring, Tiehl herded them together in a pack, pressing them nearer and nearer the mesa rim until finally they had nowhere to flee but down the steep bank of the mesa. Losing her balance, the girl fell with a frightened bark. Tiehl's ripping beak drove Verrons and the Talberonese after her. His blood sang in his ears as they crashed down the steep incline. One of the humans shouted hoarsely from far below. Then there was silence.

Retrieving the dropped heat pistol, Tiehl mounted the wall of the mountainward courtyard. He strutted it, his farsight picking at the brush and tangled vegetation below: scarlet, black, green—still. Victory swelled his chest and ruffed his plumage, uniting him with every Ehminheer who had ever defended his perch. He shrieked, gobbling back and forth the length of the wall, crest flared, beak clacking.

He maintained patrol on his own courtyard wall through the sun-warmed hours of afternoon, pausing occasionally to render screeching claim upon everything within sound of his voice. Later, however, despite his vigilance, there was a force that narrowed the boundaries of his territory. With sunset, darkness ate away the mountains, gobbled down the jungle, swallowed stone plazas, and finally turned its black teeth upon the courtyard wall. Tiehl warbled defiance but even his evensong dwindled eventually to silence and he surrendered to sleep.

As before a recurring irritant laced his night. Flutes whined reedily from the grand temple. Once he wakened briefly and caught sight of dull grey faces bathed in unreal light. Night-paralysis bound him to the wall, but simmering outrage woke him early the next morning. The wail of flutes had hardly died, the sun barely greyed the eastern sky when Tiehl cast off sleep and sprang down from the wall.

Paving stones glimmered palely. The air was heavy with anticipation of day. Tiehl clattered across the courtyard into the main temple, deliberately concentrating his possessive fury into a single virulent scarlet strand. His yellow eyes shimmered. Rage sang in his blood, an acrid blood-melody that mobilized him, limbs flexing, through the dim temple. With a shriek, he flashed at the intruding humanoids, his beak ripping, his talons tearing.

Four of the intruders wakened and grunted across the floor blindly, struggling to escape. When they tumbled out the temple entrance, Tiehl descended upon the single heedless humanoid. Rage drove him blindly. His beak tore, ripping grey hide savagely, tearing at pale muscle tissue and spattering thick blood across the floor. Only when his blood fury was fully combusted did Tiehl realize that his savaged victim had not resisted at all, had not even really bled. The blood on Tiehl's claws was already congealed, a black gel. Tiehl leapt back, his gaze fierce. The enemy was dead but a quick testing of torn flesh told Tiehl he had flayed an already cooling corpse. Some other agency—exhaustion, starvation—had made the kill hours before.

A secondary surge of anger brought his crest surging erect again. Chuckling angrily, he tugged the dead humanoid from the temple and rolled the body over the mesa wall. As it tumbled to rest far below, he dug his beak and talons into the soil to clean them. The sun rose as he returned to the temple, his emotions in flux. He had routed the intruders, all of them. But chance had stolen his single kill, and as the sun pushed morning up the sky, he was no nearer the moment when his claws would curl around the solid reality of perch. No nearer at all. Melancholy rising in his throat, he gathered up the flutes the humanoids had abandoned in their panic and hid them at the base of his perch.

CHAPTER ELEVEN

Regaining his feet at the bottom of the mesa, Sadler tottered through a psychotic's jungle of spastic greenery and epileptic vines, searching for Verrons. Before he had wandered far, dizziness and hunger gripped him, bringing cold sweat to his forehead. Testing reality with an extended hand, he stumbled to rest at the base of a moss-slimed tree. He jammed his injured wrist into his armpit and let his head sag forward against his knees.

Unexpectedly Verrons materialized beside him, his eyes redrimmed in a gaunt, mudstruck face. "Are you hurt?"

Sadler raised his head. His jiggling eyeballs anchored desperately upon Verrons' reassuring solidity. "I've hurt my wrist. Are you all right?"

"I collected a few bruises. Nothing more serious," Verrons said, kneeling to examine Sadler's injured wrist. "Seems to be a sprain," he decided. "We should probably bind it up for a few days. Do you feel like walking?"

"I don't know. I—" Sadler tongued dry lips, struggling to his feet. The effort set off fresh spasms of greenery. He touched his temples, trying to steady his vision. But more than exhaustion and hunger contributed to his giddiness. "The girl—"

Verrons' eyelids shuttered his gaze. "She's in the treetops just ahead. Doing Authority knows what."

But Sadler knew what she was doing. The first flashes had touched his mind yesterday when he dozed against the wall of the mountainward courtyard—and suddenly found himself gazing into the distance with a fierce possessiveness that jolted him awake. The young female stood at plaza's edge, her body arched in fervent proprietorship of the jungled vista below. Standing, startled, Sadler had looked upon the same vista, but from a double perspective, hers astigmatically superimposed upon his own, splintering all elements into a confusion of line and color. And today he had charted the flying male's fall with two pair of eyes: his own and hers, experiencing not just his own startled disbelief but hers as well, transmogrifying quickly to anger, then to sharp fear as the Ehminheer's shimmering glare swam air to encompass—

—*her*, not him. Sadler had sucked a sharp breath anyway, muscles mobilizing. Then the young female had fled across the plaza, snapping the strand of communication. Now Sadler directed a covert glance at Verrons. If the older man were troubled with similar phantasmic snatches of image and emotion, he apparently preferred not to discuss it.

Verrons stretched erect, his brow creased with other concerns. "This diet you mapped out, Sadler—you didn't leave out a few essential elements, did you? Or drop in something we can't metabolize? Something that gradually accumulates to a toxic level?"

Pensively Sadler stared at the jungle floor. "I worked from half a dozen texts on human nutrition, supposedly reliable ones."

"Which in turn calls into question the reliability of the tissue analysis data on local flora and fauna that you used," Verrons suggested. Certainly their condition was not reassuring: emaciation, tremor, recurring spells of dizziness and voracious hunger. In appearance Sadler and Verrons had gradually assumed the aspect of two men who had survived a pestilence—or who were about to succumb to one. Verrons shrugged. "Well, here we are. We can't return to the mesa, we don't intend to return to Selmarri Home—do we?—and in addition to all the other anomalies we've catalogued, now we have a flying male, a full-blown example of the powered race. Appearing from nowhere."

"Or we don't have him."

"Acknowledged. But if he *is* alive, he'll try to find the girl again."

"And if he's dead?" Sadler asked dully.

"That still leaves us the girl."

Reluctantly Sadler agreed. Jungle greenery in dizzy flux around him, he followed Verrons to the tree from which she cast her call to the clouds, trying angrily to command the fallen male back into the air. Sadler winced under the barrage of second-hand emotion. He squatted uneasily beneath the tree while Verrons fetched broad leaves and wrapped his injured wrist, tying it with vines.

"Wait here," Verrons instructed finally, rising. "I saw signs of lizard nestings on the mudbank. We'll lunch on fresh eggs and than catch a nap." His gaze slanted speculatively up the tree. The girl's eyes glowed down at them through the dense foliage, bright and unreadable.

"We'll know if she leaves," Sadler observed grimly.

And they did. When they had eaten, the girl's urgency withered to erratic wisps of smoldering anger and the two humans fell into uneasy sleep. At first Sadler's drowsing consciousness was as shadowed as the afternoon jungle. Then, uninvited, emotion washed across it: anger, loss, fear. Distinct images took life from the matrix of dream: fallen stone structures and fractured plazas, a dark basement, its corners deep in crumbled stone, the floor thick with dust. Sleeping forms huddled nearby, small, reassuring, their thin hair spread in the dust. Then security crumbled under Verrons' prodding hand. "Sadler, she's moving. She's running back in the direction of the city."

Reluctantly Sadler pulled himself to his feet and followed Verrons. As they trailed the young female through the jungle, her vision fractured his outlook, reducing him to dizzy stumblings when they followed too near, *déjà vu* when they let her outdistance them. At first the girl ran ahead of them. Then she tailored her pace to theirs, and snatches of emotion assailed Sadler: anger, arrogance, indulent self-aggrandizement—attitudes grown too familiar through the flutes.

Near dusk the girl halted at a rattle in the brush, spinning on long toes, her oblique eyes flaring orange. Swiftly her back arched and her long fingers climbed air; With a yap, a coarse-hided jungle piglet burst from the brush.

Sadler froze as the girl's fingertips danced, drawing visible curtains of orange light from the air. Spinning, she directed the surging draperies of energy at the startled hog. With a squeal it flopped to its side and danced a frenetic polka toward her, its feet in the air. It convulsed, joints crackling, and as she continued to irradiate it, it thumped a death-circle around her, shrilling in agony until finally its tortured muscles slackened in death.

"The power," Sadler breathed, involuntarily shrinking back into the brush.

Verrons was beside him, the two of them attempting to blend inconspicuously into the late afternoon shadows. "She's gone into strike posture before," the older man hissed, "but the result wasn't apparent to us. Now evidently the power is developing. And she's able to command it even without the focusing crystal."

Sadler nodded numbly, staring helplessly at the young female as she knelt over her prey. "It—will it be effective against us? Our nervous systems—"

"It couldn't touch us as little as three nights ago," the older man whispered. "But that was three nights ago, and the light manifestation was not visible then—at least not to us."

He didn't have to say more. Sadler hugged himself against the grip of chill, stricken with an overwhelming sense of destiny inexplicably fulfilled. Had he remained on Talberon, he would be crossing the ice plain of the northern circle now, his assignment to penetrate the fata morgana, that illusory mist-land of hills, valleys and snow-capped peaks that the great lens of the atmosphere threw up to guard the northern pole. And he would have remained at the pole, sheltering in his skin tent, until the polar sunset, to return through the aurora, surging curtains of light that turned the entire polar night sky to rainbow. Instead he hunched in the brush of Selmarri, jungle life playing its homely bush-song around him—and faced an inexplicable curtain of light summoned from the fingertips of a savage. And it roused in him a savage's fear.

The girl fed on her kill unceremoniously, darting brilliant-eyed glances toward the half-concealed humans. Then she threw aside the stripped bones, her eyes glowing against coming darkness. She stood, her long body sinuous, fingers and toes tapered, hair standing stiff from her head. Still monitoring the humans, she mounted a nearby tree. Gradually the glow of her eyes faded into dusk.

Cautiously Sadler and Verrons emerged from the brush and took shelter beneath a nearby tree. Thickening dusk isolated them one from another. "Do you still feel like sticking with her?" Verrons inquired hoarsely when twin moons rode the sky and starlight punctuated the western darkness.

Sadler nursed his sprained wrist. Despite the chill which still gripped him, his head was perceptibly clearer than it had been earlier and his muscles less tremulous. "I can't go back to Selmarri Home now," he said grimly. Men and women had walked out of the polar night months later than anticipated and had been accepted into the Academy, the final training ground for the men and women who would ultimately tame Talberon. Rega Masne had appeared from the ice plain three years after she had departed on her radius-six and had not only been enrolled in the Academy but promoted ahead of her age level. But to return prematurely, the illusory fata morgana never even challenged. . . .

Verrons grunted, lost in his own thoughts. "I'd like to know more about the power crystal," he mused.

"The flying male—"

"Exactly. He obtained a crystal somewhere." Verrons' eyes glistened palely. With a rattle of foliage, he mounted the tree.

Puzzled, Sadler followed. Verrons extracted a flute from his pocket. A shaft of moonlight brought the metal barrel alive in his hand. It was an instrument Verrons had disassembled two days before. Now he thumbnailed it open again and peered at its elements: wires, miniature ceramic units—and the crystal, small, clear, a speck of violet at its center. It refracted the cold brilliance of moonlight into their eyes. "The various internal elements are strictly products of technology," he mused. "They don't look beyond human duplication."

"But the crystal?" Sadler's nail tested its facade. Somewhere within its depths lay immortality. A fragile immortality, true, given the brittleness of the crystal—but embedded in that violet speck was the spiritual remnant of a being who had flown this world centuries before. Sadler settled back on his heels. "If we could get Authority specialists out here to study the crystals, crystallo-physicists, biospecialists—"

Verrons laughed sharply. "Sure. Any biospecialist who contracts bloodblossom will be consigned to us immediately—provided Jurgens doesn't send him to some other isolation colony. If he manages to infect his colleagues, we could see an entire laboratory staff tumbling out of the sky. Without the laboratory however."

Sadler frowned, trying to read the other man's features in the evening gloom. "Authority dropped equipment and supplies for the survey of local flora and fauna."

"But what kind of equipment?" Verrons probed.

"Discards," Sadler admitted reluctantly. "Obsolescent laboratory models and surplus and outdated supplies and reagents."

Verrons nodded. "So there we have it: a putated laboratory staff outfitted with random discards, given a nine year working life span at most and totally isolated on Selmarri—no professional crosscurrents, no computer time, nothing but a handful of crystals—which neither of us expects to do the human race any earthly good, beyond satisfying our individual curiosity."

Sadler sighed, reluctant to surrender pursuit of the fragile mirage that lay within the flute crystal. "If we could persuade the monitor ship to lift the crystals off-world for preliminary study—"

Verrons snapped the flute back together and pocketed it, shaking his head. "Dublin can call on the monitor ship in case of general emergency or in the case of a suspected remission. Otherwise the ship's activities are at the discretion of its captain—and I doubt that we have enough here to draw him out of orbit. No, it's our curiosity that's tickled. We'll have to try to satisfy it ourselves—if it can be satisfied."

Their gazes met at a common point on the ground, blunted swords. Sadler massaged his wrist, deliberately drawing pain.

"Of course it's always possible that optimistic status-of-research communique Dublin mentioned contained a grain of truth," Verrons observed finally. "Conceivably the cure *could* be isolated in the near future and then we'd have full access to Authority research facilities."

Sadler's head rose slowly, his scalp drawn painfully taut by a new and disturbing question. "Commander, if the cure is perfected—where does that leave us?"

"If we're still out here, out of contact with Selmarri Home? It leaves us lost, presumed dead. A black mark on Dublin's record and a rapidly declining life expectancy figure at the bottom of our own balance sheets." Briskly Verrons handed himself down the tree. "Only one possibility disturbs me more: returning to Selmarri Home and waiting nine years for a cure that never comes."

Sadler strained to read the older man's features. But moonlight glinted off his face without illuminating it. "But that—don't we have to assume there is a very slight chance our own people could utilize these crystals? We can't completely disallow the possibility until we know more about the crystals and about the imprintation process. And if the cure should be isolated while we're out of communication with Selmarri Home, we could have effectively blown immortality for the human race."

Verrons stepped nearer the tree, his dark eyes computing that possibility into his own personal equation. "That—that would be unfortunate. For everyone," he admitted, shrugging. "But I'll take personal sanity in the hand to immortality for the whole race in the bush." He peered up the tree, his dark eyes narrowed. "Could you reach Home alone if necessary?"

"The colony lies due east," Sadler responded reluctantly.

"Then the decision is yours, Sadler. Entirely yours. Mine is a separate matter." Turning, Verrons divorced himself from moonlight. Brush rattled.

Left alone, Sadler's gaze retreated inward. Torn, he found himself rendering a massive calculation: the human race—times possible immortality for all. And another: nine years of jungle freedom divided by the possibility that the cure *would* be isolated sometime during that period, that a normal life span could lie ahead. But what would he return to, cured, if he retreated from the only fata morgana, the only aurora-shrouded polar extreme Selmarri had to offer?

The answer was clear. His ultimate goal was Academy. But to qualify he must satisfy not only the stringent formal qualifications set by Talberon Council but also the qualifications he had set himself. And he could not do so by returning to Selmarri Home now. Silently he handed himself down the tree to find shelter for the night. As he groped through the dark jungle, dancing Mazaahr spots impeded his vision, teasing reminders of the finality of his decision.

The next morning the young female led way through the jungle with arrogant proprietorship. This was her domain, her attitude said, and she permitted them to trespass with the austere generosity of a monarch. But occasionally, through his own distraction, Sadler detected wariness in her mind, too, unease when Verrons met her challenging stare levelly, discomfiture when the older man left them to detour down a sediment-choked stream and reappear later from the jungle ahead, his dark face intent upon the brush that surrounded them.

Her occasional uncertainty was a minor ingredient of her day's mood however. Overriding it was a galling hunger for vengeance, an emotion that leapt to bright focus when she flashed small game from the brush at midday and kindled afresh in the late afternoon when she halted and drew fire from damp debris at the base of a dead tree, flushing a nest of small animals. It flared even brighter on the occasions when she rose, arched her body and from her dancing fingers appeared—nothing. Nothing at all.

"So she doesn't have total command of the power," Verrons pointed out grimly when they settled again for night. "She's apparently passing through a stage analogous to human adolescence. Capacities are unfolding and developing unevenly, erratically—but she'll have them at her fingertips soon."

"Even without the crystal?"

Verrons' brows kinked. "But the crystals *are* available—from somewhere. She may not realize their full significance yet—but unless I'm very wrong she will before long."

It was late the next morning when the jungle opened its green maw to reveal the city it had swallowed centuries before. With a forcefully broadcast surge of triumph, the girl leapt to the buckled pavement, her summons suddenly a shrill cry on the air. Advancing warily, the two humans trailed her through the time-shattered precincts of the stone city. She called twice again, striding imperiously on long, muscular toes.

Then they rounded a half-intact structure and confronted a fear-struck tableaux of small humanoids. Sadler recognized the slight bodies, the stubby limbs and underdeveloped toes, the fine hair and weak eyes instantly. "Scuttling little people," Verrons confirmed.

And they had not changed so much with time. At the girl's sinuous advance dark perspiration oozed from suddenly lax pores. Small bodies hunched defensively, faces taut with helpless dread. At the girl's yapped demand, the underpeople crept near to pay involuntary homage. Within minutes dozens of them had gathered, whining and mewing. One, an elder female, was permitted to press near and dab the girl's stiff hair with her tongue. The girl's submissive posture was that of a monarch suffering worship.

She did not suffer it long. Within minutes she stretched erect again, her hair bristling. Then her commands flew in a barking tongue and the little people scuttled to serve her. Woven mats appeared and were spread on the stone plaza. The girl sat, transforming her reed mat to a throne, and gestured Sadler and Verrons to kneel either side of her, her honor guard. Reluctantly Sadler placed himself as indicated.

Then anxious underpeople disappeared and returned bearing their offerings: fresh-skinned meat heaped on a wooden plank, eggs brittle-shelled and soft, bulbs and berries and carefully combed sheafs of tender grass. Sadler selected carefully, trying to communicate gratitude to eyes that, at contact, were immediately drowned in gouts of dark fluid. The girl, however, had little appetite for the feast she had commanded. Eating sparsely, she was on her feet again, her long body poised, her features unreadable. A sharp projection of indecision sent anxiety spiking through Sadler's nervous system. Malignant tension gripped his muscles.

Her indecision was swiftly dispersed. The girl leapt away, and jagged second-hand images of stone slashed Sadler's field of vision. Verrons was already on his feet, following her.

The odors of mold and decay were rank in the ruins of the city. Rotting vegetable debris clotted narrow thoroughfares and carpeted broader ones. Swiftly the girl raced toward the vine-infested heart of the city, Sadler and Verrons following. Here those crumbling stone structures that still stood sagged toward the pavement in ancient weariness. Soon rubble became almost impassable, its only visible denizens small thorn-tailed quadrupeds who protested the intrusion with a querulous cry repeated from throat to throat.

Then Sadler and Verrons rounded a corner and faced an intact wall. Vines tasted at it and centuries of grime were dew-plastered to its surface, but a tinge of pink was still visible. Sadler sucked a startled breath. "And where have we seen stone like this before?" Verrons demanded rhetorically, scraping at the caked surface, burnishing it with the arm of his daysuit. He was rewarded with a bold shimmer of pink stone.

The girl was already monkeying over the wall. Sadler and Verrons followed and found themselves standing on a broad plaza. Untouched by the breezes that had janitored the mesa top plazas, it was heavily carpeted in debris. The smell of decay was thick. At the center of the plaza, slowly slumping toward collapse, stood a single massive domed structure. Quickly Sadler inventoried its lines and dimensions. If he had encountered this temple on his first passage through the ruined city, he realized, he would have been stunned. But after the architectural poetry of the mesa-top complex, this was no more than massive pink doggerel, its lines undistinguished, its overall statement uninspired. Sadler kicked and rubbed at the littered surface of the plaza with his boot. Again pink stone emerged.

Verrons directed Sadler's attention to a second structure, half-hidden behind the temple. "Another stone needle. Let's have a look."

This was a needle that had snapped mid-shaft. Its massive blocks sprawled across the plaza in time-eroded chunks. "Much shorter than the mesa-top shaft, even before it fell," Verrons pointed out, prowling around the truncated structure. "The base area is smaller, the angle of taper sharper. Overall it's much less impressive—but significant."

The girl's behavior made that apparent. She dodged quickly to the interior of the shaft and crouched. Tossing back her head, she peered up the truncated shaft. Her eyes took light and orange illumination belled swiftly around her, the radiance of her own eyes reflected from the still-glossy interior shaft wall. Briefly she was lost in self-generated glare, as if she had stepped across a bridge of light to another dimension. Sadler gasped, his mind caught in a mental shriek he could not comprehend, a demand directed with emphatic virulence at forces unseen.

At forces unresponding.

He heard Verrons grunt, felt him grip his arm. He was unable to respond. Then the girl's mental shriek terminated and she sprang from the shaft. Confronting them, she leapt to her toes, her hair crackling. A cry crystallized in Sadler's throat, a massive stalactite of unreasoning fear he could neither swallow nor disgorge. But when orange veils of light leapt from the air and swathed him, when the girl whipped them around the two humans in fury ecstatic, his body did not flop helplessly to the pavement. He felt a numbing along certain nerve pathways, a cold tingle along others. His clothes were blown, his hair tugged, as if by storm. Then orange light lifted impotently. The girl raced past, the taste of her fury acrid in his mouth.

As she ran, an image filled Sadler's mind, brilliant, flashing—a crystal of orange. She raised her head, and the crystal was framed against the sky, clouds billowing around it, sunlight shafting through it. Without volition, Sadler followed Verrons around the side of the ancient temple. The girl turned and whipped a scorching gaze over them. With writhing fingers, she drew orange fire from the debris that littered the plaza. She swept the material into the air, a tornado-column of burning litter. Sparks zipped from the upper extremity of the column of burning litter, dispersed by skirling wind currents.

Sadler's mouth dried. With Verrons, he dodged to cover of the temple. Tensely they charted the progress of the firestorm from plaza to rubbled city beyond, the girl at its center. Sadler tongued crackling lips. "She—she knows about the crystal now."

"She does," Verrons agreed tautly. "Apparently the knowledge simply made transition from one level of awareness to another, stimulated by light."

Sadler followed Verrons from the musty temple and over the wall. Ash and incinerated debris marked the girl's trail through the city. The path led back toward the plaza where they had feasted. As they neared, yelping cries guided them.

In the plaza, the girl reigned from the center of turbulence, light veils dancing around her, tumbling little underpeople across the stone, drawing dark liquid from their pores and pale blood from their nostrils and eyes. The girl arched like a deadly spider at the center of her energy web, her prey convulsing helplessly around her, bones rattling against stone.

As Sadler and Verrons pounded near, she narrowed her attention to two elder males, permitting the others to fall limp from her web. The two little males she brought rolling to her feet. Peering down at them through veils of light, she shrieked a demand.

Their mouths worked desperately, but the seizures that racked their small bodies would not permit them to speak. Arms falling, the girl let light die. Bending, she tangled long fingers into the males' hair, pulling their heads back sharply.

Again she met the futile inability to answer. Sadler tasted her fiery anger before he saw it leap from the air, bouncing the two old males back across the stone pavement to pound their convulsing bodies against a heap of rubble. Releasing them, the girl turned on the two humans with a snarl. But her oblique eyes did not fire orange again. Abruptly she turned and raced away.

Verrons crossed the plaza and bent over the still males. He probed their battered flesh, then stood, his brows pulled taut. "Dead."

"Both of them?" Sadler demanded, unbelieving.

"Both." Verrons' lips pursed grimly. "Apparently she wanted information about the crystal and either they had none or they failed to communicate what they did know." He glanced around. Wet eyes peered fearfully at them from the shadows. With a summoning gesture, Verrons led Sadler away from the scene of death.

They watched from shelter of a half-fallen structure as the underpeople huddled around their dead. A whining cry united the group. Then woven mats were brought and the dead were wrapped and carried away. Only the stones remained, mute witness. Later the underpeople returned to huddle together against the somber backdrop of fallen stone. Occasionally a whining plaint began at one point in the group and traversed its ranks. As the group enlarged, there was a constant scampering of individuals through the group, whispering furtively from ear to ear, casting uneasy glances toward the jungle where the girl had disappeared.

Both whispers and plaints halted abruptly when the girl reappeared at dusk, her hair caked with mud, an intricately knotted rope of vines twisted around her body. There was crystal neither upon her forehead nor in her mind. Charting her sinuous advance toward the band, Sadler picked up no overtone of emotion.

The girl seated herself at the center of the plaza, prepared to suffer homage again. The little people obliged her with patent reluctance, their eyes streaming, the effluvia of fear misting the dusky air. When their whimpering obsequies had satisfied the girl, she jumped up and led way to an underground warren. She claimed the center of the floor, motioning Sadler and Verrons to flank her. At her command the underpeople spread sleeping mats for them. A short time later Sadler lay on woven reeds and stared up into musky darkness, tasting the mingled odors of dust, mold and fear.

"We'll return to the local temple tomorrow," Verrons said

quietly. "We can pace it off and have a look for stray relics. We could find anything under that debris."

It was a long time before Sadler slept. Then, sometime deep in the night, a splash of liquid upon his face woke him. Within the same moment, a surge of fury burst across the surface of his mind. Looking up, he distinguished an oozing little face suspended above him. In the stubby-fingered hand, even in the dark, Sadler caught the flash of sharpened bone. Nearby someone screamed in rage and pain. He knew it was not himself because the voice was not human.

Was it?

CHAPTER TWELVE

Driven from the stonewarren, Aleida hurled herself into the maw of night, fury and frustration twin switches she used to mortify her own flesh. *Attacked in her sleep*—but that she took as homage to the power. The others recognized her ascendancy and feared it—with reason. For she would show no mercy to animals just because she had been whelped from among them. What drove her in fury was her impotence to wield the power she had scourged them with today in her defense tonight. Flinging herself up at the bite of sharpened bone, she had arched and writhed—and the dark warren had remained just that. Dark. She had escaped with her life only by battling her attackers as an animal fights animals, tooth and nail. The taste of blood was still thick in her mouth.

Mortified, she threw herself up a shadow-shrouded tree. It was a night as oppressive as Aleida's mood, as dark as the powers that had failed her. Dense cloud hung low. Only toward the mountains was there the starry hint of light. And shrill voices yapped on her trail. Quickly Aleida scrambled down the tree and raced ahead.

When she was certain she had outrun pursuit, she mounted another tree and glared at the sullen sky. Even when sleep claimed her, she retained vestigial awareness, her teeth clenched, her skeletal muscles taut, ready for flight.

Consequently she woke at daylight with pain in every joint, a bony ache infecting her jaw and lower skull. But the power, she knew with fierce elation, rode her fingertips again. She could feel it there, tingling, ready. And the time had come for decision. Twice, guided by instinct, she had sought out and employed the reflective interior surface of a stone shaft to irradiate herself with the light of her own eyes. The first time Bright-Feather had prematurely derailed the train of information she had felt winding to the surface of her mind, stimulated by light.

But yesterday? Images of the crystal with which her unconscious had presented her broke light in her mind again, driving gaudy shards deep into soft brain tissue. The crystal's light was orange, as orange as the veils of power she had festooned herself with, as orange as the light she had beamed into her own eyes. She had seen a similar crystal, but green, at the male's forehead. Was that why he flew and she did not? Was the crystal the tool she must possess to shape the power into proper strength and coherence? And if so, where lay the path to possession?

She jumped down from the tree. Certainly it did not lead back to the broken shaft in the debris-ridden temple square, not when there were nine pink temples ahead, every glossy stone laid to receive her, and at their climax a shaft that touched cloud. But as she pictured that shaft blue plumage flashed to mind and gall soured her. Bright-Feather—not only was he immune to her power, he controlled power of his own now, life-threatening in its reach and capability. Aleida's teeth ground vengefully. Clearly Bright-Feather's power was grounded in the instruments he had stolen from the other intruders. If she stole those instruments and activated them with her own hand. . . .

Now the taste in her mouth grew sweeter. Fiercely Aleida drew her own power from the air and used it to storm a path through brush and vine. Her fingers brought down wind and fire, and as she ran, devastation stretched behind her. But to the insensate giant of rock, soil and tree that gave her life, the injury was no more than the mark of a fingernail across her own flank.

She was child of this soil. Would it grant her license to the power if it resented the free exercise of that same power? *Never.* She had her answer in the flurry of orange veils, in the storm-shriek of wind and fire.

When she reached the base of the mesa next afternoon, she had further answer. She scrambled to the treetops, and from the mesa the pink shaft fractured sunlight and hurled rainbow swords at her, a piercing welcome.

Night seemed the most auspicious time to return to the temple area. Accordingly Aleida circled the mesa, and at dusk she dared its western wall. Soon she clung near the upper rim of the mesa, the sun dyeing the sky purple behind her, her marrow chilling as Bright-Feather's evening song penetrated the darkening air. But tonight the notes were less a celebration than a raw discord cast against night. When she peered over the rim of the mesa, Bright-Feather hunched on the courtyard wall, the threat of his beak-weapon diminished by the patent lack of vigor in his posture. She studied him warily, trying to discern some reason for the change.

Soon the sun set. Briefly Bright-Feather's head remained erect, silhouetted against a backdrop of swiftly gathering darkness, occasionally jerking around, signalling up harsh chuckles from his throat. Aleida hugged ground, her toes tingling impatiently. The stone shaft beckoned, looming up out of night, imperious, obsessing. But when the first moon surfaced upon the horizon and Bright-Feather finally tucked his beak to rest, when no one moved and no one watched—except Aleida—a strange transformation glowed across the complex. Alerted by the unexpected crackle of her hair, Aleida crept over the rim of the mesa and whipped a burning gaze from temple to temple.

A faint halo of color misted each structure: the grand temple, red; its nearest sisters, violet and green; the next two, gold—and orange, the color of her own glowing eyes! Aleida's wiry body tightened. As she watched, 'a gathering cloud of brilliance seemed to condense from the very air. Aleida responded by jumping to her feet and running toward the temple shrouded in orange light.

She had entered this temple before, by daylight. She had entered it when intruders walked the plaza beyond. Now she entered it alone, in silence, in darkness, running. But it was not dark within the temple. When Aleida crossed the portal, faint halo became fierce glare. And overhead the ceiling, featureless until now, was suddenly alive. Radiant forms darted across its flat surface, flexing and flowing, a dizzying evolution of color and line. And at the center of the ceiling hung a single bright figure, an orange wheel of light, arms flickering as it spun.

Aleida ran to the center of the floor, turning her face to the brilliant wheel of light. Immediately the orange of her eyes met answering illumination. Instantly a column of light was extruded from the glowing ceiling. It pillared her, hands at her side, head thrown back. Then, without volition, she found herself turning, impaled upon the axis of the world. She *was* the world, a dark body, a mute body, its every inert particle aching with the possibility of life. Her own body contained the realization. Slowly her arms belled out. A sexless voice whispered into her mind. *You live, sister. Resurrection has come from destruction and now in you, living in the cells of your body, is the all. You are everything. We have nothing to give but your past—and the future. Claim them, sister.*

Light died. Aleida reeled dizzily from the center of the floor. At her feet a stone sheet slid aside, revealing a rectangular opening in the floor. A broad stone staircase led down, orange railings flanking it. Aleida's eyes flared wide. She dropped to her knees. Below light glowed alive. Corridor walls were polished metal, the floor glazed stone.

We have nothing to give but your past—and the future. Rising, her hair crackling, Aleida put hand to railing, foot to stair. She descended to her destiny.

When the small temple suddenly darkened again, Sadler hauled himself over the rim of the plaza and stared into the unaccountably empty structure. "She—she's gone. She walked right through the floor."

Frowning, Verrons topped the mesa wall and came to his knees, the forged metal spear he had unearthed as they fled through the rubbled back lanes of the stone city gripped tight. The gash on his jaw was black by moonlight, a badge of their narrow escape from the underpeople's midnight offensive. He peered at the suddenly empty temple, then darted a glance across the plaza to where the Ehminheer roosted. "Let's see if we can make it happen to us, too."

Sadler hesitated only momentarily. Together they slipped silently across the plaza. On the horizon, twin moons dazzled the face of night. The air was cool, the early evening breeze light. When they entered, the small temple did not welcome the two humans with light, but at the center of the floor they found a large rectangular opening and leading from it stairs with ornate metal railings. Startled, Sadler knelt. Below he saw a lighted corridor, metal walls bright, glazed floor glossy.

"Don't ask me," Verrons said. "Every structure dark. Then our heroine steps into this one, it lights like a star gone nova, she vanishes—and suddenly we're offered free access to the nether regions." His dark eyes scanned the ceiling. "There must be a scanning beam here similar to the one we wrung flutes from in the grand temple. But the light was so totally diffused through the structure—"

Puzzled, Sadler followed Verrons' gaze. The temple ceiling was flat, featureless, bearing neither motif nor device. "Maybe she used her own power to light the structure."

"Possible. And to open the door?"

Sadler peered down the ornate stairs, a frown darkening his gaze. "I don't know. I—all I caught from her was a brief image of light. We—"

"We could be *persona non grata* below the surface," Verrons suggested thoughtfully.

Sadler burnished damp palms on his daysuit. "There's one way to find out." Before he could renege, he set boot to stair.

At the bottom of the staircase, glazed stone floor stretched ten meters to a blank wall. Before Sadler had taken five steps, the metal walls glided aside and he stood within a chamber of the same proportions as the temple above. The ceiling was low, illuminated by glowing panels. Sadler's head snapped around. His gaze traveled sixty degrees and was captured by a life-size figure of stone. Long and bronze she stood, head raised, orange eyes cast up. An orange crystal was recessed into her petrified brow. Her long arms were flung backward around an oblong white crystal as tall as she. She grasped the polished stone floor with muscular toes, ready to spring.

Stunned, Sadler stared up into her stone face. The questing spirit recorded there was familiar. Only subtle disparities of feature differentiated her from the young female whose storm trail they had followed through the jungle.

"Sadler—here." Verrons' voice was urgent.

The dancer reappeared on the opposite face of the crystal, this time vividly orange, her body subtly recontoured to suggest energy flow. Her arms reached upward. The air around her head was softly illuminated. "The crystal passage," Verrons breathed, radiant flecks of orange blazing upon his pupils.

Sadler stared up at the glowing face. Slowly he swung and peered around the chamber. A chill of apprehension gripped him. "Commander, the girl." She had descended the stairs before them but she was nowhere in sight.

Verrons frowned. Quickly he paced off the nearest metal wall, tapping lightly at its surface. When he reached its midpoint, panels slid and they looked down a second featureless corridor. He grunted appreciatively. "Let's see if we can locate other exits." Circuiting the chamber, tapping, he keyed open two additional corridors. "North, east and west—I vote we explore to the west."

Cautiously they stepped into the indicated corridor. Sadler wheeled as metal paneling closed behind them. Verrons ignored the sound, however, stepping ahead. When he had traversed most of the length of the corridor, the metal wall ahead moved. Sadler hurried after him and they entered a second underground chamber slightly larger than the first. This time the resident dancer regarded the illuminated ceiling with radiant violet eyes. On the southern wall, a stone staircase identical to the previous one led to the ceiling.

"At a guess we're beneath the temple directly west of the one where we entered the subground," Verrons speculated. "And another guess." He arced a gesture at the stone dancer. "We're going to find a chamber under each temple—and represented in each, a dancer of a different order."

"Order?" Sadler demanded, peering up into the violet dancer's imperious features.

"Of light. As determined by crystal color." He mounted the staircase and probed at the stone ceiling, pressing upward with his palms without effect. He retreated, frowning abstractedly. "But I think we have something more immediate to worry about than which corridor yields a blue dancer, which green. The wall panels roll for us, but this exit panel doesn't. No more than it ever opened for us when we were exploring the surface complex."

Sadler's eyes flickered across the indicated square of ceiling, unwelcome possibilities flashing to mind. "But if the entry panels only respond to the girl—"

Verrons nodded. "We could very easily find ourselves trapped down here, unless we keep her in sight."

Sadler's eyes glanced off metal walls. Quickly he stepped off the three walls that did not house stairs. Each slid to offer a corridor. "But we have no idea which of the first three corridors she chose," he realized in dismay.

"She may never have entered this particular chamber at all," Verrons agreed. "Which leaves us a choice. We can go on exploring at random and hope we encounter her. We can return to the first chamber and retreat to surface level immediately, before we find ourselves trapped. Or we can return there and try to pick up the girl's trail. Barefoot, she should leave some trace on these floors."

Frowning, Sadler realized that all reasonable alternatives led back to the first chamber. But when they hurried back down the corridor, the ceiling panel in the first chamber had closed. Verrons climbed the stairs and tested the panel vigorously, without success. "It's anyone's guess," he concluded, descending the stairs, rubbing his gashed jaw. "There could be a time-delay mechanism that closes the hatch a certain interval after it was opened, in which case the girl may still be down here. Or we could be up against a system sophisticated enough to close *this* entry when she exists by another. In which case, we're trapped." He paced the floor, peering up at the featureless ceiling. "On the other hand there is a scant possibility that this entry opens only to the members of the order of orange—and that every other hatch down here is keyed to a single order. So that if she *is* still down here and this *was* a time-delayed closure, she can only leave the substructure by this staircase."

Sadler stared at him, trying to forge some productive course of action from a welter of alternatives.

Verrons paced around the small chamber restlessly. "A few days ago I felt like one-half to two-thirds of a normal healthy human male. I would have been happy to curl up in a corner and nap here for a few hours. But tonight I feel inclined to keep moving. Of course you're welcome to keep the stairs warm while I chart corridors to get a better idea of the extent and layout of the substructure."

Sadler glanced pensively at the staircase and shook his head.

Whatever the cause of their previous inanition—infection, malnutrition, simple fatigue—it had passed soon after the Ehminheer had routed them from the mesa top. "I'll come with you."

"Good. Let's see if we can find any trace of the girl." Deliberately Verrons paced the walls, opening corridors. They scanned polished floors, finding no trace of the girl's feet, but some meters down the corridor leading north, the polished wall bore an unmistakable handprint. Verrons extended his spear, testing the blank wall ahead.

In response it slid and they peered into a long hall. Its burnished walls and brightly illuminated ceiling were an imposing expanse. The glazed floor was set with a series of free-form display cases. Verrons' dark pupils dilated.

But they had no time to explore their new surroundings. On the opposite side of the chamber, the wall opened and the girl appeared, her hair bristling, her oblique eyes luminescent. At sight of them, she rose swiftly to her toes, and Sadler caught a disconcerting internalized image of himself, eyes frozen, with Verrons' face superimposed upon his own.

Verrons' features thawed quickly. "We'd better not lose sight of her again."

Sensing challenge, she toed the length of the hall, flashing corridors from polished walls, dodging finally into one. As she raced down the passage, she swung her head in an exaggerated arc, bouncing orange light from panel to panel, mirroring it back into the humans' eyes. Sadler heard mocking laughter echo not from her throat but from her mind.

Running after her, they looped in and out of the long display hall. Sadler caught brief glimpses of a carefully arranged collection of art objects, fragile bowls and vessels, containers intricately wrought, delicate implements, imposing statuettes, objects woven of gleaming wire. The collection, exquisite, extensive, flew past swiftly. So did the stone occupants of the sub-temple chambers.

Then a panel glided open at the western end of the display hall and the girl halted, arching to her toes. Suddenly, as he peered past her, a surging red fog clouded Sadler's field of vision, at its center a flute. He stepped back hastily, attempting to retreat. But the attraction of the silver instrument was compelling.

Possessed, Sadler trailed the girl into the final underground chamber. The flute mounted there was larger than those dispensed by the mechanism of the grand temple. Its barrel was broad and elaborately engraved, tapering to a slender mouthpiece. Cradled upon a stand of bright metal, it faced into a chamber as long, as wide as the grand temple—beneath which, Sadler realized, they now stood. His gaze panned the hall. Its walls were restless with veined fire, the streaking brilliance of opal.

Trailing him, Verrons slanted a narrowing gaze at the flute. "It's securely mounted. They obviously didn't intend anyone to drop this one."

Sadler grunted, only half aware of Verrons' comment. Energy leapt from the opalescent walls and parched him, a streaking scarlet predator. He rasped his hand across suddenly crackling lips. His tongue had dried to leather. By contrast, the mouthpiece of the flute assumed a shimmering liquid brilliance.

Sadler took a single step toward the instrument, simultaneously moving beyond the physical limitations of his body. Suddenly—*the girl was poised against the far wall, her long body arched, her glowing eyes upon him*—he existed upon a higher plane and he knew, his muscles knew, that he had only to make his hands dance the proper demand in the air and his long toes would gently relinquish their grip on the floor. His twining fingers would cleave the ceiling—*the girl writhed now, and energy leapt from the walls to flow into her slowly undulating fingertips*—and he would quiver upward, an arrow drawn to the sky. And as he darted at the underbelly of cloud, his throat would open with a thick cry. Moisture would slap his face, sunlight would bristle his naked body. . . .

Dizzily Sadler tried to reconcile duality. With one body he sliced cloud, while the other tottered weakly, reluctantly, toward the bright oasis of flute. The metal mouthpiece was water and wine, cool, sweet, intoxicating. Parched, he pulled at it, nursing it, but instead of drawing its reviving liquor into himself, he felt his breath being sucked down the broad barrel. Like a physical extrusion of himself, the stream of exhalate threaded the mouthpiece and snaked into the unseen interior of the instrument.

It emerged as a cloud of red that blotted out dancing girl and bedazzled humans, submerging awareness, drowning it. Soon the gathering cloud spawned a single red presence who stalked the length of the hall on muscular toes, rending the charged air. As he strode, he summoned lesser copies of himself from the fire-streaked walls, fiery little phantasms who danced attendance, his demon court.

Now I am again, in my all and in my power. It was the voice of the firestorm, explosive and deep. With a grandiose gesture he swept his spectral court into the air. As they arced down, he caught them on his flaming chest, absorbing them and swelling mightily. A crown of fire burst from his head. *Now I am, and now you see what once was.*

With a leap, he spun into the air and became the sun, his crown a series of fierce solar eruptions. Far below, at his gesture, other light dancers flared alive upon the face of a barren globe: Selmarri. Dancing, they spread their colors, whipping them out, forming them into grandiose shapes of fancy and fantasy—which promptly, when the dancers swept on, became the reality of a jungled world swept by breezes, served by streams and lit by red-being sun and silver-entity moons. All were at once separate and conjoined: dancers, rock, soil and sky. They existed in unity, animate and inanimate, sensate and insensate, willed and un-willed. Yet each retained its identity.

Sadler nourished the flute and life crawled across the face of the world in the tornado-path of the rainbow dancers. Small people appeared from the trees, limp hair trailing down their fragile shoulders, their weak eyes puddling. *From the power came life. From life came the powers.* For soon into each band of under-people babes with bristling manes were born. In their cherub fists they clutched rays of light, and when infant innocence deserted them, those rays became swords. Their bodies grew tall and brown, legs powerful, toes and fingers long, eyes oblique and glowing. In every band rough hair was carried above fine, and when the one crackled, the other burned.

Life was dedicated to power, power to life. To the steam pools the gifted babes were borne. Into the deep cavern where the forces of the world joined, where water, air and mineral were fused by time, they were carried. There, with the light of their eyes, they shattered free raw accretions of mineral. Deep within these cloudy masses were the bright gems that would bring the power to tight focus. *For it was the will of this world that they wield light-swords, that they strike and cleave, create and enforce.*

But death was never defeated, death the return of matter to the eternal cycle. Only the electrical patterns of the spirit could be saved, cast in crystal and preserved to inspire and inform. So it happened that more were born into their ranks to take up the sword of light when the death crystal fell from cooling fingers. They were born to the powered and they were born to the weak, but all commanded the powers of this world.

Sadler watched civilization grow across the jungled face of the world. Swiftly cities shouldered aside trees. Stone structures tunneled into the earth and arched into the sky. Scattered bands of underpeople became urban masses. Mercilessly the powered race molded them into a work force. Small bodies scuttled and served, their little faces oozing with desperate anxiety to please, to forestall the paralyzing sword and the convulsing curtain of light. And above the scene, brown bodies flew, long fingers cleaving cloud, wiry hair sparking.

But it happened that after many score generations, the deep caverns became sterile. Too many raw masses had been carried away and refined to power foci. Now the babes were brought and the light of their eyes found no answering gleam in the walls of the caverns. At the insistence of the elders, mineral masses were broken down and carried back anyway. They proved useless. Under stress of refining, they crumbled to dust.

With them crumbled the future. Without gem focus, the power was a sword that buckled on contact, an arcing body that tumbled from the clouds mid-flight, a will that could be imposed only sporadically, unpredictably. Without gem focus, the power was nothing.

It was worse. When babes whose power could not be focused were left in care of the underpeople, they were abused in secret and died of mysterious causes. They could not protect themselves from the new boldness which moved in the ranks of the lesser people. It was, it became apparent, a killing boldness—a boldness which could not be permitted to survive.

But first every possible means of obtaining foci was pursued. Seekers thrust deep into the mountains. They sought every smallest cavern in every smallest ridge for sign of foci. A scattered few were unearthed—very few. In our impatience to seed the clouds with our presence, we had overdrawn the reserves of the caverns. We had tapped them until they were exhausted. Now they must be given time to replenish. Water and mineral must have centuries at the heart of the mountains to combine into suitable structures. Only then would foci be available to baby hands again, power to adult ones.

We were willing to give time its hand in our behalf. In the underpeople lay the danger. Weak, powerless, they cringed before the swords of our power now. They appeared as required to give our ancestors light with their breath. Glowing spirits danced the dark night of a hundred temples, recreating every time since the beginning. But when our power was gone, not only would the underpeople desert their proper worship, they would viciously destroy the flutes that are our immortality. The ancestors would perish every one in their crystalline shells. The past would be destroyed, co-victim with the future. This could not be permitted.

Dimly Sadler was aware of the girl, an orange whirlwind sweeping through surging clouds of red. Her fingertips rose and fell as streaks of fire from the opalescent walls arced through her. Her body, flesh when she slowed, became light as she spun faster.

First we sought to safely house the ancestors. We had erected cities and we had erected temples and consecration shafts. Now we must erect the ultimate structure. Endlessly Sadler's breath flowed as he audited the debates that raged the ranks of the powered. Thereafter he lived the first steps of temple construction. A site far from any population center was selected and the mesa raised. A storage vault was created to house the collection of flutes, receptacles of the revered ancestors.

And there was more, much more. The narrative was not done. But as temples rose on the mesa, the saga grew distant, only echoes bearing the tale to Sadler. Gradually dizzying numbness gripped him. His arms hung uselessly at his sides. His legs became columns of dead tissue, devoid of sensation. Although he labored to draw breath, breath with which to nourish all the panoramic history of the dancers' race, his ribs had become a bony girdle that prevented his chest from expanding. Dumbly he fought to retain consciousness. Then slowly, totally exhausted, he felt himself dropping to the polished floor.

In the underground chamber the drama continued without him. Once, reviving briefly, he found light in the air, the girl in motion and Verrons at the flute, his face lost in glare. The firestorm roar of the red being's voice still sundered the chamber, but the fleeting nature of consciousness negated comprehension. Although Sadler struggled to raise his head, to croak some incoherent demand to be returned to his station at the flute, his scalp tingled malevolently and his senses faded, leached away.

Sometime later he struggled back to consciousness again. Verrons hovered over him, his body swaying dangerously, his speech thick. "Sadler, she—the girl's on her way to the surface. We've got to keep her in sight."

Weakly Sadler struggled to his feet, fighting nauseous surges of dizziness. Peering around he found the fire opal walls dead.

Unsteadily Verrons led way to the display hall. He rubbed his forehead, his eyes drained of vitality. "I'm receiving just enough to know that she has entered the nearest small chamber. And to know the hatch she wants to exit by refuses to open for her."

As if in confirmation the girl appeared from a corridor to their left. She rose to her toes, eyes blazing, then raced down the long hall to disappear into the next corridor that opened. Verrons hesitated, swaying. "She—another dead end," he whispered hoarsely. "The mechanism is definitely keyed to order of light. She won't be able to leave by any door other than the one she entered by."

Muzzily Sadler assembled a single coherent conclusion. "Then if we can reach the orange chamber before her—"

"We have to," Verrons groaned, and launched himself unevenly the length of the display hall.

Despite their halting progress, they waited at the foot of the stairs in the chamber of orange light when the girl finally appeared. At sight of them her eyes flared bright. With a snarl she leapt past them up the stairs.

This time stone slid and the girl scrambled through the opening into the dark temple. Compelling images cascaded from her mind: pounding gouts of steam, tortuous underground passages and, gleaming from a cloudy mineral matrix, the crystal, object of obsession.

Desperately Sadler and Verrons hauled themselves up the stairs before the sliding door could close. They emerged to hear a rattle of rocks as the girl vanished over the mesa wall. Numbly Sadler followed Verrons to the plaza and peered into pre-dawn mist. "She—she knows now."

Slumping to the chill stone, Verrons gazed planet west. "She knows where to get the power crystal," he said, his voice flat with exhaustion. "There is—or was—a volcanic plateau east of the mountains, an area of geophysical disturbance. The caverns lay there—once. If they still do—"

Sadler nodded, images from the flute experience flickering to mind: shimmering mineral pools, yellow-crusted steam vents, expanses of laval sand. He touched his lips. They were cracked, as if the heat, the thirst he had experienced had been real, not illusion. "I—I missed out on the later developments," he said reluctantly.

Verrons turned to face him, his dark eyes dull. "You can guess, can't you?"

Bleakly, refusing to meet the other man's eyes, Sadler did. "The powered race constructed safe storage for the flutes—and exterminated the underpeople."

"Not totally of course." Verrons' voice, as he peered across the complex, was distant, embedded in another time, another milieu. "They allowed a certain minute percentage to escape the killing ray. But they scattered the survivors in the jungles, isolated and disorganized—and until their deaths the remaining dancers kept them that way. There was no point in encouraging the regeneration of either the underpeople or the powered form prematurely, before the necessary geological activity had regenerated the crystal crop."

Morning came slowly in shades of grey. Sadler stared into the distance, fighting numbing fatigue. "The crop—has it regenerated now?"

"Who knows? Who knows how much time has passed since the red flute was mounted? If she has definite bearings—and she may have gathered data from the experience we missed—the girl may reach the region to find it still sterile. Or she may find the caverns have been closed by earth tremors or that more recent volcanic flows have blocked entrance to the caverns."

"But the flying male—"

"He may have originated on the far side of the continent. There were cavern areas associated with other mountain ranges. And if he found his way into those caverns, if he sighted even a single crystal mass, I expect instinct would guide him to break it down and utilize it. But this is the only major temple complex—designed not only to protect the flutes but to dispense them to custody of later powered individuals. After regeneration the powered were to shepherd parties of underpeople to the complex. The mechanism would dispense an appropriate number of flutes.

Under supervision of powered overseers, the underpeople would flute—they would worship. Then, as the cities were revived, as local temples were rebuilt, the ancestors could be distributed back across the continent again." He drew a shuddering breath, drained by the effort of speech.

"And whatever the criteria for receiving flutes, we met them," Sadler murmured.

"And we worshipped," the older man admitted. "And now?"

Sadler peered at him. "We—aren't we going to follow the girl? To the caverns?"

Verrons grunted, his eyes slowly sliding shut. With effort he opened them and turned to study the Ehminheer perched on his courtyard wall. "I don't think I can make it down the gully. But if the Ehminheer finds us here—"

Sadler peered at the avian silhouetted against a sky stained with the first scarlet streamers of dawn. They couldn't sleep here. But the pre-dawn chill had numbed his legs, sapping what little strength remained in his body. With effort he stood, but he was not particularly surprised to note that Verrons had stretched out on the cold stone instead, his dark eyes closed, his jaw slack. Hopelessly Sadler sank back to the plaza and huddled beside him. When his eyes closed, even the Mazaahr spots that danced to greet him were dim, little more than pale dots of light.

Later he swam to momentary awareness as the Ehminheer's morning song burst from the western extreme of the complex, a raucous medley of chortles and shrieks. When the song died, Sadler closed his eyes again and surrendered to the coming warmth of day.

CHAPTER THIRTEEN

Dawn drove darkness to its mountain fastness, a pale victory, and the pink stones of the complex glimmered back to life. Tiehl's morning song shrieked to a strident climax and died abruptly. For when he wheeled and peered back over the plaza, he saw familiar human forms sprawled on the glistening stone, twin disfigurations. Momentarily Tiehl puffed himself large, anger a rising whine in his blood. But a spike of anxiety deflated him and he huddled warily on the wall, his gaze haunted. This week Tiehl's metabolic calendar had delivered him again to brittling season, that period when the horny layers of an Ehminheer's beak and talons separate and crack away at the slightest pressure, leaving him defenseless.

Morbidly Tiehl chewed a foretalon, snapping back the stiff surface rind. He had hidden the pistols nearby. But until brittling season passed and his horny tissues began to regenerate, he faced a time of spiritual impotence, an involuntary withering of gamecock audacity. Necessarily feeding entirely upon vegetable matter for eight to ten days, he could perform only an empty pantomime of the ferocity that had grown on him in the shadow of perch.

Uneasily Tiehl paced his wall, threatened by the presence of the humans, yet unable to launch himself against them. Soon the sun escaped its jungle bonds and bobbed up the sky, a rosy ovoid trailing stratus. Still Tiehl patrolled his wall, uttering an occasional anxious shriek that did nothing to relieve his tension.

At midmorning his voice shriveled into silence as the humans stirred and sat. Their appearance was unprepossessing. The snow savage's pale jaws were frosted with beard and his eyes were red-rimmed, as if he had stared too intently into an angry sun. Verrons was emaciated, his sinews straining against his leathery flesh. Tiehl puffed his plumage and huddled watchfully.

Wakened, the two humans conferred briefly, glancing toward Tiehl's wall. Then the younger stood and, gripping a corroded metal spear, moved stiffly toward the gully. When he had disappeared, Verrons stretched to his feet, too. He paused, seeming to consciously gather strength, and then approached Tiehl with deliberate firmness.

Tiehl's plumage rippled, blue fire. Uneasily he paced away down the wall. "You trespass," he cried, the warning harsh, blood-gilded with sharp chuckles.

But Verrons did not halt. Defensively Tiehl curled his useless talons under, concealing them. "I did not give you permission to return here," he warned, but even he recognized the querulous tone of the threat.

"That may be," Verrons admitted, halting a short distance from the wall. "But we've picked up some interesting facts over the past few days. I thought you might be willing to help us follow up on them." Briefly his gaze slid away to catalogue the grey on grey panorama of the jungle below. "But I don't suppose you pick out detail as far as the mountains, even with your far-vision."

Tiehl's crest erected at the challenge. He quelled the instinctive response with an uneasy chortle, his beak clacking. He sensed unstated purpose in the human's approach. And if Verrons realized Tiehl's beak was no more than useless horn today, that his talons were peeling, if Verrons intended to try to displace Tiehl from perch. . . .

Shrugging, Verrons strode the length of the wall, peering into the distance. The mountains were a series of fractured spines this morning, anesthetized by haze, their recovery a distant prospect. "We seem to have unearthed a unique racial form here," he said slowly, paying the words out deliberately. "Most of the higher indigenes we have encountered are primitive, relatively unsophisticated. They function roughly at a stone age level. A few members of the race, however, develop highly specialized nervous systems with which they are able to focus and employ solar energy. But in order to do so, they must obtain use of a crystal device. We have every indication that the young female belongs to the latter group. Apparently when she obtains a crystal—"

Tiehl's mind made an intuitive leap. "She will fly," he squawked, his pupils flaring involuntarily.

"When she gains use of a crystal, yes, apparently so," Verrons said slowly, studying Tiehl closely. "The device is nothing more than a curiosity to any species but the girl's, but Sadler and I plan to investigate anyway. Apparently the crystals are located in mountain caverns near a geyser area. But if your farsight doesn't bring in detail at that range—"

Irresistibly Tiehl's farsight flared toward the distant range. With a weak clack of his beak, he reeled it back. "If it does?" he demanded suspiciously.

Verrons' dark eyes engaged his. "Does it, Ehminheer?"

Tiehl's plumage rippled again, a bristling tide of distrust. He hopped the length of the wall and hunched defensively, drawing his beak to his chest. If the human thought he could employ Tiehl as a telescope, teasing him with information, wheedling his assistance. . . . "You are trespassing," Tiehl reminded him harshly.

Verrons' dark eyebrows peaked thoughtfully. "Ehminheer, I thought you might be interested in helping us learn more about the crystal device. The male may be dead but if the girl succeeds in finding a crystal—"

Mention of the flying male brought gall to Tiehl's tongue. A bitter caw throbbed up from his chest. He glared down his beak at the human, his throat rattling warning.

Warily Verrons paced away from the wall. "If you would prefer to talk later—"

Tiehl shrieked an inarticulate rejection, and with a shrug the human retreated. When he had descended two levels, Tiehl hurled an angry tirade after him. Then he sprang from the wall and retrieved the heat pistols from hiding at the base of the perch. Gingerly he buckled them on, careful not to sacrifice brittle finger talons prematurely. There was trickery in Verrons' proposal, even treachery. The fact that Tiehl could not pinpoint its exact dimensions did not mean that the human's approach had been innocent. Restlessly Tiehl paced around the base of the towering stone shaft, mustering up vitality for a show of strength.

When he returned to the wall, Verrons lay stretched out in the sun at the lowest point of the plaza. Tiehl cackled at him indignantly, daring him to flaunt his treachery again. But the human did not respond and gradually as the sun evaporated early morning haze, his words returned to haunt Tiehl: a crystal device that focused solar energy, yielding command of the air. Hunched on his wall, Tiehl summoned back vivid images of the flying male. A brilliant gem flashed from a cradle of flesh, dyeing the air with promise.

And the device derived from the geyser region. Urgently Tiehl flared his farsight to the mountains. They were shoulders now, hulking black on the horizon, mist settling heavily in their hollows. Morning cloud-faces barely began to build from their neck-stumps. But somewhere, enfolded in those rocky black arms. . . .

With a jubilant squawk, Tiehl located the steam plumes he had sighted the day he claimed perch. They flashed lacy white against the distant black of mountain. Tiehl's reaching vision strained to resolve detail, but he could not bring the area to sharp focus. It was too distant, the intervening air too thick—but he had pinpointed the key to flight and now his shimmering gaze cast up hard Ehminhee walls against the Selmarri sky. Never mind Verrons' disclaimer. There were crystal wings in the mountains, wings cold, hard and brilliant, sturdy pinions he could close palm around, wings that would dispatch him against the sky like an expertly tossed dart, arcing and soaring—and shrieking low, a blaze of blue, to make proper claim upon perch. Tiehl's heart seized.

But he was not alone on the mesa top. With a swift surge of suspicion, he flattened his rising crest, drawing in his farvision, then flaring it at the human. Verrons sat, peering the length of the plaza at Tiehl. Assessingly, human gaze met Ehminheer, yellow and black fusing at the midpoint of the complex.

With an angry squawk, Tiehl hopped to shelter of the courtyard wall. If Verrons had deliberately tricked him into betraying the coordinates of the geyser zone, if the humans intended to seize the crystal wings for themselves and claim the sky. . . . Tensely Tiehl hopped back to the wall and paced its length, studying Verrons closely. When the human finally stretched back out on the stone, Tiehl hunched on his wall, carefully balancing Verrons' gain against his own. He had betrayed the general coordinates of the geyser zone—but Verrons had betrayed the significance of the crystals. And if he had hoped his disclaimer that only the girl could coax flight from the gems would discourage Tiehl, he had misjudged. Tiehl ruffed his plumage, his pupils scoring beady calculations on sun-warmed stone as he weighed temporary desertion of his perch against the promise of gaudy crystal wings to carry him fire-plumed against the Selmarri sky.

And as the sun approached the midpoint of the sky, he found it not a difficult choice to make. Not at all. . . .

As the sun passed zenith, Verrons' brief morning briskness decomposed and he stretched slack-limbed on the plaza. Dream crested and troughed across the warm stones, a tidal system that eroded reality. Briefly Selmarri was a solid matter-sphere governed by the laws of the physical universe. Then the Ehminheer strutted the length of his wall and became a creature of phantasm, bright crest burning against a surging red sky, his glare the hell-gaze of a mutant demon. The heat of sunlight on Verrons' back intensified malevolently.

Weakly he struggled from stomach to back. For a few moments the effort rendered the sky clear, the air cool. Then his vision blurred, and the man-leopard of Rumar prowled a wind-teased skyplain on legs of cloud. A single misty form stalked the beast, its cloud-face unresolved but its identity immediately clear. Verrons' pupils widened. His lips labored desperately, struggling to birth warning—but as he lay pinned to stone, the stalking form of the miner slowly separated into a series of puffy little clouds, each immediately swelling into another predatory human form, determined to hunt the man-leopard from his plain. Paralyzed, Verrons failed to utter a single syllable of warning. He could only lie helpless while the scene progressed to its logical climax, man and leopard fusing silently into a single bubbling cloudhead that slowly drifted away, leaving the sky-plain barren of life.

Desperately Verrons broke the hold of dream and struggled awake. Sadler's boots clattered across the plaza. Verrons sat stiffly and noted that the Talberonese's hands were empty except for the spear. "No game?"

Sadler's face was taut. "I had both our game bags full but I had to throw them to the humanoids. You—I think you'd better come down for a look, Commander."

"At the humanoids?" When had they ever been mobile by daylight?

"Yes. They—I didn't think much about it at the time, but I didn't hear them up here fluting last night. Judging from the slashes and burns on their hides and the fact that one of them is missing, I think the Ehminheer drove them off the mesa top, probably at about the same time he drove us away." Briefly Sadler's gaze flickered to the top level of the complex. "Did you learn anything from the Ehminheer?"

Standing, Verrons shook his head. "I questioned him but he's not willing to help." He peered at the Ehminheer, preternaturally alert on his high wall. "If we want to let him simmer for a day or two before we head toward the mountains—" Shrugging, he let the thought complete itself. "Let's go see what transpires with the humanoids."

Near the lower mouth of the gully, Sadler paused, scanning the foliage that partially shielded view of the stream. "I was hunting downstream when I came across them. They saw me spear a piglet and they went wild. They chased me as far as the streambank. I threw them game but it was the spear they wanted. I wouldn't be surprised—" Abruptly, his pale eyes narrowing, he handed Verrons the spear. With a quick nod, he indicated the mudbank upstream of the gully mouth.

Verrons met the tallest humanoid's eye at the same instant it picked him from the vegetation of the mesa side. Verrons sucked a startled breath. Today the humanoid's deep eyes glinted with unexpected vitality and his lacy lip veil switched emphatically, living tissue. With a swift flexing of limbs, the humanoid moved to obstruct the gully mouth. His three lieutenants flanked him, grunting excitedly. The coarse-hided bodies were still starvling gaunt, but it was obvious to Verrons that the humanoids no longer tottered on the verge of sudden extinction.

As for why. . . ?

Holding Verrons' gaze, the tallest humanoid rolled back thin lips to expose a double rank of horny yellow chewing surfaces. The grimace, underscored by a series of harsh grunts, was clearly threatening. Lacerations scored the coarse grey hide, creating an epidermal crazy quilt. "The wounds weren't too recently inflicted. They're closing and healing," Verrons pointed out.

Sadler agreed. "The Ehminheer must have driven them off the mesa top almost immediately after he drove us away. And apparently so long as we stay within the gully, they won't come after us."

Verrons frowned. "Let's test it." He pushed past Sadler and advanced down the gully. The humanoids' agitation at his approach was marked. Lip veils flopped, grey limbs flexed, horny teeth gnawed ostentatiously. Verrons halted a couple of meters short of the gully mouth, deliberately teasing. None of the four, despite their marked excitement, lunged into the gully.

Or more accurately, none lunged after the spear in his hand. Because there, it became apparent, lay the focus of their agitation. To the accompaniment of indignant grunts, Verrons retreated. "So we're all right so long as we stay this side of the gully mouth," he said thoughtfully. "If you call hungry enough to digest your own boots all right."

Sadler's expression soured. "We can go back to the mesa top and pick our way down the opposite wall."

"Granted. Or we can stay and try to use their interest in the spear as a basis for establishing communication. Unfortunately the spear is the only bauble we have to offer—and once we yield that, it could become too late for communication very suddenly."

Sadler's white brows conferred at the bridge of his nose. "You've never established communication with members of an alien species before?"

"Initial communication? No. Exploration Service seldom permits study parties to encroach upon known intelligent or semi-intelligent races. I did observe a couple of contact specialists at work several years ago, but I'm afraid their process consisted primarily of grunting and hawing and drawing pictures in the dirt."

"Wasn't it effective?"

"Not especially, at least not in the cases I observed. There has to be intelligence comparable in type if not in level in both species before communication can proceed far."

Sadler evaluated the clutch of humanoids critically. "And you wouldn't classify this an intelligent—or semi-intelligent—species?"

Verrons studied the leader of the humanoids, painfully aware of ambivalence. "A few days ago I would have given you an unequivocal no. But today? Even a dog, if it's hungry enough, will try to snatch game from your hands. But go for the spear that brought it down?" He shook his head. He simply could not fit the humanoids into the Selmarri picture. Were they the last tailings of a semi-intelligent species, barreling swiftly downhill into extinction? If so, had their forebears hidden in some jungle fastness, isolated, invulnerable to conquest and exploitation, when the light dancers ruled Selmarri? Difficult to credit, given the power the dancers commanded. But clearly these four were not the establishing seed of a developing race.

Was that really so clear—today? But if this were a race destined to survive even on a very modest scale, where were the young? As cleverly sequestered as the forebears? And who could attribute even minimal cleverness to this breed? Whichever way he tried to turn, Verrons tangled himself in his own theoretical traces. "One thing I would like to know: what brought them to this pitch of activity in the first place? What prepared them to respond to our spear with anything more vigorous than snores? The only stimulus that obtained a comparable result was my stealing their flutes."

"The Ehminheer may have their flutes now," Sadler ventured.

Verrons grunted. "You think he confiscated them when he drove the humanoids off the mesa top? Then I suppose even if they dared make a foray to the temple, the mechanism would refuse to issue them new instruments—for reasons we still don't understand. All of which may or may not relate to what brought them out of their torpor." Verrons' gaze sought back up the gully, discontent. Flutes or no flutes, intelligent indigenes or dullards, more immediate matters demanded attention. Dispassionately Verrons noted the recurrence of symptoms he had not suffered for several days: tremor, weakness, an occasional disturbing sense of disorientation—and agonizing hunger. He held out a hand. It quivered. He stumped the spear haft against the rocky soil. "Let's pull our retreat."

The humanoids objected passionately to the humans' withdrawal. And reaching the mesa top, Verrons' own expectations were jarred when he found the Ehminheer neither upon his wall nor anywhere upon the mesa top. When they had searched every structure, Verrons stood at the western edge of the plaza peering intently toward the mountains. "If he was able to pick out the geyser area even from this distance—"

"He may have just gone for game," Sadler suggested, his face drawn.

"Granted." But Verrons remembered the Ehminheer's jubilant outcry shortly before noon. He remembered too how the avian had stifled the outburst upon realizing Verrons was watching him. "If we set out after him now—"

"We'll never catch him if he's already started toward the mountains."

Verrons nodded, hunger gripping him in a fresh spasm. "Let's go feed ourselves. We should feel stronger tomorrow. We can travel then." Cautiously he led way down the treacherous mesa wall.

Three days' practice with the spear served them well. Despite their weakness, they soon fed on berries, bulbs and tender jungle pig. "A menu I could appreciate better if we had a cookfire," Verrons observed when the involuntary tremor of his hands was finally dampened. He peered around the dense undergrowth. "I suppose that if we want to conduct a communications seminar before we leave the area, we should stock up on game."

Moving cautiously, watchful for sign of the humanoids, they tracked down small game and lashed it into bundles with vine-cord. However when they made their way to the top of the mesa and ventured down the gully again, the humanoids were no longer in evidence at the foot of the mesa. Verrons' eyes narrowed critically upon the unoccupied mudbank. A confusion of tracks marked its glossy surface. "Do you feel like carrying the effort into their territory?"

Reluctantly Sadler assented. However they found the humanoids neither in their mud wallow nor in the vicinity of their feeding grounds. As they rattled through the much-ravaged briars of the berry bog, dusk was their only companion under the trees. The earthen musk of mud and vegetation was heavy in the sunset silence of the jungle.

Sadler's eyes were shadow-clouded, unreadable. "Maybe the Ehminheer has returned to the mesa top by now."

Verrons nodded abstractedly. Whether or not the avian had returned, they would be more secure at the mesa top than in the jungle tonight. And no matter what phenomenon the temples teased them with, Verrons for one intended to sleep. Let them spit flutes; let them flaunt staircases; let light-dancers rend the night with the thunder-voice of their ancient arrogance. Verrons' muscles were lax with fatigue.

His intention proved unexpectedly easy of execution. The two men stretched out in the temple of orange dancers. Soon darkness dulled pink stone and no Ehminheer appeared to shred the silence with his evensong. No humanoids came to flute the night. When Verrons closed his eyes, darkness was total, undisturbed even by the phantom flash of Mazaahr spots. Nor did Verrons' private night sky torment him with dream images of the man-leopard and its relentless stalker.

It was early morning when Verrons led way back down the gully, his share of the previous day's bundled game slung stiffly over his shoulder. Mist gathered in bouldered pockets and swelled from behind clumps of scarlet and black vegetation. "If we don't find the humanoids in any of their usual haunts, we'll head directly for the mountains," Verrons said. But as they neared the lower mouth of the gully, grey bodies materialized from cover of dew-stained foliage. Verrons threw back a restraining arm.

A metal object gleamed in the tallest humanoid's grasp. Tensely human eye met humanoid across a span of meters. The humanoid's split nostrils flared. With an emphatic grunt, the humanoid altared the metal object on a moss-furred boulder at the base of the gully and retreated.

Verrons' eyes drank the gleam of polished metal. He tongued suddenly dry lips, silently passing the spear to Sadler. Cautiously he descended and closed his hand around the object. It was a small sturdy metal barrel, both ends open, its interior surface set with lightweight metal paddles. Suspended at its center was a round instrument face marked with needled dials. The metal of the barrel was lightly pitted, the clear face of the instrument pack completely unmarked.

The humanoid gestured at the object with splayed fingers and grunted. "Trade?" Verrons guessed incredulously. "For meat?" he formed the words roundly, pointing to his open mouth.

Incredibly the humanoid responded with a like gesture, his lip-veil flopping emphatically.

Verrons' jaws rippled. Quickly he slung bundled game off his shoulder. "Meat," he pronounced, placing a single bundle on the mossed rock and retreating.

The four humanoids snatched their booty with eager grunts and disappeared into the brush, leaving Verrons and Sadler to examine their own prize. Verrons elevated it. Dial hands moved as thin metal paddles caught the light breeze and rotated within the barrel. "Offhand I'd guess it's a weather instrument, an anemometer. Quite a sophisticated offering from this crew." More puzzling, the instrument was in excellent condition. "You didn't dig out anything comparable when you took your trek from Selmarri Home to the jungle village?"

"No more than you and I came across anything like it in the stone city."

Verrons nodded abstractedly. A barrel anemometer—several giant steps up the developmental ladder from a forged metal spear. "There must be artifact stores out here we simply haven't stumbled across yet. Probably a depot for items not unique or precious enough to be placed in the sub-complex display hall but too significant simply to be abandoned." His eyes narrowed. "Logically the facility might even house technological master flutes comparable to the red flute mounted under the grand temple." Verrons directed a harsh breath into the barrel of the anemometer. Paddles spun. His jaw setting, he turned his attention back to the brush at the foot of the mesa. "Our grey-hided friends aren't going to be satisfied with their handout for long. If we can persuade them to lead us to wherever they found the anemometer—"

Sadler and Verrons crouched in the gully to wait. Soon brush rattled. The humanoids' second advance was less militant than their advance of the previous day, but as they blocked the gully mouth, their deep eyes converged again on the spear in Verrons' hand. Setting the anemometer on a rock nearby, he selected a second bundle of game from his stock and held it up. "Meat!" he pronounced emphatically.

For reply he received a series of rejective grunts. The tallest humanoid glowered at the offering. Then his gaze flashed to the spear in Verrons' hand. Splayed fingers indicated first the anemometer, then the spear.

Verrons tensed, unwilling to believe they had moved so swiftly from basic communication to basic haggling. He shook his head, driving the haft of the spear into the ground beside him. "Meat." He directed an emphatic gesture at the instrument on the rock beside him. "*Trade—*for *meat.*"

The humanoids crouched and gazed from game to weather instrument to spear, their lip veils fluttering. Guttural utterances punctuated their consideration of the alternatives Verrons offered.

"They have language?" Sadler demanded in a half-whisper.

"I'm past guessing," Verrons admitted, alert for the humanoids' next move. He began to feel like the preschool instructor who came to class with a stack of primers and found himself embroiled in a discussion of molecular physics—unprepared.

Finally the tallest humanoid took his feet again. He bared his horny teeth, apparently in declaration. Verrons' hand tightened on the spear haft. But instead of charging the humans, the humanoid turned. His three lieutenants followed him into the brush, stalks crackling underfoot.

Warily Verrons descended the gully to watch the four disappear into the jungle. "Apparently they realize they'll have to fetch something more impressive to trade for the spear. Let's give them a few minutes' lead."

They followed the humanoids' trail vigilantly, falling back twice when their own faster pace brought them too near. "They travel like turtles," Verrons commented. And fortunately a little like elephants, their path clearly marked by trampled vegetation. Nevertheless he moved with his spear at the ready, seeking the bending stalks and swaying shadows for sign of ambush. Underfoot the soil was damp and black, rich with decay.

It was midmorning when the jungle march halted. Ahead the humanoids' heavy tread was silenced. Verrons and Sadler waited, then moved forward cautiously. A small dome sat on the jungle floor, half overgrown with vines. Its door stood open. From the interior Verrons heard the unmistakable grunt of their humanoid guides. And beyond the first dome were others of similar size and construction, a double rank of pale jungle pearls.

Verrons exchanged a startled glance with Sadler. Cautiously they edged past the first dome and around the first of the second rank. Verrons tapped the translucent paneling lightly. It was a plaston material, virtually untouched by deterioration. He pressed his forehead to the paneling. Within the dome shadowy forms were stranded in silent immobility.

Sadler was as unprepared as Verrons. He molded his forehead against plaston paneling. Then, glancing away, he touched Verrons' arm. "Over there."

Through dense vegetation, Verrons spotted a second cluster of domes. He flared a glance back at the structure the humanoids had entered. "Keep an eye on them. If they head my way, warn me." Quickly he dodged away.

The second cluster was more extensive than the first and more varied. It included a single longhouse, several small domes and half a dozen larger ones. Again the exterior paneling, although assaulted by vine, was unmarked by deterioration. Cautiously Verrons pushed through a hinged door into the longhouse.

The dim interior held deserted stillness—and chaos. Containers and debris were strewn across the floor and across every other horizontal surface of the structure. Freeform smears and stains lent the walls dubious distinction. Verrons forded the length of the structure: tables, chairs, cook units, water tanks—all of alien design and manufacture, but recognizable in their function, granted a humanoid context. He had stumbled into a communal cookshack, a devastated one. Pulling at a cabinet door, he found stacked plaston mess trays, their fastidious arrangement an ironic counterpoint to the unmannered chaos around him.

Disturbed, he emerged at the far end of the structure and entered one of the larger circular domes. Again light was dim but contents recognizable: cots, tables, chairs, chests, miscellany. This time everything was in fair order.

He was sifting miscellany when Sadler appeared. "They're headed back toward the mesa, Commander."

Verrons' head snapped up. "Taking what?"

"Another meteorological instrument, I think. I took a look through that first dome before coming for you. It's evidently a storage lab for weather instruments and meteorological records and supplies. None of them precisely like anything I've encountered before, but close enough. And there are logs, too. Not very extensive, lots of empty pages. I couldn't read the script, of course, or the numbering system—"

"Just like I can't read this?" Verrons interrupted. The item he thrust at Sadler consisted of long limp plastic pages bound with

adhesive. They were covered with an incomprehensible interlac-
ing of line and curve. "As bad as my own handwriting."

Sadler's grey eyes flashed down the limp page. "Meaning
we're dealing here with someone who has hands?"

Verrons indicated the furnishings of the dome. "And someone
who has arms and legs and torsos and heads—like our humanoids. Or some other humanoid race."

"There are only two humanoid races on Selmarri," Sadler said
slowy, "unless you want to classify either the light dancers or
the underpeople as a separate third race."

"But the underpeople have been living at a pre-stone age level
for centuries. And this cluster of domes hasn't been here more
than a few years." He sifted through the contents of a locker. A
spill of brilliant fabric ran through his hands. "No mildew, no
rot, no deterioration of any kind—yet. Leaving the humanoids?
But if they were coming up the evolutionary scale anywhere
near creating this sophisticated a layout, the light dancers would
have known about them. We would have sighted them through
the flutes. But even the master flute offered no hint that a second
intelligent race shared this world."

Sadler nodded thoughtfully. "Then there is one other possibility."

"Correct. The race that created this outpost came from
offworld, just as we did."

"And this has to be just that—an outpost."

"Agreed. But let's look around some more before we carry
speculation any farther." Verrons found he needed time to assimilate the abruptly altered constellation of facts and assumptions.

They tackled miscellany together. Almost too quickly they uncovered their key. Verrons spread it on a table and they bent
over it together. Silence stretched between them, insulating them
from the jungle world beyond the dome.

"A photo log," Sadler said finally, softly.

"Of the folks back home. Or of themselves before they left
home." The faces that looked up at him from printed plastic
pages were familiar in conformation: bifurcate nostrils, round
oral orifices, fleshy violet veils cascading from lower lip arcs. The
forked hands were familiar, too. The physiques might have been,
starved of fat and muscle, bared of gowns, robes, trousers and
brilliant swathings, the coarse grey flesh smeared instead with
mud. Verrons flicked quickly through the volume. Their human-

oids appeared against the background of some unidentifiable other world, patron-masters of science and technology. Even though Sadler and Verrons could not decipher the script that laced the page backs, they read substantial fact from the printed photo presentation.

They reached the last page of the album and Verrons slapped it shut. "They were either surveying Selmarri or actually settling it," he said finally. "A quick look around should tell us which. And a bed count should tell us how many of them there were originally."

Sadler nodded somberly.

The original party, they soon determined from survey of the pearlescent domes, had consisted of better than four dozen members. And they had come prepared to farm. Equipment and implements stood mute witness to that fact in a second longhouse a distance through the trees. Well-oiled metal blades gleamed. "Everything uncrated but apparently never used." In a smaller dome nearby, bags and barrels had been opened and thrown about. Verrons retrieved a single flat green seed from a crevice in the flooring. "At a guess they consumed their seed stores instead of planting them."

Sadler stared at him blankly. "But—why?"

Verrons shrugged tautly. "For the same reason they tore the cookshack apart? Because they were starving?"

"But you would expect them to bring supplies to last them at least through their first growing season. Even through their first two or three years, as insurance against crop failure. They didn't come here from a background of poverty."

But poverty was their background now: dormitories abandoned, personal possessions forgotten, the majority of their party dead or missing. The four dozen members of the settling party were four now, naked, emaciated, dull.

Dull—*sometimes!* Just as he and Sadler were dull *sometimes,* weak *sometimes,* dizzy, disorganized, ravenous—*sometimes.* Verrons recalled the morning he had watched the humanoids feed in the berry bog, stuffing themselves until their grey bellies bulged tumorously. "Sadler, let's have a look at that cookshack again."

They looked. It had the aspect of a facility ravaged by a localized storm of hunger. And sorting through heaped debris and refuse, Verrons found the gleam of metal. Reluctantly he retrieved a single flute, its silver barrel cool to his fingertips.

The flute was not an instrument of fascination today. "Sadler, the light phenomenon—" Grimly Verrons thumbnailed open the metal barrel and flicked out a white crystal, a speck of green at its center. Even in the filtered dimness of the dome, the crystal caught light. Verrons stared at the flashing gem, repelled by its unnatural brilliance and by the intuitive realization that gripped him. "These crystals contain no energy supply, Sadler. And there's no source here either." Driven by unwelcome insight, he probed the miniaturized components packed into the upper barrel. "The energy that feeds the light dancers—it has to come directly from us. From our own nervous systems." When he put flute to lips, it was his own energy that brought light to the air, that enabled long-dead dancers to speak and move again. His golden dancer had drawn her life directly from him. And the stumbling fatigue, the voracious hunger, the dizzy faintness—those were not simply the penalties assessed for irregular hours and poorly balanced nutrition. Those were the symptoms of an exhausted human power cell—as his repeated fainting spells should have warned him. As they surely would have warned him, he realized grimly, given a few more nights in the temple, flute to mouth. But by then he would have been too weak, too disorganized to act on the realization, to withdraw himself from the compelling web of light and motion, to let screaming dancers die from the night.

Sadler stared at him, Verrons' insight mirrored in his pale eyes, his lips drawn tight. "Then the humanoids—"

"They came to settle, to establish a colony. But curiosity drew them to the mesa and they triggered the dispensing mechanism. They met its criteria purely by chance—just as we did. And then they became so involved in the flute experience and so weakened by it that they ran through their food stocks and never planted the seed they brought. When both those sources of nutrition were exhausted, they were forced to live off the land. Which may or may not provide an adequate diet for their species. With the flutes sapping them, leaving them too weak and disorganized to do more than stuff themselves with berries, the result was starvation.

"Sadler, the dancers didn't expect the underpeople to rebel against flute worship simply because it was a form of subjection —but because it was a form of slow death. The light dancers used the underpeople like disposable power cells to keep the ancestors alive—and that's how the humanoids were used too."

"And us," Sadler amplified grimly.

"Yes." But even if he had known, could he have denied his golden dancer second life? Troubled, Verrons paced away, his eyes narrowing. "And as soon as the humanoids find the Ehminheer has gone, my bet is that they'll be back up the gully, trying to solicit fresh flutes from the temple mechanism. As to whether it will dispense them. . . ." He frowned, rubbing his beard. "At a guess, prolonged exposure to the flutes damaged their nervous systems sufficiently that by the time we arrived, they were no longer able to trigger the mechanism. Just as a depleted power cell will be rejected by testing equipment even though it may contain enough energy to function for a short while longer."

"But now? Now that they've had time to recover?"

Verrons shrugged. "How far have they recovered? To what extent was the damage reversible?" He and Sadler had bounced back, given a brief period of rest and adequate diet. But their exposure to the flutes had not been prolonged. "Some of the equipment we've seen here—"

"There are several more storage domes near the meteorological lab," Sadler reminded him.

"Which I suggest we explore now, because I'm willing to bet we'll find equipment there far more effective for jungle survival than this spear—equipment the humanoids' damaged brains no longer even recognize as survival tools. They had to see you bring down a piglet with the spear to recognize its possibilities." And the anemometer the humanoids had tried to trade for the spear? It probably represented nothing more than a chunk of shiny metal to their damaged brains.

Grimly Verrons led way through the brush and vines that strained to swallow the abandoned settlement. "If we find anything we can use, we'll leave them the spear—in trade," he vowed.

CHAPTER FOURTEEN

Days passed beneath Aleida's feet, days fired by visions of a flashing orange crystal, until finally the mountain range rose sharply ahead, its every ridge and pinnacle joined in a concerted thrust against the mid-morning sky. Aleida had run the line of the foothills for two days now, sampling their topographic eccentricity impatiently, alert for some clue that she could not even name, some subtle suggestion that the caverns lay near. Finally at dawn today she had risen from the rocky shelf where she had slept and an almost imperceptible scent had reached her, bringing her hair crackling alive. Her eyes had flared, casting a halo of light around her. Instinctively she had run southward along the line of foothills, and soon she had been rewarded by a thickening stench on the cool air. Now she paused again, measuring the stinging effluvium against a barely-apprehended strand of flute memory.

It was the sulphur-smell of the caverns! Her hair crackling, Aleida raced up the rising slope and topped the crest of a strangely domed hill. Beyond, a broad plateau gradually sloped upward to the base of the mountains. Above and to her northwest, where plateau met mountain, a lacy finger of steam rose, arched gracefully, then slowly spilled back to earth. In the foreground Aleida spotted a lesser geyser playing into a yellow-crusted pool.

Pausing, Aleida surveyed the area keenly. The plateau was sparsely vegetated, pocked with bizarre accretions of mineral, punctuated with crescent flows of black sand. A broad stream cut a swift crystal swath across it. And beyond? Squinting, Aleida tried to pick detail from the dense shadows at the base of the mountains. Instead she found a moving streak of blue. Her body stiffened. Her hair crackling, she rose to her toes.

Bright-Feather had already sighted her. He shrieked warning, the cry acrid on the thin air as he ran toward her. A swift spike of fear lanced Aleida, primitive, unreasoning. Her hands fell. Cowed, she shriveled back over the crest of the hill and crouched behind a boulder.

Entry to the caverns—frustration burst from her fingertips in orange sparks—she had to find entry to the caverns. She had come too far to turn back now, no matter how primal the fear Bright-Feather stimulated in her. And he held no license here where mountains met sky. These mountains had not risen out of the earth to receive him. No crystal grew for him deep within the rocky womb. He was an intruder.

A delayed surge of rage mobilized her. Swiftly Aleida sprang from hiding and dared the crest of the hill again. Ignoring Bright-Feather's indignant shriek, she raced down the rugged slope and ran westward across the mineral-pocked plateau. As she drew nearer the mountains, the smell of sulphur quickly became choking-thick. It seemed to hang in a chalky yellow veil over a landscape drawn directly from dream. Her toes carried her past brush-shaded basins where mud bubbled glossy and brown, past yellow-caked steam vents, past glimmering pools of unnaturally brilliant water. As she ran, Bright-Feather charged flex-limbed down the course of the stream.

Aleida glared at him, her eyes blazing with orange fire. As he neared, however, she realized with shock that today his gaudy eyes flashed yellow above—nothing, nothing at all but a fleshy pink welt where his beak had been. His extremities were just as bare. He was armed with nothing but the fire-tools he brandished at her. But despite his lack of natural weaponry, he was charged with possessive ferocity. And within minutes they faced each other across the tumbling stream. Instinctively Aleida surged to her toes, flashing curtains of light from the air and hurling them across the water.

Steam rose, but Bright-Feather neither retreated nor fell. Instead he raised his hand and the fire-tool spat across the breadth of the stream. Its beam scorched Aleida's thigh. With an agonized shriek, she raced away upstream, dodging toward the shadows of the mountains as if toward shelter.

Bright-Feather's weapon spat again and his beam seared her shoulder and crackled at her hair. At the second assault, Aleida whirled with an indignant scream. Again she instinctively arched to her toes. But this time instinct led her to direct the storm-force of her power against the surface of the stream. Spinning icy water up into a whirling spout, she threw it at Bright-Feather as he triggered his fire-tool again. Water and heat intersected and steam exploded the length of his beam of fire. With a frenzied shriek, Bright-Feather hurled the weapon away.

Aleida's eyes flared bright. But she had not totally disarmed Bright-Feather. There was a second weapon in his other hand. Blue crest erect, he brought the weapon to bear.

Before he could fire, Aleida directed a second funnel of icy water at him. It spun through the cool air and splashed across his bristling plumage. A flying vortex, it wrenched the weapon from his grasp, spun it away, and dropped it in a shallow pool nearby. Bright-Feather stared in astonishment. Then he shook his plumage and launched himself after his weapons.

Aleida did not wait for a second engagement. She raced away upstream. When she darted a glance back, Bright-Feather had retrieved both weapons. Aleida blew a warning sheet of water from the stream surface. With a truncated squawk, Bright-Feather holstered his weapons and ran after her.

His pace upstream matched hers, and the swift waters led them quickly to the area where geysers played against the dark shoulders of the mountains. Their lacy plumes dared the chill air intermittently, curling out of the ground, hanging breeze-whipped in the air, then sinking back to earth. Despite Bright-Feather's repeated shriek of warning, Aleida's glance darted at the shadows, seeking possible entry into the caverns.

As they reached the base of the mountains, the stream narrowed and split into half a dozen sparkling rivulets. Aleida
halted, eyeing Bright-Feather warily across the suddenly insub-
stantial barricade of water. His yellow eyes shimmied wildly.
But before the encounter could take any more ominous turn,
Bright-Feather's gaudy gaze was distracted. His head spinning,
he peered into the sky above the foothills. Aleida followed the
direction of his gaze. She saw nothing. But obviously from
Bright-Feather's sudden agitation, someone or something rode
the sky. The male? Hope surged through her but she felt no rising sense of excitation, no engorging of organs. She felt nothing.

Nothing at all, not even when Bright-Feather abandoned their
confrontation, racing away downstream with a tearing shriek.
Aleida surveyed the sky again, fruitlessly. But whatever Bright-
Feather saw, apparently it represented a greater threat than she
did. And if she could find entry to the caverns while he was distracted. . . . Quickly she turned back and danced across the
narrow rivulets of the stream. Rock and coarse sand shifted underfoot as she dashed along the uneven ground at the base of the
mountains, her eyes probing every shadow. The rock of the
mountains was black and rugged, rising steeply to the sky. Far
above the mountain peaks were capped with white. Once as she
ran, a gout of steam exploded from its vent and showered her
with mist. Peering down, Aleida saw Bright-Feather streaking
wildly back across the plateau, his eyes still on the sky.

She ran until a crevice in the mountainside, half hidden by
fallen stone, caught her eye. Halting, she measured herself
against it. The crevice extended little higher than eye level and
was broad at its base, tapering quickly to no more than a crack.
Urgently she kicked away rocky rubble and wedged herself into
the crevice, her fingers groping inward for passage to the heart
of the mountain. As she inched forward, her eyes flared bright,
but their light was quickly lost in the rugged maw of rock.
Crawling deeper into the narrow crevice, rock scraping her flesh,
she probed ahead of herself with her fingertips. But although the
smell of sulphur grew stronger, the crevice quickly narrowed to
impassibility. Impatiently Aleida backed out and flashed a
glance back over the plateau.

Two bodies rode low on the afternoon sky, bobbing over the
crest of the oddly domed hill she had topped not long before.
The palehands—airborne? Aleida stared incredulously as they

floated down the slope toward the protesting Bright-Feather. Her indignation almost matched his. This world was hers: jungle, mountains and sky, even if she weren't able to press her rightful claim to the upper strata yet. Now the palehands violated her airspace as well as her firmament. Instinctively Aleida's back arched.

She quelled her writhing arms. The power would not carry her from the ground, not without the crystal. And the crystal—she turned, as if drawn by it. Fiercely, her hair crackling, Aleida launched herself northward again.

She had not run far before the floating palehands skimmed up the slope and hovered near her, bulky black packs strapped to their backs. The packs emitted an airy humming sound. Briefly the taller blocked Aleida's path and the smaller bobbed lightly back and forth behind him. Aleida halted, glaring at them. Then they spoke to each other in their unemphatic tongue, the taller nodded, and both lifted into the air and skimmed ahead to the north.

Aleida forced a fierce epithet through her bared teeth and Bright-Feather screeched an answer from below, racing mountainward again. Vengefully Aleida reversed course and dashed southward along the rugged base of the mountain. There was entry here somewhere—not for the palehands, not for Bright-Feather, but entry for her. So let the others search to the north. If she ran south, that was where entry to the mountains would lie.

That was where entry did lie, a second crevice in the mountainside hardly more promising than the first. Again Aleida had to kick aside rocky rubble, again she had to wedge herself into a small opening. But this time, although jagged rock drew blood from her flanks, although at some points she had to snake through the tortuous fissure on her side, the crevice never closed entirely. She advanced painfully, struggling, her fingers always finding promise ahead. And the palehands? The smaller might squeeze through here but never the larger. She paused, listening for pursuit anyway. She heard nothing.

She moved ahead again. Soon she lost all sense of time. She struggled endlessly through the mountain, the choking sweetness of perspiration mingling with the harsh tang of sulphur. Then, without warning, the passage grew shorter and broader. Aleida dropped and crawled forward on her stomach. Soon she was unable to raise her head although her groping hands met resistance on neither side. Panic seized her. Desperately she pressed haunch and shoulder muscles up against the resisting roof of the mountain. Her reaching hands told her that although she could not stand, could not even crouch, she could crawl in any direction from here. But which would be the right direction?

Deliberately she relaxed her straining muscles and squeezed her eyes shut, trying to recapture images from the night beneath the temple. Was this the mountain she had been intended to enter? Or had she let herself be lured into the demon's own domain? Did he even now wrest the mountain off its foundations, preparing to smash it down upon her? Startled by the vividness of her own fantasy, she yelped with fear.

Painfully she forced herself to struggle forward again. Soon she had become totally disoriented. Whether she crawled ahead toward the heart of the mountain or back toward the geyser area, she did not know. She only knew that her flesh was scrubbed raw against rock, that her body was slick with perspiration, that its odor sickened her.

Her oppression ended abruptly. One moment she inched forward beneath the crushing weight of the mountain. The next her probing hands reported a cold draught. She wriggled forward and to her astonishment found she could raise her head. Another writhing of muscles, and her entire body emerged from beneath the roof of stone.

Her jubilation was brief. She scrambled to her haunches and with one long-toed foot explored the rocky floor ahead. The length of one foreleg, the length of two—and the floor fell away to nothing. Aleida pulled her foot back and dropped to her knees, groping forward with her fingers. They relayed the same message: she faced a steep drop directly ahead. Shivering, Aleida explored an arm's length to her left, to her right. From all indications she was crouched on a narrow ledge of rock that overhung—what? An internal abyss? Cautiously Aleida straightened to her feet and arched her back. Almost reluctantly she raised her arms and let the fingers dance.

The gesture brought faint orange veils rippling from her fingertips. She cast them on the air, assessing her position by their weakly surging light. She found that she stood on a high ledge of rock overhanging a deep internal crevasse. Several arm lengths away, the opposite face of the crevasse rose, steep, featureless. Flinging veils of light wide, Aleida peered to either side of her position. Ledge and crevasse appeared to extend indefinitely.

Her arms fell. And now? Crawl back the way she had come? Or edge cautiously down the ledge? She had neither instinct nor information to guide her. She shivered, a single and suddenly very vulnerable living mote stranded in the dark mountain. Slowly, her breath held, she moved to her right.

As she progressed, the wall behind her was polished smooth in spots by running water and the ledge was slick underfoot. Then both became rough and dry again. As Aleida continued her cautious sidewise progress, the stinging odor of sulphur grew stronger. Her eyes watered and her skin drew tight with dried perspiration.

Much later she squatted to rest. Absently she tongued dried perspiration from the back of her hand. The muscles of her calves quivered weakly. When she was ready to continue, she could bring only weak veils of light from the air.

Good news was that the ledge widened again directly ahead. Bad was that it was blocked at its widest point by a barricade of rock that had broken from the wall of the crevasse and lodged on the ledge. Grimly Aleida advanced, her light winking out. She worked in complete darkness to clear passage, rolling rock and boulder into the crevasse. The distant roar of impact was a deep voice bellowing from the center of the mountain.

From that point the ledge gradually narrowed until finally Aleida's toes protruded over its rim. She halted and, arching, brought weak light from the air. A short distance ahead, she saw, the ledge disappeared entirely. But so, she saw with a gust of relief, did the crevasse. Lowering herself through a narrow, rubble-choked crevice, she found herself in a winding passage in which she could stand upright.

It descended steeply and soon Aleida lost all sense of direction. At times, the passage seemed to lead directly down into the underbelly of the mountain. At other times, it seemed to coil upward and outward. An endless interval later, her hand probed an apparent dead end. Lighting the air, she found that directly before her the passage abruptly narrowed to a crawl hole, while to her right, it wound upward again. She dodged quickly into the second passage.

She dodged as quickly out again. Because from somewhere

above came the sound of voices—unmistakable voices. The pale-hands had found their way into the mountain, Bright-Feather accompanying them. How? A second entry somewhere, one capacious enough to accommodate even the tall palehand? Quickly Aleida bolted down the crawl hole, her heart pounding a jealous rhythm. The palehands—rock scraped her tender flanks—could the palehands pass here? She wanted to think not, but a sweeping survey told her the passage was not restrictively narrow.

She did not hear voices again as she scuttled forward, knees and palms bleeding. Nor did she hear them when the crawl tunnel gradually expanded and she was able to run at a half crouch. She pattered quickly through the mountains until she faced a series of branching passages. Straightening erect, she veered, as nearly as she could determine, in the direction of the mountain's center, tossing faint veils of light before her. Once, pausing, she thought she heard voices again. She listened intently, her legs quivering with fatigue. The sound did not recur.

Soon, as she wound through the mountain she began to encounter passages half-barricaded with loose rock that had broken from the passage walls. The smell of sulphur was stronger here, and her pounding heart, her rushing blood, told her she drew near the place where the powers of this world were united in the form of a bright crystal.

When she felt a smooth surface beneath her toes, she arched her back, and this time the veils of light she flung into the air were brilliant and surging. They danced around her, illuminating walls and floor of artificially glazed stone. Even the vaulted ceiling gleamed. With an exultant cry, Aleida raced forward. The passage widened and, encased in light, she ran down a broad glazed thoroughfare. Ahead the sound of running water was faint, evocative. How many years had it been since long toes had raced this pavement? How many since stiff hair had belled out crackling, since glowing eyes had dashed brilliance from wall to polished wall? How many of her powered ancestors had passed this way in ages past to grasp power in still-infant hands, to make the forces of earth and sky finally and irrevocably their own? It seemed to Aleida that she did not run this corridor alone, that others ran it with her, a hundred others, a thousand others, and all of them—herself!

Then the passage ended in a glazed wall containing a single narrow arch. A sheet of running water curtained the arch. Aleida halted, her pulse pounding drunkenly. Instinctively she arched her back and strode through the flowing curtain on her toes, hands raised high, fingers twining.

The veils of light that burst from her fingertips were superfluous in the deep cavern. Because here where the subterranean river crashed noisily through a channel of black rock, here where cavern walls steepled high into the heart of the mountain, the rocks themselves were crusted with light of every order. It glowed from the walls, only partially dimmed by the thick mineral accretions that overlaid its multiple crystalline sources. It shone with a vibrant promise that almost seemed to speak aloud.

You have come, our own. You are here to claim what the forces of our world have wrought for you. You are here to break light from the wall with the force of your gaze, here to grow in power, in command and presence.

Claim what you will, our own.

Aleida strode forward, body arched, fingers moving sinuously. From every side fire glowed: blue fire, silver fire, indigo, gold—orange fire! Her eyes blazed answer, and raw energy arced from eyes to wall in a crackling flow.

Or did energy flow from wall to eyes? How could Aleida know when its electrical force crackled her spine, convulsing her, and her arms suddenly flailed helplessly against the chill air? How could she know when her feet carried her forward unbidden? Helpless, Aleida puppet-danced toward the river. With bleeding knees, scraped palms, lacerated flanks and backside, she waded the icy rapids. Black rock slashed at the soles of her feet, drawing blood.

Although the subterranean river was both broad and swift, Aleida was not swept from her feet. The arc of energy drew her unerringly through the water to the opposite bank. There, from high on the mineral-crusted wall, a certain crystal glowed more brightly than any other. Aleida's arms rose smoothly again. Instinctively her fingers wove the pattern that would produce the desired alteration in the energy flow of her nervous system. She threw back her head, and the altered rhythm of her brain waves intensified the light that flowed between eyes and rock. Slowly rock crumbled from around the embedded crystal. Aleida's hands extended and into them fell a fist-sized mass of matter: crystal, matrix and mineral encrustation.

Aleida backed away toward the river, the weight of the world cradled in her palm, burning. She hardly realized her legs moved, but within minutes she had forded the subterranean river and passed back under the water-curtained arch. Dimly she heard the slap of her feet, and glazed walls and floor flowed past. She ran, her attention entirely invested in the crystal mass in her hands.

Her concentration shattered when she neared the end of the glazed passageway. Voices reached her there, both near and clear. Aleida's head snapped up. A low growl sounded in her throat. She paused momentarily, then raced toward the sound of voices.

She confronted the three intruders in a narrow passage, its floors rubbed with fallen stone. At sight of her, they froze. Immediately Aleida arched to her toes, and the crystal in her hand heated. It was not necessary for her hands to rise now, for her fingers to dance. The crystal focused tight the power that even here in the mountain flowed both within and without her, shaping it into a bright beam, a sword of light. It was only necessary for Aleida to arch back her head and let the sword sweep from her eyes.

But even crystal-focused, her power inflicted no trauma upon the intruders. Bright-Feather screeched with fury and the tallest palehand leapt forward. Quickly Aleida snapped her head erect and sprang past them to run down the rough-walled passage. A short distance away she turned, and again her head arched back and the crystal in her hand glowed.

This time she directed the sword of her power not against the intruders but against the passage wall. Under stress of her power, rock broke free and shuddered from the passage wall in a rumbling avalanche. Dust rose, a choking cloud. When it cleared, the passage was solidly blocked.

Aleida's head fell. She listened intently, the crystal cooling in her hand. If the intruders had survived the avalanche, her ears did not report the fact to her. Her lips quivered in a fierce, meaningless grin. Then she was running again, crystal in hand, running up twisting passages, running toward view of the sky that was hers now. Running toward the universe of sunlight and cloud that had waited long dead years for her appearance.

CHAPTER FIFTEEN

Verrons was momentarily paralyzed when the young female turned her swordlike gaze against the passage wall. Then, at the jarring impact of falling stone, he regained control of shock-deadened muscles and retreated down the passage, throwing himself to shelter beneath a jagged outcropping of rock. The deafening rumble of falling rock seemed to go on forever before it faded into a clattering rattle of loose stone that ended in silence. Stiffly Verrons stood and peered into total darkness. He drew his hand across his eyes and was briefly distracted when brilliant Mazaahr moths failed to dance across his field of vision. If he had accurately pinpointed the moment when he had first noted their absence. . . .

Distractedly he groped for the light unit he had brought from the humanoid settlement. At his touch, the beam glowed alive, activated by the pressure of his fingers on the sturdy handle. Apprehensively he flashed the beam up the obstructed passage. To his relief he picked out Sadler and the Ehminheer crouched a short distance away. Blinded by his beam, they groped to their feet. Verrons' voice seemed to echo back into his own ears. "Are you all right?"

The Ehminheer flexed erect with a squawk, apparently uninjured. Sadler stood and retrieved his own light unit with a numbed slowness of reflex. The beam failed to activate at his touch. Turning, he peered directly into Verrons' light, his pale features almost erased in the flat glare of Verrons' beam. "I—I must have dropped my unit. I can't trigger the beam."

Quickly Verrons brought his own beam to bear on the light unit Sadler had selected from the equipment shed at the abandoned humanoid settlement. "Apparently the element shattered." Frowning, he peered toward the rock slide that obstructed their passage. His voice seemed muffled. "And apparently we have a choice. We can try to dig our way out—or we can continue down this passage and hope to locate a connecting branch to lead us back out around the obstructed area." Given the number of branching corridors they had encountered in their long trek through the mountain, the latter possibility seemed promising.

"How extensive do you think the rockfall is?" Sadler asked. His pale hair was speckled with dust.

Verrons shook his head. "No way to tell. She may have blocked our passage for tens of meters. Even if we dig through the rubble, the rockfall may have weakened the passage walls enough to make this section permanently hazardous."

Sadler nodded. "Finding a connecting passage may be our only hope then."

Assessingly Verrons turned his beam on the Ehminheer. "Ehminheer?"

K'Obrohms' blue crest stood fully erect, and his gaze was giddy above the fleshy welt where his beak had been. Grimly Verrons' grip on the light unit tightened. At brittling season the Ehminheer should have been vulnerable, indecisive. But k'Obrohms was driven by visions of crystal wings, his hands taloned with the heat pistols he had stolen from Sadler and Verrons. Earlier the sight of the two humans airborne, propelled by liftpacks they had taken from the humanoid settlement, had driven him into fury ecstatic. When they shed the packs, his overriding obsession with the flight crystal had drawn him into uneasy alliance with them. His behavior had grown increasingly more erratic as they followed the tunnel through the mountain, however. Now his gaze danced fiercely in the beam of Verrons' light. "I want the crystal," he uttered, a demand.

Uneasily Verrons turned and peered up the passage the way the girl had come. "Let's have a look." Briefly he closed his eyes and again noted the absence of dancing light specks. "Sadler. . . ."

But the Ehminheer had already plunged past him down the dark mountain corridor. Reluctantly Verrons followed, swinging his beam wide in search for side passages.

They encountered no connecting passageway. Instead the corridor led almost immediately into a widening underground passage with brightly glazed floor, walls and ceilings. Verrons' lips tightened as his light played across glossy surfaces. Wordlessly he slipped past the Ehminheer and led way down a broadening underground thoroughfare. As they progressed the sound of flowing water gradually drowned the clatter of their heels.

A few minutes later they faced a high glazed wall containing a single narrow archway. From beyond the sound of water was distinct. Verrons flared a glance back at Sadler, whose face hung palely against the glossy corridor wall. Then, shielding his light unit under one arm, Verrons dodged through the sheet of running water that curtained the archway. He emerged in a high-vaulted cavern where the walls glowed with a light of their own, muted, multi-colored. Crystal water flowed swiftly down a broad channel of rock. On the far bank of the subterranean river, there was a raw gouge in the wall.

"There," Sadler said in a low voice. "She took the crystal from there."

Verrons nodded. Obviously the crystal crop had regenerated. In fact, if they had some way of determining the period required for crystal formation, they might even be able to estimate how long the flute society had lain dead. Frowning, Verrons surveyed the light-studded walls. Every order of light was represented, the crystals' tantalizing brilliance dimmed by overlaying milky accretions of mineral. Verrons peered back at the agitated Ehminheer. "What effect do your heat pistols have on this rock?"

The gaudy gaze flashed at Verrons. K'Obrohms' facial conformation, naked of jutting yellow beak, was reptilian. Pistols leapt to his untaloned hands. Fiercely the Ehminheer directed twin beams at the damp wall. The only perceptible result was a sizzling conversion of moisture to steam. When stone did not crumble, he strafed the wall vengefully, swinging the pistols wide.

Still stone did not yield to his heat beams. Briefly, his crest flaring, an angry chuckle trapped in his throat, he appeared on the verge of irrational rage. But he choked back his fury with an angry cluck and turned to Verrons, his stringy body taut. "So now we have just one route out of here, Verrons," he squawked.

Back the way they had come. "We can return later with tools from the humanoid settlement," Verrons suggested, studying the crystal-set walls. But the fanatic shimmer of Tiehl's gaze told him Tiehl's thoughts lay instead with the crystal mass the young female had broken loose from the wall. Verrons directed his beam of light back through the water-curtained arch.

Minutes later they faced the blocked passageway again. Verrons studied the situation thoughtfully. "Ehminheer, you'd better stand well back and direct the beam for us. If our work sets off even a minor avalanche, move back immediately—your bones are much more fragile than ours—but keep the light directed our way."

The two humans tackled the blocked passage cautiously, the single light unit providing uneven illumination. Initially the Ehminheer followed Verrons' instructions. However as the two men worked and it became apparent that the removal of rubble was not merely a prelude to a second rockfall, the Ehminheer gradually skirted the work area.

Verrons eyed him uneasily. Once they had breached the barricade of rubble, the Ehminheer would have little use for them. Their liftpacks, however, abandoned near the mouth of the tunnel, would provide him a welcome boost in pursuit of the young female. And the Ehminheer held not just weapons but necessarily the only functional light unit. Verrons palmed a large rock, weighing it thoughtfully. Expertly tossed, it might disable the Ehminheer long enough for the humans to disarm him.

Expertly tossed, it might also shatter the avian's fragile skull. And in the absence of open threat to their own lives, Verrons could not rule that a permissible casualty. Verrons paused to wipe perspiration from his face. "Ehminheer, when we dig out of here—"

"Then I will go for the crystal," k'Obrohms declared flatly, dancing back from him, light unit in one hand, heat pistol in the other.

Verrons' lips tightened. "If you're thinking of taking the lift-packs, there are a few things you should consider." When Tiehl's dancing gaze affirmed Verrons' guess, Verrons went on. "We have no idea what their performance limitations may be. Sadler and I elected not to test them at risk. And they're powered by energy cells which are at least partially depleted. They have no more than a few air-hours left in them."

"They will have enough," Tiehl asserted.

Verrons shrugged. "If you stick close to the ground—no farther than you would want to fall in case of an energy fade—you may be in no danger. But frankly I'm not convinced you can restrict yourself that closely, are you?"

The avian did not reply, although the fleshy pink welt of his mouth parted slightly at the challenge.

"And if you take altitude before you're fully familiar with the controls, you may unintentionally outfly your oxygen level. And anoxia is just as fatal as a fall."

"I will manage," k'Obrohms asserted.

"You'd manage best by sticking with us once we've cleared passage out of here," Verrons said curtly.

The Ehminheer's response was an angry chortle and an impatient gesture of the heat pistol in his hand.

Verrons sighed, recognizing the futility of argument. From that point, the humans' labor at the barricade became a task supervised by a blue-crested slavemaster. When the Ehminheer's light beam finally probed over the reduced pile of stone into the passage beyond, Sadler glanced to Verrons for some signal. Grimly Verrons shook his head. Heat pistols at close range constituted a very convincing argument against direct confrontation. "Ehminheer—"

K'Obrohms refused the appeal. With a warning shriek, he launched himself over the rubble heap and squeezed through the narrow opening Verrons and Sadler had created. As the untaloned feet disappeared, Verrons pulled Sadler back from the area. "If he sets off a secondary slide. . . ."

Their ears detected only a minor rattle of rock from the other side of the barricade. Then the Ehminheer shrieked from the passage beyond and the two humans stood alone in complete darkness. "So now all we have to do is finish digging free and grope our way back to the surface," Verrons said grimly.

"And hope he leaves one liftpack for us," Sadler added.

"Agreed. Otherwise we have a long walk ahead of us." But to the humanoid settlement? To the temple complex? Or to Selmarri Home? Once again Verrons drew his hand across his eyes. Again alien light failed to flutter and dance in telltale patterns. "Sadler—"

Rock shifted as Sadler tested the narrow opening in the rocky barricade. "I think I could almost squeeze through now. If we had a light—"

"Sadler," Verrons persisted, "are you still seeing Mazaahr spots?"

The other's silence was startled. "I—" He seemed to grope for an answer. "Yes, I'm—aren't you?"

"They haven't decreased in intensity or frequency?" Verrons pressed.

Again Sadler's silence held a shocked quality. "They—*yes*," he said finally. "They faded several days ago. And they don't seem to be reintensifying. It's almost as if—"

Don't say it, Verrons pleaded silently. Don't do more than admit the bare possibility. And hold it loosely, ready to surrender it at a moment's notice. "I noticed the change soon after we blew the master flute," Verrons said, reluctant to reveal that for him the spots had disappeared entirely. "I know Authority has done extensive research into radiation therapy. Without any particular success to date. The organism is resistant to everything they've subjected it to. But what we encountered in the red dancer's hall may be unique, something our scientists haven't come near duplicating under laboratory conditions."

Sadler moved closer, his voice lowered. "That—the master flute. That's when I noticed the change. Commander, if we can get back to the red hall and see if the spots will yield entirely to a second irradiation—"

"Exactly," Verrons said crisply. Upon original exposure, he had spent a somewhat longer time transfixed at the center of the red dancer's power web than Sadler had. If a second exposure cleared the Mazaahr spots from Sadler's field of vision, too, that in itself should be indicative. "We just may be able to provide Dublin with ample cause to invoke the remission clause."

Sadler's voice sharpened. "Remission clause?"

"Suspected remission is the only condition other than general emergency under which the Head Resident is authorized to summon the monitor ship below patrol altitude. Of course given the subjective nature of the spots, Dublin may be reluctant to take our word for it. But if we can persuade him to draw blood samples and have them dispatched up to the ship—" Groping forward, he began kicking aside fallen stone again. "But first things first."

They set to work in silence at the rocky barricade, each insulated by his own thoughts. As they rolled away stone, the chill of the mountain became an insidious force that turned first bone, then muscle and flesh to stone. When they judged they had cleared safe passage, they rested briefly. "If we had tools we could chop free a couple of crystal masses to light our way out of here," Verrons mused. But tools, of course, were exactly what they did not have.

What they had were booted feet, blinded eyes and searching fingertips. They moved cautiously through the cleared section of passageway into the pitch black corridor beyond. Verrons' voice was lost in the stone passage. "Any estimate how long it took us to get this far from the surface?"

"A couple of hours?" Sadler guessed hollowly. "My chronom gave up days ago."

As had Verrons'. Blindly they inched their way down winding and branching passages, instinct and intuition their only navigational aids. Twice brief rests degenerated into impromptu naps. Each time they shook themselves awake and pressed forward again, realizing that without food, without water, without anything to offer protection against cold, time could only work against them.

A silent enemy, time weighted their feet, time dulled their senses and paralyzed their minds. They stumbled endlessly through tortuous mountain corridors, nothing but their probing fingertips to guide them. Then, unexpectedly, far ahead the quality of blackness altered. Disoriented by the unanticipated deepening of his visual field, Verrons stumbled.

Night peered into the mountain, its star-speckled face impassive. Unbelievingly Verrons staggered toward it, stumbling on numb feet until he stood staring out at the stars. His relief was physical balm. Minutes passed before he thought to look for the liftpacks they had abandoned at the cave entrance. Although both packs were gone, the Ehminheer had left behind the single functioning light unit. Silently Verrons hefted the unit and cut darkness with its beam. He hardly recognized the grit-masked face he picked up in the beam as Sadler's. The white of his eyes glistened beneath the black-caked ledge of his brow. "Looks like we walk," the Talberonese said dully.

That night however they walked only far enough to take shelter within a cluster of vegetation. There they slept, their bodies lax, their minds still restlessly seeking the mountain corridors of nightmare for escape—from darkness, from disease.

And with morning they faced decision. "If we want to return to the temple and test the master flute, our logical next step is to get back to the humanoid settlement and reequip ourselves with liftpacks. And this time we should probably pick up a few tools and implements—and perhaps those viewing glasses." Verrons frowned into the morning sun, considering. The glasses had been engineered to accommodate eyes very different from their own. While they yielded fair distant vision, they also yielded vertigo and nausea.

Sadler followed Verrons' gaze. "We don't want to meet the Ehminheer in the air," he said slowly.

Verrons nodded. Yesterday they had evaded the Ehminheer's initial jealous fury by dint of their pack-enhanced maneuverability. But now the Ehminheer had purchase on the air, too. And they must assume that with the freedom of the skies, he had shed the final restraints of civilization. "Once we have packs, we'll stay close to cover." Verrons brushed at his daysuit, glancing out over the vale of wonders they were preparing to abandon without even cursory exploration. "Of course it's possible he's already come to terms with reality in its most solid form. But we can't assume his power cells have failed this soon."

Nor, he realized an hour later, when they saw a distant form silhouetted against the sky, could they assume it was the Ehminheer. Verrons narrowed his eyes, trying to define the figure more clearly. K'Obrohms? The flying male? Or the girl, soaring the sky on crystal wings?

Too quickly the form was lost in cloud. Pausing, Verrons let his contemplative gaze ride the line of foothills. He found he had developed very little feeling of kinship with this world. He felt its breezes at his jaw, he drank its waters, he hunted and foraged its brush. But on some level, Selmarri refused to incorporate his presence into its scheme of existence. It excluded him from the timeless balance of its existence. "Estimates again," he said.

"How long will it take us to hike back to the humanoid settlement?"

Reluctantly Sadler withdrew his own gaze from the clouds. "Up to four days," he guessed.

But neither of them was disappointed when at midafternoon of the third day, pearl grey domes showed through dense jungle vegetation. They approached the abandoned settlement cautiously, encountering neither humanoid nor other guardian. The domes sat pale and silent beneath encroaching jungle growth. Skirting through the shadows, ragged and weary, Sadler and Verrons headed for the row of storage domes where they had previously uncovered a cache of technological treasures.

Verrons paused within the deserted dome briefly, wiping perspiration from his forehead. Their three-day jungle trek had stimulated no return of Mazaahr spots, but their accelerated pace had driven them both to the verge of exhaustion. "We'll definitely want the glasses," he said finally, sorting through the first cluttered storage locker. "We'll simply make it firm policy to have solid ground underfoot when we use them." Stepping back, he peered down the row of lockers. "I'd feel better if we could pick up a few hand weapons, too." Whatever the balance of power between the Ehminheer and the young female, their own arrival at the mesa top would be unwelcome. And if they were to force passage into the chamber of the red dancer in the face of opposition. . . . "Anything we can operate safely that might put us on par with the Ehminheer and the girl."

At dusk Verrons regarded their haul with the beginnings of discouragement. They had isolated several mysterious devices, a long metal barrel with an activating device located mid-barrel, a smaller slimmer model of the same device and a lozenge shaped object with fingergrips and a series of small protruding barrels. Additionally there were several sets of long plaston darts, metal tipped. "Completely useless against a heat spear," Verrons concluded. Hand thrown, they would provide nothing more than target practice for the Ehminheer. And once he had melted the plaston shafts, the tips would fall to ground, useless.

"There's that rack of hatchets in the farm tool shed," Sadler suggested unenthusiastically.

"They might be useful for hand to hand combat," Verrons admitted. "But with the degree of mobility the Ehminheer has now, I doubt we'll find ourselves in that situation." He hefted the longest of the metal barrels. "Let's field test these."

The barrels, they quickly determined in a scorching of jungle vegetation, were flame throwers. Their reach however was not sufficient to be of use against either the Ehminheer or the girl. "Which leaves us this one possibility," Verrons mused, studying the five-barreled lozenge in his hand. The case was of plaston, the barrels', metal. He pried up a hinged cover to study the small array of what appeared to be activating buttons. Holding the device at arm's length, all barrels directed jungleward, Verrons pressed first one button, then a second, finally a third. The device failed to perform.

"Whatever it's meant to do," Sadler pointed out, "the Ehminheer could disable it simply by melting the case."

Leaving them with a handful of hot plaston—and third-degree burns. Discontentedly Verrons peered around the small clearing. Shadows already deepened under the trees. "If you want to stay here tomorrow morning while I scout out the temple area—"

Sadler's head snapped up. "Alone?"

Tossing aside the barreled lozenge, Verrons paced back toward the row of domes. "Just a thought." Pausing, he peered up at the darkening sky. The form he had seen against the clouds three days ago was momentarily reimposed upon his mind's eye and his sense of alienation from Selmarri reasserted itself. Not far from here by liftpack lived the underpeople: small, vulnerable. Whether or not the flying male had survived the Ehminheer's heat beam, their way of life would be radically altered soon—perhaps already had been. Because the girl had the focusing crystal now and there was no compassion in her soul: there was only fire.

Selmarri: a world where the innocent were enslaved and the savage elevated, where the living died and the dead lived. Selmarri: the world from which they unexpectedly found themselves seeking salvation from the microorganism which stalked their race across the stars.

The next day they launched themselves into the dewy morning air, skimming the treetops. They had not traveled far before the first streaks of fire touched Verrons' mind, searing across his awareness. He glanced at Sadler and received a crisp nod in return. From somewhere ahead the girl was broadcasting with fierce clarity. Before they had skimmed much farther, they were receiving visual images, bright, disconnected shards of color: glimmering pink stone, veils of orange light, brilliant blue plumage. "At least we don't have to worry about the Ehminheer so long as we see flashes of him through her eyes," Verrons observed.

But the flashes did not tell them much beyond the fact that both girl and avian occupied the temple complex and that the girl was angry. Emboldened, Verrons and Sadler bobbed above the treetops and flew swiftly toward the mesa, drawn on a thread of fire. When they sighted sunlight lancing from the stone needle, they settled into a treetop. Verrons permitted the buoyance of his liftpack to support most of his weight. "What do the glasses give us?"

Quickly Sadler put the binoculars they had salvaged from the humanoid settlement to his eyes. His lips blanched. "The—the Ehminheer is on his perch," he said finally, extending one hand to steady himself.

"At the top of the stone needle?"

"Yes . . . and. . . ." His voice fading, Sadler proffered the glasses.

Unwisely Verrons clapped them directly to his eyes. His vision was swiftly sundered, its two components wrenched away in opposite directions. Nausea precipitated in the pit of his stomach. Verrons sucked a quick breath, pulling the glasses from his eyes. Then, cautiously, he eased his gaze back down the twin barrels. Breathing raggedly, he distinguished the Ehminheer atop the stone needle. Vaguely he could see the beginnings of the avian's new beak. On his back, k'Obrohms wore the two liftpacks he had taken from the cavern mouth. But the Ehminheer did not strut his perch. Instead he huddled on the upper rim of the towering stone chimney like a storm-tossed waterfowl, his scrawny body hunched, his head tucked sideways, his plumage ruffed and blown. Grimly Verrons lowered the glasses. "I think I can guess the origin of this particular storm."

The two launched themselves again immediately, skimming just above the treetops. But by the time they reached the mesa area, the girl's transmission of visual images told them the situation on the mesa top had become at least temporarily quiescent. She had retired to the interior of one of the small temples and their glasses brought in the Ehminheer standing tall on his perch, his gaze giddy with indignation.

Sadler and Verrons took the side of the mesa cautiously, setting their liftpacks to yield minimal buoyancy. "We'll surface near the south-westernmost of the lesser temples, one level down from the grand temple. We'd better take shelter there until we see how the situation develops."

"The girl—"

"She's probably gone to ground in the temple of her own order, directly east of the temple where we'll surface."

Ultimately Verrons' guess proved correct. When they neared the upper rim of the mesa, however, the Ehminheer sighted them and shrieked from his perch. Swiftly he arced off the stone chimney, diving toward them. "Hit the ground!"

Verrons' warning was unnecessary. Sadler had already deactivated his liftpack and he hugged the rocky soil of the mesa side. Gobbling, the Ehminheer swooped overhead. Both his talons and his beak had begun to regenerate, emerging razor-sharp from the blue-plumed flesh. And all trace of Fleet Technician k'Obrohms had vanished. It was a predatory forest-lord who swept overhead, sunlight glinting from his full plumage, his savage gaze penetrating.

Three screaming dives and the Ehminheer abruptly swept back toward his perch. Verrons and Sadler scrambled up the last meters of the incline and dodged across pink stone to cover of the selected temple. They peered from its entry arch to see the girl scamper from the temple a level below theirs and skirt around the side of the grand temple.

Screaming, the Ehminheer settled to perch, heat pistols appearing in hand. Before he could direct tongues of heat at the girl, she dodged to cover of the courtyard wall. She hunkered there, the crystal, still encased in matrix, in her outstretched palms. Briefly, as pistol fire scorched the pavement before her, the crystal blazed, and the projected force of her anger drove needles of light into Verrons' eyes. He gasped, shielding his eyes with a forearm.

Anger. She had the crystal, she carried it in hand—but she was not satisfied. She was not satisfied at all. And the Ehminheer—he held his perch now. But he held it against the girl. Painfully Verrons tried to grasp the rationale that underlay their fiery confrontation, the Ehminheer blazing the pavement with both pistols, the girl circling within shelter of the courtyard wall, her hair crackling, in her stride the smooth-muscled stealth of a predator.

But he viewed the scene through too many eyes, his own, hers, the details splintered and scattered incomprehensibly, his wit scattered with them.

Then he realized that the tone of the Ehminheer's tirade had altered. Heat pistols ceased to blaze. Through the girl's eyes, through his own, Verrons peered up the stone shaft at the avian. The Ehminheer had stretched erect. His cry dying to a gobble, he peered into the eastern sky.

Sadler's voice was strangled. "Commander—"

And Verrons saw it, too, a glint of metal in the distant sky. "The glasses!" he snapped. But they were at his own neck. Quickly throwing off the confusion of splintered vision, he backed from shelter and put the glasses to his eyes. Dizziness, nausea—and then an image of bright metal, the Authority emblem glimmering blue on its silver side, swam across his field of vision. It was an Authority ship, not a drop-ship, not a drone, but the monitor ship itself, forging its way cautiously across the sky toward the mesa top.

He dropped the glasses, his mouth drying. "Radiation—" he gasped. Crystal-enhanced, the girl's developing power had reached out to register upon the monitor ship's radiation screens. Now the ship approached, its commander intent upon evaluating the unexpected phenomenon. And if Sadler and Verrons could reach the master flute, if the red dancer could extinguish the Mazaahr spots from Sadler's field of vision as well as Verrons', if they could subsequently signal the monitor ship to pick them up for definitive testing. . . .

Urgently his gaze swung back to the plaza. The Ehminheer, he saw, had not had opportunity to analyze the significance of the ship's appearance. Because in the initial moment of his inattention, the girl had leapt from cover of the wall. Now she held the crystal mass before her on one palm, her other hand rising into the air, fingers dancing. And around and from her swept storm. The wind currents she generated and dispersed up the stone shaft shrieked, almost visible in their whirlwind intensity.

This time the storm caught the Ehminheer off guard. Before he could huddle tight to the upper rim of the shaft, winds whipped his gaudy body free and tossed it toward the pavement. With a startled shriek, he engaged his liftpacks. But the turbulence of the winds the girl spun at him prevented him from gaining a foothold on the air. Instead, limbs tumbling, he was spun slow-motion over the northern wall of the courtyard.

Swiftly the girl darted back around the courtyard wall and into the grand temple. Tossing a beckoning gesture at Sadler, Verrons raced after her.

They halted at the courtyard entry as, from beyond the wall, the avian's stringy form reappeared, bounding vengefully into the air toward the top of the stone shaft.

He was swept back down as the girl pulled wind from the air again, creating a furious vortex that shrieked around him, tugging loose bright feathers and whirling them upward in its funnel. The Ehminheer squawked indignantly as the winds whipped him back over the wall toward the pavement. Immediately the girl darted past Sadler and Verrons, racing from the temple. They followed to see her draw fresh turbulence from the air and dance the lightweight Ehminheer frenetically across the plaza toward the verge of the mesa. He re-activated his liftpacks, but their force seemed only to add to the power turbulence held over him. His scrawny body arced wildly into the air and swooped away over the side of the mesa.

There was no sound of impact. Nevertheless the girl turned immediately to Sadler and Verrons. She rose to her toes, her head thrown back to level the fire of her eyes directly at them. Her vision of Verrons—a bearded outcast ringed in fire—was imposed sharply upon his mind. At the same time, Verrons felt heat scorch his flesh. His lips were suddenly cracked, his eyes seared.

"Sadler—"

"She—can she ignite us?"

"I don't know," Verrons said painfully. "But we can't let her see she's affecting us." Because once she realized her crystal-enhanced power had found vulnerability, once she realized she could inflict pain, whether accompanied by visible physical trauma or not—

Did it even matter to her whether pain stemmed from tissue damage? Once she knew she held a weapon against them, she would wield it mercilessly. *And this was the founding mother of the new race of light dancers?* As she sank back to the pavement, her head rising erect, Verrons experienced profound pessimism about the future of Selmarri, about the fate that even now stalked away across the pink stones toward the grand temple. He stroked his face and found it tender. Sadler's features were flushed, as if the flesh had been scorched. "The crystal—"

"We can't leave now," Verrons said. Because when he peered up, the monitor ship had moved perceptibly nearer, like a cautious metal behemoth gliding silently across the sky to satisfy its curiosity. "If we can't get to the master flute—" And if they couldn't successfully signal the ship to lift them for testing afterward. . . .

Abruptly the Ehminheer bobbed over the mesa wall, a vengeful streak of blue, heat pistols in hand. There was no sanity in his yellow eyes. There was only the fierce passion of inflamed instincts, the fury of the displaced lord of the stone perch. Startled, Verrons stared into unreasoning yellow eyes. "Ehminheer—"

For answer he drew fire. The Ehminheer's pistol blast slashed between the two humans. Almost without volition, Verrons broke and ran for shelter of the grand temple. He was dimly aware of Sadler running after him.

The Ehminheer hurtled into the temple after them, his regenerated talons chattering against polished stone. Halting, he glared through the broad arch into the courtyard. There the girl crouched within the stone shaft, radiance boiling around her in a surging orange cloud. Shrieking, the Ehminheer flung a beam of heat against the cloud of her power.

The two forces, heat and light, met with a flash of violet light and a deep, jarring *crump!* The explosive report shook the temple twice again in rapid succession before an unseen force jarred both heat pistols from the avian's grasp. The weapons clattered against stone. Triumphant, the girl leapt erect and glared from the heart of her surging cloud with luminous eyes.

Frustrated anger rattled in the Ehminheer's throat. As the girl advanced from the base of the stone shaft, he snatched up both heat pistols and retreated from the temple. She stalked after him to frame herself in the broad entryway. Her posture, back arched, head thrown back, proclaimed the quality of her menace. She held the pose for several minutes, then turned and strode back through the temple to the courtyard.

Cautiously Verrons inched along the wall toward the entry arch and peered out. In the plaza the Ehminheer screamed in rage. At Verrons' appearance, the avian spit a beam of heat at him. Verrons dodged back. "We couldn't leave now if we wanted to," he realized.

"If we wait until dusk—"

Verrons shook his head tautly. "Our best chance of reaching the master flute is after dark. Just hope the girl cooperates with us." Only at her presence would the floor of the temple of orange dancers glide freely open, offering unobstructed passage to the underground.

Uneasily his gaze returned to the courtyard. The girl crouched within the stone shaft again, her head thrown back. Reflected from the polished inner surface of the shaft, the light of her eyes burgeoned into a cloud of power that swirled around her, almost obscuring her. Slowly she raised the crystal mass on her outstretched palms until she held it level with her glowing eyes. With a blazing crackle, mineral encrustation and rocky matrix were reduced to dry powder that crumbled away. The brief flare of light was blindingly intense.

When he looked again, the girl stood within a dispersing cloud. The crystal lay in the palm of one hand, a thing of incredible beauty. Doubly possessed, Verrons peered into its orange depths with her eyes as well as his own. Briefly it shone at the very center of his being and from it he drew the compelling promise of what now could be, of what now *would* be. . . .

Would be? But the crystal was not recessed into the flesh of her brow. Instead it lay hard and cold in the palm of her hand. *Why?* And whose was that fierce demand? His—or hers? Whose was the rage that rose swiftly, like a floodtide of lava welling from an unseen vent? At the center of its hellfire flow the crystal glittered and shone. But when the girl crouched again, when she sent veils of power swirling up the stone shaft again and pressed the glowing crystal against her forehead, no protective niche opened in the bone of her brow. The crystal remained stubbornly, brilliantly a thing apart.

And that mattered. That mattered very much. The refined crystal was not meant to be carried awkwardly in hand. It was meant to be securely cradled in close proximity to the critical brain areas where rapidly altering wave patterns directed and channeled the flow of power.

Dizzily Verrons stood ground as the girl stalked from the base of the stone shaft to confront Sadler and himself. He clenched his teeth, trying to expunge her passions from his mind, trying to reclaim the inviolability of his own perceptions. It was a futile effort. Her frustration, her rage flowed through him like a current. And it quickly became apparent that now she had intentions, intentions that included Sadler and himself. She stalked a wide circle around them, orange eyes brilliant, hair bristling stiffly from her head. And in her hand, if only figuratively, she clutched a pair of tools: Sadler and Verrons.

"Commander—"

Verrons touched his temples as mental images swiftly formed and clarified: a swath of misty red, the flash of an opaline wall, a gleaming silver flute solidly mounted. Meeting the girl's brilliant eyes, Verrons barely concealed a surge of elation. "The underground chamber," he breathed. "She intends to take us back there with her." And studying Sadler's suddenly taut features, Verrons knew the Talberonese read the same intention in her mind.

CHAPTER SIXTEEN

From her vantage point near the temple of orange dancers, Aleida watched night stalk across the temple complex. Soon Bright-Feather uttered a last sleepy warning from the summit of the stone needle, which she had permitted him to reclaim that afternoon after she swept the palehands with her to the smaller temple. Periodically through the afternoon, he had launched himself to circle the mesa, broadcasting warning shrieks on the empty air. And at the moments of his greatest agitation, Aleida had noted familiar twinges of excitation.

The male? Arcing near, his approach hidden by cloud? But peering up, Aleida had detected no sign of him. There had only been the strange metal disk in the distance, floating high in the sky. Earlier in the day it had approached closely enough for her to study the symbol painted on its underside. Then it had retreated, hovering against the distant clouds, anomalous but apparently not threatening.

Restlessly Aleida paced back across the plaza. That afternoon, entering the temple of orange dancers, she had swept the pale-hands into one corner and arched herself at the center of the floor, her head falling back, her eyes glowing. But the ceiling had not answered her demand with light, the floor with passage.

It was not a denial she had accepted with grace. She had leapt from the center of the floor, hair bristling indignantly. She was so near, the refined crystal in hand, the secret of its implantation already recorded somewhere in the tissues of her brain. But she could not retrieve that information without appropriate stimulation, and stimulation lay below, in the hall of the master flute—beneath the solid stone floor.

The floor however refused to open for her by daylight, and she had no recourse but to wait for night. So wait she did, through the long sunwashed hours of afternoon, one eye always on the palehands. Vaguely it troubled her that they did not actively contest their captivity. In fact there was a vigilant quality to their stillness as they sat against the stone wall, dark eyes and light leveled on her—a waiting quality.

Now, returning to the temple, she sensed a new, coiled alertness in the palehands. More significantly, she sensed a change in the atmosphere of the temple itself. She paused, slowly rising to her toes. In response, orange radiance glowed from the dark air. Swiftly Aleida advanced to the center of the floor, and the ceiling came alive above her head. Light figures danced, a flowing, glowing evolution of line and curve. Then the orange wheel of light flared into prominence and began to rotate at the center of the ceiling, its multiple arms raining brilliance down through the air. Aleida's hair crackled and ecstasy gripped her arching body. She hung helpless in the thrall of light until the voice of the temple spoke. *Enter, sister, and learn of what was. For what was will be again.*

At her feet, the floor opened and Aleida stood at the top of the railed stairs, her eyes flooded with light. Bedazzled, her gaze fell across the palehands. They were poised half-erect against the far wall, faces taut, animal readiness drawing every muscle. Momentarily Aleida was displeased. It was hers to initiate the pilgrimage to the font of knowledge, theirs merely to dumbly accede to her wishes. Quickly Aleida rose to her toes, commanded wind from the glowing air and curled it at them. It carried ragged tails of light with it, enveloping the palehands in whipping brilliance.

Her winds shrieked swiftly to near-tornado fury and the pale-hands let themselves be tugged across the floor to the staircase. Reaching the bottom of the stairs, they peered back at Aleida. She rose to her toes, indicating with her chin the direction they were to take.

Walls slid as they routed themselves through underground corridors to the grand hall. There energy streaked opaline walls in a compelling flow and the master flute beckoned, an instrument of liquid fascination. Gusting the palehands into the hall, Aleida strode to the center of the floor. She rose to her toes, her fingers drawing energy from the air to flare along the pathways of her nervous system and spark from her hair and fingertips. His eyes glazing, the fairest palehand stumbled toward the flute. Again Aleida was displeased that he seemed to move with his own purpose rather than hers. But he put his mouth to the mouthpiece and with his breath the voice of the firestorm bellowed. *Now I am again in my power and in my all.*

Now the red dancer was and now he danced. Now he spoke the history of this world and of the light dancers who ruled it. He spoke their first appearance, their ascendancy and, in a voice crackling and deep, the fate that ultimately extinguished them from earth and sky. But when the caverns glowed again with crystal foci, when long-limbed saviors were born again from the ranks of the underpeople. . . .

The crystal! Aleida shrieked impatiently, polished gem blazing in hand. *Tell me how to fuse this crystal by my brow. Tell me how to become what I must be to live as I will.*

The firestorm voice died abruptly despite the palehand's continued effort. When the red dancer spoke again, his tone was altered. In syllables crisp and dry, he told her what she needed to know—more than she needed to know. He told her how to bring the necessary powers to focus to cause the very bone of her brow to part to receive the gem she held in hand. He told her then how she must channel the energy that flowed within her to bring external energy to optimum coherence, that her will be done. He told her how she must cause the world to serve her power, that she might best serve the power of the world. And he told her how, one day many years in the future, she must return to the cavern and blaze free a second orange crystal, from which she must refine a clear kernel of brilliance to contain her living will at the death of her body. Then, finally, his voice died from the chamber. Slowly Aleida's body stopped spinning and the opaline walls faded.

She knew how to fuse the crystal. But the knowledge was useless tonight, she realized, useless for many hours to come. Turning, she found that the palehands peered at her warily. With a perverse stirring, Aleida arched her body again and held the gleaming crystal high. Radiance surged into the air and mingled with the light of the crystal. *I will hear the story of creation again*, she commanded.

Again, before the younger palehand gave his breath to the firestorm, she suffered the unsettling feeling that in some way she was serving the palehands' purpose. But the roar of storm, the dance of light was her own desire, too. And so the night passed in an ecstasy that gave birth finally to exhaustion. Aleida slumped to the floor, her body drinking the cold of the earth. The fairer palehand lay in a torpor nearby. Briefly she had the impression that the other palehand left the chamber, that she heard him moving through the display hall beyond. But exhaustion prevented her from investigating.

Much later some instinct prompted her to jump up to make her way back to the surface. The palehands followed, the fairer one stumbling with fatigue. But as she ran gleaming corridors, she realized the palehands had fallen behind, even that they had evaded her. She spun, the beginnings of fury building in her fingertips. They were her instrument; she was not theirs. Quickly, she turned back to find them in the hall of displays, each of them running toward her now, the darker carrying an elongated metal statuette under one arm, a second, bulkier statuette in his hand, the fairer stumbling after him bearing a heavy stone vase.

Disconcerted, she rose briefly to her toes. But the palehands did not wield the objects as weapons. They simply halted, waiting for her to lead way again.

And urgency drove her, urgency to sample daylight again, to begin drawing from the sun the power she coveted, the power she craved. With a warning snarl, she turned and ran down branching corridors until she reached the chamber of orange dancers.

She emerged from the underground in a rush, hardly noticing that the palehands lingered in the small temple, wedging their booty into the opening from which they had emerged, prevent-

ing the stone door from closing completely. Drawn, Aleida raced
from the small temple on long toes and ran under the morning
sky. Soon, very soon, the sun would soar to the zenith and the
union of crystal and flesh would be complete. Exultant, Aleida
raced the perimeters of the complex. Mingled with Bright-
Feather's warning shriek, she heard the cry of the upper strata,
distant, beckoning. And as she ran, engorging organs lanced her
with sweet agony. Seeking high, seeking wide, it seemed to
Aleida that the source of her torment was near, as near as the
sky. And soon, reaching, she would hold that in her hands.

She would hold it if she could first reclaim the stone needle
from Bright-Feather. Aleida halted abruptly and spun. Bright-
Feather glared from the upper lip of the needle. With a cry,
Aleida launched herself up the five levels of the plaza, gathering
wind as she ran. She raced through the grand temple at the center of storm and emerged in the walled courtyard. With a flick of
her head, she sent turbulence bellowing up the exterior shaft of
the stone needle. Bright horsetails of orange light rode the wind.

Bright-Feather hunched on the upper rim of the shaft. The
winds tore at his plumage, stripping away gaudy blue feathers.
Suddenly, with an angry squawk, he darted straight up into the
air. Swiftly Aleida rushed the base of the shaft. She knelt inside,
peering up, alert for any attempt to reclaim the perch. Twice
Bright-Feather streaked across the sky above the needle. Aleida
dispatched a howl of wind at him, sweeping him from sight.

Then she knelt alone at the bottom of a deep well of stone, intensely aware of the sun's slow approach to the zenith, of the
growing heat of the crystal she cradled in her palms. Bright-
Feather shrieked from the periphery of the complex and the
palehands loomed out of the shadows of the grand temple. But
they kept their distance, regarding her with unreadable eyes.
More distracting were the scalding surges of excitation that
sporadically brought Aleida to her feet, a growl in her throat.

Then the sun's rim appeared at the edge of the shaft above.
Aleida's head dropped back, and she raised the crystal, balancing it on her extended fingertips, elevating it until it was centered upon the vertical axis of the stone needle, directly above
her brow.

Slowly, ringed in fire, the sun centered itself in the orifice of
the shaft. A single pencil of light extended down the shaft, penetrating the crystal, searing the flesh of Aleida's brow. Her hair

belled out from her head, and it seemed to Aleida, as light
etched her brow, that she knelt alone at the center of a slowly rotating universe, its axis extending directly through her, im-
mobilizing her. For an endless period, the universe moved
around her, stately, slow. Then, as the sun passed from the zenith, the shaft of light that pinned her dissolved. Aleida lowered
her hands until the crystal dropped into the newly created inden-
tation in her brow.

The final process of fusion sent a series of convulsions crackling down her spine. She was briefly blinded by an interior vision of fire, her own face at its center. Then her hands fell to her
side and she stood.

Slowly she drifted from the shaft into the sunlit courtyard. For
with the crystal cradled securely in the bone of her brow, her
perception of time, of distance, was radically altered. The pavement appeared farther, glossier, and her limbs seemed to move
with a peculiar floating grace. Certainly the distant clouds were
whiter, the vault of the sky deeper, bluer. And now it was neither imagination nor dream that the sky summoned her. As she
crossed the pavement, the sky uttered not the mocking cry of
nightmare but a compelling call, deep throated, that tugged at
the muscles of her calves and brought her floating in great,
weightless bounds through the grand temple to the plaza beyond.

Fly, sister, the clouds cried, and Aleida's muscles moved sinuously, subcutaneous serpents writhing after sunlight. She leapt
across the shimmering reaches of the plaza, pink stone dissolving
beneath her feet.

But even as gravity released her, she became aware, as if from
a distance, of Bright-Feather's infuriated scream, of his hurtling
approach, fire instruments in hand. Her anger was swift and
powerful. Dropping back to the pavement, she faced him. She
uttered a single sharp warning. When it went unheeded, a sword
of light slashed with merciless brilliance from the crystal at her
brow, and the smell of scorched flesh tainted the air. Both
Bright-Feather's fire instruments clattered to the pavement. He
darted away gobbling in pain, the flesh of his hands crisped
black.

Black—as black as the form that suddenly appeared from the
southern sky, riding the air in long, swooping arcs. Turning,
Aleida was paralyzed, her body poised, arms reaching. A bellow-

ing cry broke from her throat, a demand uttered in a language she had never spoken before.

He dove air toward her. The scar on his side was ashen grey against the black of his flesh, a badge of honor. His eyes were green, as brilliant as the crystal at his brow. Aleida shot fiery-eyed scorn at the screaming Bright-Feather. Then, running, she launched herself again from the stone pavement. Automatically her arms rose, her fingers twined, and the air parted before her.

Aleida executed her initial flight in exultant swoops, first circling the stone needle, then arcing away toward the distant clouds. Air slapped her face and tugged her hair, and the male flew after her, his path of flight describing a series of complex whorls about hers. With fierce joy, Aleida aimed her hurtling body directly at the billowing midday clouds. Within minutes, she tasted cold moisture on every skin surface. She threw back her head and hurtled up through the dense clouds.

When she emerged on the lower cloudplain, she tossed back her head, her cry of triumph blending with the cry of the clouds. She suffered no sense of separateness now. She was conjoined with sunlight and wind, a force among forces. The light of her eyes was a solar radiance, and when she inhaled, her lungs drew at the breath-wind of the sky. A being infinite and tall, she arrowed across the field of cloud, casting upon it an aura of orange light.

But this was only the lowliest of the cloudplains that hung like islands of white in the vault of the sky. Beyond the mountains lay others, broad and high. And above her the male flew, lancing the air with a sword of green light, beckoning her—not just to the far regions of the sky but to the destiny that waited for them both in the energy-washed upper air. For within them they bore the seed of generations destined to reclaim all the kingdoms of earth and sky. Within them they bore the future of their kind.

The air rippled noisily as Aleida arrowed toward him, after him. At a distance she heard Bright-Feather shriek. She glanced down to see him tumble erratically up the sky, looping and lunging out of control. Legs flailing, he struggled at the controls of his buoyancy packs with useless charred hands. His efforts at adjustment were obviously painful, just as obviously futile.

And he was obviously harmless now as he tumbled away in the direction of the metal vessel that had appeared from the distance again. Briefly however Aleida paused in her headlong flight through her reclaimed kingdom. For as the gleaming vessel glided near the mesa area, she heard the cry of the red dancer. His voice reached her almost subliminally, strained through muffling layers of soil and stone. He seemed to speak in regular pulses of energy, as if someone supplied him life in briefly measured bursts, permitting him to do no more than utter repeated strangled cries. There was a scheme to the pattern of his cries, as if his voice were being forced to carry some message imposed by the will of another.

But Aleida could not deal with the puzzle of his strangely truncated cries now. Swiftly she darted away after the male, her laughter as mocking as the laughter of the clouds. Together they rode the air currents toward the mountains, looping and diving, hair crackling. Aleida's fingertips bristled with new nerve endings that flooded her with data she had never before realized existed. For the air had flavor, the air had weight: it was an ever-fluctuating system of currents and troughs, eddies and pools. And its every transitory characteristic was of significance to a being who merged herself with the sky.

As they soared, the world below was gradually transformed into a landscape brilliant with the light of a hundred long-toed dancers. Red, violet, green; orange, gold, blue; indigo, silver and yellow, they unfurled their billowing colors, swaddling rock, soil and water in them, making of the jungle panorama a pattern of swiftly flowing color. To Aleida it seemed that each dancer was at once her ancestor and herself. And as she flew, the sky spoke softly in her ear. *What was, is, sister.*

Aleida's lips formed the exultant response. *And will be!*

And far below, her exultation was echoed by Verrons' as he emerged from the underground temple and hurried out to peer into the early afternoon sky. Sadler wedged the stone door open and ran after him. As the Talberonese raised his head, the monitor ship's gleaming profile came to quick focus upon the reflective surfaces of his eyes. At the ship's underbelly a small port slid open and a finned metal dart emerged, to arc swiftly in their direction. Verrons recognized its function immediately from the markings on its cylindrical barrel. "They read our signal," he said almost reverently as the communications drone sped toward them. "They read our signal. They're going to give us a chance to prove we've isolated the cure."

EPILOGUE

It was midmorning when Verrons dropped the hovercraft to polished stone for the last time, settling lightly near the colonnade that bordered the northern perimeter of the plaza. Beyond the grand temple the mountains were mist-cloaked giants, dark guardians of the strange powers that animated Selmarri. During the past two weeks every resident of Selmarri Home had been scheduled through the chamber of the red dancer and every one had subsequently tested free of bloodblossom microorganism. But now Verrons touched the commset controls with a tightening frown. "Remote hygiene craft querying mission coordinator. There is still no sign of the humanoids in the temple vicinity and no sign of the Ehminheer. Did the final search sweep turn up any sign of them?"

The dispassionate voice responded immediately. "Negative. However when contingents from the other isolation worlds arrive, they will be instructed to survey the area closely. Have you begun foaming the temples, Commander?"

Verrons sighed. "We're getting to it immediately."

"Good. Demolition time for Selmarri Home remains as previously set. Final evacuation time likewise. Schedule yourself back to the monitor craft accordingly."

"We will," Verrons responded. Heavily he embarked from the small craft. As he did, the sheen of pink stone keyed to life a series of vivid images: the girl arching within the stone shaft, impaled on an axis of light; the flying male silhouetted against the sky; the Ehminheer in uncoordinated ascent, his burned hands helpless at the liftpack controls. It was barely possible k'Obrohms had managed to adjust his lift settings before he hit the upper atmosphere and lost consciousness. But if the Ehminheer had survived, he would exercise every wile to avoid being sighted.

Turning, Verrons found Sadler had already opened the cargo hatch and was stacking cannisters of disinfecting foam on the plaza. Verrons checked cannister pressure readings, silently numbering his own regrets. The radiation web of the red dancer had granted them all the gift of a normal lifespan. Now Rumar and the man-leopard waited again. But here on the mesa top, flute in hand, he had caught a tantalizing glimpse of eternity. And he had caught an even more compelling glimpse of an existence that knew no bounds, of an existence that held all the earthen globe in one hand, all the airy skies in the other. Although he had realized even then that he would never cradle a gleaming crystal in the furrow of his own brow, that his own mortality could never be invested in a shining crystal, to become virtual immortality, he still felt the attraction of the light dancers who waited in the temple mechanism to live again.

At that moment a cloud of dark smoke blossomed upon the eastern horizon. Verrons snatched glasses from the craft and trained them. The sound of multiple explosions crackled faintly through the morning air. Selmarri Home had been rendered into debris—debris scattered with explosive force to the hungry maw of the jungle. Verrons' narrowing gaze returned to the temple complex. Pink stone shimmered in the morning sun. "We'd better get moving."

Silently they made their final tour of the complex, sterilizing every accessible surface. Working their way back to the hovercraft, they loaded aboard spent cannisters. Almost reluctantly Verrons set the hovercraft into the air again. As they lofted, the disinfecting foam had already evaporated from the upper levels of the complex and the grand temple was poetry again, wrought in glossy pink stone. To the south, puffy white clouds grew upon the horizon and a single hazy light dancer seemed to stride the sky, haughty in a gown of clouds.

But darkness moved in her wake, the darkness of an entire generation of light dancers waiting to be born and to rule. His jaw setting, Verrons set course toward the threatening cloud formation. As he flew, he forced the winds of imagery to transmute the distant cloud dancer, to bring her from two legs to four, to replace her haughty face with a softly spotted muzzle. Only when the distant clouds finally offered him the promise of golden skies, rippling grassplains and the man-leopards, glossy-pelted beasts of obscure promise, did he alter course toward the monitor ship. Then the two men flew into the sun, one bound to challenge mirage, the other to probe the faint shadow of intelligence that fell across a distant world.